Count d'Orsay.
After a painting by Sir Francis Grant, P.R.A.

D'Orsay

D'ORSAY

OR

The Complete Dandy

By

W. Teignmouth Shore

WITH PHOTOGRAVURE AND SIXTEEN OTHER PORTRAITS

London

John Long, Limited

Norris Street, Haymarket

First Published in 1911

Contents

Contents

List of Illustrations

Dandiacal

WHAT a delightful fellow is your complete dandy. No mere clothes' prop he, the coat does not make the dandy; no mere *flâneur* in fine garments; far more than that is our true dandy.

Though there is not any authority for making the statement, we do not think that we are wrong in asserting that on the day when Adam first complained to Eve that she had not cut his fig-leaf breeches according to the latest fashion dandyism was born. It is not dead yet, only moribund, palsied, shaking and decrepit with old age, blown upon by an over-practical world of money-spinners and money-spenders. Joy seems to have become a thing of which it is necessary to go in pursuit; in the golden days of the dandies it was a good comrade which came almost without hailing to those who desired its company. A real dandy would wither and wilt in a world where joy is so much of a stranger as it is now to most folk.

It is curious that there does not exist any history of the Rise, Decline and Fall of Dandyism, a subject fit for the pen of Gibbon. But the reason is, that to write it with anything approaching to accuracy and completeness, or with sufficient sympathy and insight, would stagger the painstaking pedantry of a German philosopher and tax the wit and wisdom of George Meredith. Perhaps some day the University of Oxford or of Cambridge, when it has finished trifling with ponderous records of kings and queens, of statesmen and soldiers, of men of science and of writers of books, will gather together a happy band of scholars and men of the world, and will issue to us a joint-stock history of Dandyism. Reform is in the University air; let us hope. Might not the Academic authorities go even further with profit to themselves and to the nation? Ought they not to found and well endow a Chair of Dandyism? Should there not be a Professor of Dandyism to teach the young idea how to distinguish between dress and mere clothes? Between those two there is as great a gulf fixed as between the gentle art of the *gourmet* and the mere feeding of the *gourmand.* To teach also the art of living and the history of dandies and of dandyism? In these prosaic days we are only too ready to learn how to obtain the means of living without acquiring also a knowledge of how to use those means to good purpose. The Universities should likewise institute scholarships of dandyism, to encourage the study of dandyism in our Public and Board Schools, in both of which it is so grossly neglected. These scholarships must not be of meagre twenties and thirties of pounds, but of several hundreds per annum, so as to enable the scholar to practise the arts that he studies. We commend this outlet for money to millionaires of a practical turn of mind. The future happiness of our race depends upon its dandyism.

The dandy has played a conspicuous part upon the stage of history: Alcibiades, Marc Antony, Buckingham, Claude Duval, Benjamin Disraeli prove the truth of this statement. It would be a nice point to decide how far their dandyism was part and parcel of their equipment for attaining greatness. At one period of English history the whole population of the country was divided between dandies and anti-dandies, Cavaliers and Puritans, the former dandified in dress, religion, methods of fighting and in morals. They were great dandies those martial Cavaliers, and so were a few of their successors, who flirted and frivoled at Whitehall under Charles II.

The literature of dandyism is varied, vast and interesting, but space forbids our doing more than briefly alluding to two of its lighter branches in English letters. The drama—or rather the comedy—of dandyism holds a very high place in the history of the British Stage. Lyly, the Euphuist, was a literary dandy of the first water, and his euphuism the height of dandyism in literary style. Shakespeare in *Love's Labour Lost* has given us a whole comedy of dandyism, and in Mercutio a portrait of the complete Elizabethan dandy. But the comedy of dandyism was at its zenith in the days of Charles II. Congreve and Wycherley were its high priests, who preached through the mouths of their brilliant puppets the gospel of joy which the Court so ably practised. We have in *The School for Scandal* another bright flash of dandyism, though Charles Surface has too much heart for a true and perfect dandy.

In fiction we have many striking examples of dandiacal literature, notably *Vivian Grey* and *Pelham*, both written by dandies.

Dandies vary in kind as well as in degree, there being some who play at dandyism in the days of their youth, such for example as Disraeli; others who are pinchbeck dandies, falling into the slough of overdressing, such for example as Charles Dickens, who was a mere colourist in garments. There are the born dandies, Brummel, D'Orsay, George Bernard Shaw for examples, the last of whom was born at least 200 years behind his time; he would have been delightful at the Court of Charles the Merry. It is not necessary to be in the fashion to achieve the dignity of dandyism; G. B. S. sets the fashion himself and is the only one who can follow it.

The psychology of the dandy has been much misunderstood, probably because it has been so little studied. What dandies have done has been told to us in many a biography, but what they have been—upon that point silence reigns almost supreme. Yet the mind of the complete dandy is well worth plumbing. Those who know him not will perchance advance the theory that a man possessed of a mind cannot be a dandy ; as a matter of fact the reverse is the truth ; he must possess mind, but not a heart.

Even so profound a philosopher and student of human nature—the two are seldom found in conjunction, which accounts for the inefficacy of most philosophy—as Professor Teufelsdröckh of Weissnichtwo has defined a dandy as " a Clothes-wearing Man, a Man whose trade, office and existence consists in the wearing of Clothes. Every faculty of his soul, spirit, purse and person is heroically consecrated to this one object, the wearing of clothes wisely and well : so that others dress to live, he lives to dress."

Which proves that though undoubtedly German philosophers know most things in Heaven and on Earth they do not know all, though they themselves would never make this admission. Teufelsdröckh's definition of a dandy is preposterously incomplete, showing that he did not possess insight into the heart and soul of dandyism. He perceived the clothes, but not the man.

The proper wearing of proper clothes is but part of the whole duty of a dandy-man. A complete dandy is dandified in all his modes of life ; his sense of honour and his conceptions of morality are dandified ; he is an epicure in

all the arts of fine living, in all forms of fashionable and expensive amusement, in all luxurious
accomplishments. He must be endowed with
wit, or at least gifted with a tongue of sprightliness sufficient to pass muster as witty. He must
be perfect in the amiable art of polite conversation and expert in the language of love.
He must own "the courtier's, soldier's, scholar's
eye, tongue, sword"; he must be "the glass of
fashion and the mould of form, the observed of
all observers."

How far did D'Orsay fulfil these requirements? It is the aim of the following pages to
answer that question.

D'Orsay

I

IT is the habit of historians to pay little heed to the childhood and the training of the kings, conquerors, statesmen and the other big folk whose achievements they record and whose characters they seldom fathom or portray. But perhaps they are right just as perhaps sometimes they are accurate. It is easier to judge correctly and with understanding the boy and what really were the influences that affected his development, when we know the performances of his maturity, than it is to trace in the child the father of the man. By what the man was we may know what the boy had been. Which brings us to this point, that we need not very deeply regret that the records of D'Orsay's early years are but scanty. Such as they are they suffice to give us all that we require—a fugitive glimpse here and there of a childhood as great in promise as the manhood was in performance.

Gédéon Gaspard Alfred de Grimaud, Count d'Orsay and du Saint-Empire, Prince of Dandies, was born upon the 4th of September, in the year 1801. Whether or not he came into the world under the influence of a lucky star we can find no record ; upon that point each of us may draw his own conclusion in accordance with his judgment of D'Orsay's career and character.

He sprang from a noble and distinguished family, his father Albert, Count d'Orsay, being a soldier of the Empire and accepted as one of the handsomest men of his day, Napoleon saying of him that he was "*aussi brave que beau.*" It has been written of the son, "Il est le fils d'un général de nos armées héroiques, aussi célèbre par sa beauté que par ses faits d'armes." Alfred inherited his father's good looks and his accomplishment with the sword.

Writing in 1828, Lady Blessington says: "General d'Orsay, known from his youth as Le Beau d'Orsay, still justifies the appellation, for he is the handsomest man of his age that I have ever beheld . . . ;" and Lady Blessington was an experienced judge of manly beauty.

His mother, a beautiful woman, was Eléanore, Baroness de Franquemont, a daughter of the King of Würtemberg by his marriage with Madame Crawford, also needless to say a beautiful woman; also apparently dowered handsomely with wit and worldly wisdom. Her marriage with the King who, it has been neatly said, "baptised with French names his dogs, his castles and his bastards," was of course a left-handed affair, and on his right-handedly marrying within his own rank, she retired in dudgeon to France. Later she married an Irishman of large means, a Mr O'Sullivan, with whom she resided for some time in India, surviving him and dying at the advanced age of eighty-four, full of youthfulness and ardour. The grandson inherited her accomplishment in love.

So alluring, indeed, were her charms, that on her return from the East one of her many admirers presented her with a bottle of otto of Roses, outdone in sweetness by the following Mooreish compliment :—

> "Quand la 'belle Sullivan' quitta l'Asie,
> La Rose, amoureuse de ses charmes,
> Pleura le départ de sa belle amie,
> Et ce flacon contient ses larmes."

The fragrance of the otto has long departed but that of the compliment remains. A pretty compliment deserves to attain immortality.

When in Paris in 1828 Lady Blessington was upon terms of intimacy with the D'Orsays, and was greatly impressed by *la belle Sullivan*, or, as she preferred to be called, Madame Crawford. She visited her in a charming hôtel, "*entre Cour et Jardin*"; and decided that she was the most "exquisite person of her age" that she had ever seen. She was then in her eightieth year, but we are told that she did not look more than fifty-five, and was full of good-humour and vivacity. "Scrupulously exact in her person, and dressed with the utmost care as well as good taste, she gives me a notion of the appearance which the celebrated Ninon de l'Enclos must have presented at the same age, and has much of the charm of manner said to have belonged to that remarkable woman."

There is considerable mystery about this good lady's career.

B

It was a foregone conclusion that a woman
of this style would dote upon and do her best
endeavour to spoil a bright, handsome boy such
as was her grandson Alfred.　Being an only son,
an elder brother having died in infancy, the child
was made much of on all sides.　His good looks,
his smartness, even his early developed taste for
extravagant luxuries, charmed his accomplished
grandmother, whom when later on he entered the
army we find presenting him with a magnificent
service of plate, which brought upon him more
ridicule than envy from his brother officers.

In 1815 Paris was in a ferment of excitements
and entertainments, all the great men and many
of the great ladies of Europe were there gathered
together — where the spoil is there shall the
vultures be gathered together.　Young D'Orsay,
mere lad though he was, came very much to
the front; even thus early his immaculate dress
was noticeable; his spirited English hunter and
his superb horsemanship attracted attention.
Though he probably did not particularly relish
the occurrence, he was presented to the Duke
of Wellington.　A great meeting this, the conqueror of the men of France and the future
conqueror of the women of England.

Lord William Pitt Lennox, himself only sixteen, relates that he met D'Orsay in Paris in
1814, and he goes on to state that "in the hours
of recreation, he showed me all the sights of the
'City of Frivolity,' as Paris has been not in-
aptly named."　Pretty good for two such mere lads!

"One of our first visits was to the Café des

Milles Colonnes, which was, at the period I write of, the most attractive café in Paris. Large as it was, it was scarcely capable of containing the vast crowds who besieged it every evening, to admire its saloons decorated with unprecedented magnificence. . . .

"Wellington had a private box at the Théâtre Français, which D'Orsay and myself constantly occupied to witness the splendid acting of Talma, Madame Georges, Mademoiselle Duchesnois in tragedy, and of that daughter of Nature, Mademoiselle Mars, in comedy. . . .

"Upon witnessing Perlet in *Le Comédien d'Etampes*, D'Orsay said—

"'Is not Perlet *superlative*?'"

In another of his numerous voluminous and often highly entertaining memoirs, Lord William writes of this same visit to Paris :—

"One youth attracted great attention that day"—it was a royal hunt in the Bois de Boulogne—"from his handsome appearance, his gentlemanlike bearing, his faultless dress and the splendid English hunter he was mounted upon. This was Count Alfred d'Orsay, afterwards so well known in London society. De Grammont,* who some few years after married his sister, had sent him from England a first-rate Leicestershire hunter, whose fine shape, simple saddle and bridle contrasted favourably with the heavy animals and smart caparisons then in fashion with the Parisian Nimrods.

"The Count was presented to Wellington

* De Guiche. See p. 35.

and his staff, and from that moment he became a constant guest at the Hôtel Borghese. . . ."

Of another hunt, or rather of the return from it, we read :—

"Nothing occurred during the day's sport to merit any particular comment; perhaps the most amusing part of it was our 'lark' home across the country, when myself, Fremantle, and other *attachés* of the English Embassy, led some half dozen Frenchmen a rather stiffish line of stone walls and brooks. Among the latter was D'Orsay, who, albeit unaccustomed to go 'across country,' was always in the 'first flight,' making up by hard riding whatever he may have lacked in judgment; he afterwards lived to be an excellent sportsman and a good rider to hounds."

As became the son of his father, though scarcely fitting in the grandson of a king, D'Orsay was ever a staunch Bonapartist, feeling the full strength of the glamour of Napoleon. But the Emperor and the Empire vanished in cannon smoke; the Bourbons occupied rather uncomfortably the throne of France, and D'Orsay, much against the grain, entered the King's *garde-du-corps*. But so ardent was his devotion to Bonapartism, that when the new monarch made his state entry into his capital, the lad refused to be a witness of his triumph, would not add his voice to the general acclamation, and indulged in the luxury of tears in a back room.

His inherited instincts and his education gave him a taste for all the fine arts of life, and Nature endowed him with exceptionally good looks. An upstanding man he became, over six feet in stature; broad-shouldered and slim-waisted; hands and feet of unusual beauty; long, curly, dark chestnut hair; forehead high and wide; lips rather full; eyes large, and light hazel in colour. Though there was something almost femininely soft about his beauty he was nowise effeminate; in fact, he was a superb athlete, and highly skilled in almost every form of manly exercise and sport. We are told that he was a wit; a capital companion at all hours of the day and night; a quite capable amateur artist, who, as is the way of amateurs, received assistance from his professional friends, and—which is unusual at any rate among amateurs in art if not in sport—took pay for his work. In short, he was a very highly-gifted and accomplished young man.

D'Orsay was born in an age when the atmosphere was electric with adventure; when nobodies rapidly became somebodies, and many who had been brought up to consider themselves very considerable somebodies were shocked at being told that in truth they were nobodies, or at best but the thin shadows of great names. It was an age when even the discomforts of a throne were not an unreasonable aspiration for the most humbly born. With his beauty of face and figure, fascinating manners and high family influence, young D'Orsay must have looked upon the world as a fine fat oyster which he could easily open and from which he could pluck the pearl of success. He possessed a winning tongue that would have made him a great diplomat; the daring and skill at arms that would have stood him in good stead as a soldier of fortune ; a power of raising money in most desperate straits that would have rendered him an unrivalled minister of finance. From all these roads to distinction he turned aside ; he was born to a greater fate ; his was the genius of a complete dandy. Few great men have been able so justly to appraise their abilities; still fewer to attain so surely their ambition.

During his short service in the army he proved himself a good officer and made himself popular with his men by looking to their comfort and welfare. Naturally he assumed the lead in all the gaieties of the garrison town, the assemblies, the dances, the dinners, the promenadings, but how petty they must have been to him, and how often he must have wistfully repined for Paris. He could not play his great part on so circumscribed a stage and with so poor a company of players. But if he could not find sufficient social sport, he could fight, and did. On one occasion the cause of the duel was noteworthy. It happened only a few days after he had joined his regiment that at mess one of his brother officers made use of an offensive expression in connection with the name of the Blessed Virgin. D'Orsay, as became a devout Catholic gentleman, expostulated. The offence was offensively repeated, upon which D'Orsay, evidently feeling that a verbal retort would not suffice to meet the gravity of the occasion, threw a plateful of spinach in the face of the transgressor. Thereupon a challenge and a duel fought that evening upon the town ramparts.

With what result? Alas, as so often upon important affairs, history holds her tongue. The historic muse is an arrant jade, who chatters unceasingly upon matters of no moment, and is silent upon points concerning which we thirst for information. That is one of the ways of women.

On the occasion of a later duel, D'Orsay remarked to his second before the encounter :—

"You know, my dear friend, I am not on a par with my antagonist; he is a very ugly fellow, and if I wound him in the face he won't look much the worse for it; but on my side it ought to be agreed that he should not aim higher than my chest, for if my face should be spoiled *ce serait vraiment dommage.*"

A dandy with a damaged nose or deprived of one eye would be a figure of fun.

From remote ancestors D'Orsay inherited the spirit of chivalry, setting woman upon a lofty pedestal and then asking her to step down and make love to him. He was always ready to rescue a woman—not merely a beauty—in distress, of which a fine example is an event which befell while he was living out of barracks in apartments, which were kept by a widow, who had one son and two daughters. The son was a muscular young man of robust temper, and attracted—or rather distracted—one day by the sounds of tumult rising from below, D'Orsay hastened downstairs to find this youth employed in bullying his mother. The blood of D'Orsay was inflamed; the dandy thrashed the lout, promising still heavier punishment should occasion arise.

II

SHE

EVEN the ardent D'Orsay, while he was thus preparing himself for his life-work and laying the foundation upon which he was to raise so superb a fame, could not in the hours of his highest inspiration have dreamed that Fate was deciding his future in the person of a lovely Irish peeress, the cynosure of London society. Such, in fact, was the case. In the year 1821 he visited England and met with the woman who held his fortunes in her beautiful arms.

Margaret, or as she preferred to be called, and when a lady expresses a preference that should suffice, Marguerite Power was born at Knockbrit, near Clonmel, on the 1st of September 1789, being the third of the six children of Edmund Power, a Tipperary squireen of extravagant propensities and of a violent temper and overbearing tyranny which rendered him a curse to his family. He was a good-looking, swaggering fellow, with a showy air, fond of fine clothes, fine wine, fine horses, and various other fine things, indulgence in which his income did not justify. His were a handsome set of children : the two sons, Michael and Robert, attained the army rank of captain ; Marguerite—and two sisters, Ellen and Mary Anne ; the eldest child died young. Of a quieter disposition than her brothers and sisters, Marguerite as a child was rather weak and ailing, sensitive and reflective. At that time of her life her beauty was not obvious; indeed few then seem to have realised that there was any charm in the soft, round, clear-complexioned face, with its pretty dimples and large, grey eyes shielded by long, drooping lashes. Her voice was low, soft, caressing; her movements unstudiedly graceful. A dreamy child, who lived in fancy-land; strange to her comrades, who awarded her little else than ridicule and misunderstanding.

In 1796 the Powers moved into Clonmel, which change was welcomed by all the family save Marguerite, who looked forward to it with a foreboding that was only too fully fulfilled. In some ways this move wrought good for the child, awakening her to the realities of life, arousing an interest in the ways and doings of the society into which she was thrown; her health improved, and with it her spirits, both mental and physical.

Her father's pecuniary affairs now went rapidly from worse to much worse, and his adventures in politics rendered him highly unpopular with those of his own rank and station. He was a hospitable soul in his reckless, feckless way while he had a penny to spend, and often when he had not, filling his house with guests, many of whom were military men, and emptying his purse.

When only fifteen years old Marguerite began to go out into society, as did her sister Ellen, her junior by more than a year. The rackety society of a small, Irish garrison town can scarcely have been wholesome for a young, impressionable girl, and to its influence may be attributed the develop-

ment in Lady Blessington's character of many evil
traits which healthful surroundings and judicious
restraint might have held in check. The two
graceful, pretty children quickly became popular.

Among the familiar guests at the father's
house in 1804 were two officers of the 47th
Regiment of Foot, then stationed in Clonmel,
Captain Murray and Captain Maurice St Leger
Farmer, the latter a man of considerable means,
which was quite sufficient in Power's eyes to
make him an excellent match for Marguerite, to
whom both the officers were paying attention.
Though Farmer was young, good - looking,
plausible, the child's fancy turned toward his
rival, who wooed and would have won her had
a fair field been granted him. He warned
Marguerite that Farmer had proposed for her
hand to her father, the news coming to her
entirely unexpected, most unwelcome, difficult to
credit. But in a few days the information was
proved conclusively to be true, her father in-
forming her that Farmer had approached him in
the matter, and that he had given his cordial
consent to his addresses. Marguerite was
dismayed, at first stunned. She fully understood the strong inducements which the prospect
of her marriage with Farmer had for a man in
her father's embarrassed circumstances, and knew
only too well from bitter experience how intoler-
ant he was of opposition to any of his whims or
wishes, and how little weight the desires of any of
his children bore with him. From her mother she
expected some sympathy, but to her dismay re-

ceived scant consideration for her plea to be spared, her unwillingness being counted the romantic notion of a child too young to be able to form a right judgment of the advantages offered by this proposed marriage. Tears and entreaties availed not, and the child was married to a man whom she held in detestation and in fear.

That the outcome of this inhuman mating was misery is not wonderful; there was not in it any possibility of happiness. The one a very turbulent man who, though not actually insane, was subject to paroxysms of rage that were terrifying; the other a child not yet sixteen years of age, with a nature very sensitive, impressionable, and with that intense longing for love, sympathy and understanding so common among Irish women and men. We know what Marguerite Power did become; it is idle to conjecture what she might have been had not this abominable marriage been thrust upon her.

From her own account, which seems trustworthy, we learn that her husband treated his child-wife outrageously, not even refraining from physical violence. Her arms were meanly pinched till black and blue; her face struck. When he went abroad, not infrequently he would lock her into her room, sometimes leaving her for hours without nourishment.

Three months after their marriage Farmer was ordered to rejoin his regiment at Kildare, and his wife took the bold, determined step of refusing to go with him. A separation being arranged, Marguerite returned to her father's house, where she received a welcome the reverse of kind. Home was made utterly distasteful to her, and sympathy—

the one thing that might have saved her—was withheld by her father and mother. It was given to her from an alien quarter, and she accepted the "protection" offered to her by Captain Thomas Jenkins of the 11th Light Dragoons, a Hampshire man of considerable property. The astonishing thing is that she acted on the advice given to her by Major, afterwards Sir Edward Blakeney, her supposed friend and well-wisher. Meanwhile Farmer had gone out to India in the East India Company's service.

When Lord Mountjoy, better known as Lord Blessington, first met with the fascinating Marguerite is not quite clear, but in all probability he did so in or about 1804, when serving as Lieutenant-Colonel of the Tyrone Militia when stationed at Clonmel.

Blessington plays a considerable and mysterious part in the life of D'Orsay. His father, the Right Hon. Luke Gardiner, was born in the year 1745, and did his duty by his country and possibly by his conscience in various ways. He married the daughter of a Scotch baronet, who presented him with several daughters and two sons, one of these latter dying in infancy, the other, Charles John, entering the world on July 19, 1782. He was educated at Eton and at Christ Church, Oxford, and succeeded his father in the titles of Viscount and Baron Mountjoy in 1798. In 1809 he was elected, upon what qualifications it is difficult to imagine, a representative peer of Ireland, and in 1816 was created Earl of Blessington. In this same year we hear of his visiting Marguerite in Manchester Square, London.

LADY BLESSINGTON

(*From a Water-Colour Drawing by A. E. Chalon, R.A.*)

[TO FACE PAGE 28

As far as wealth was concerned Blessington certainly was granted a fine start in life, but it may
well be doubted if he were well endowed or endowed
at all with brains of any value, though we are informed by a lukewarm but still possibly too warm
biographer that he was "possessed of some talents."
Let us hope so ; but if so, he contrived with great
skill to bury them. We do hear of him speaking
in the House of Lords in support of a motion for
a vote of thanks to Lord Wellington, and as a
specimen of his eloquence we quote :—

"No general was better skilled in war, none
more enlightened than Lord Viscount Wellington.
The choice of a position at Talavera reflected lustre
on his talents ; the victory was as brilliant and as
glorious as any on record. It was entitled to the
unanimous approbation of their lordships, and the
eternal gratitude of Spain and of this country."

It is also recorded that his lordship spoke but
seldom, which may be counted to him for a saving
grace.

He seems to have been more at home in the
green-room than in the neighbourhood of the
woolsack. He was very wealthy, very prodigal,
vastly futile. Byron relates of him :—"Mountjoy . . . seems very good-natured, but is much
tamed since I recollect him in all the glory
of gems and snuff-boxes, and uniforms and
theatricals, sitting to Strolling, the painter, to be
depicted as one of the heroes of Agincourt."

In another portrait he appears as Achilles,
dragging at his chariot-tail the body of Hector, a
friend "sitting" for the corpse. Physically he was

vigorous ; a tall, bright-looking man ; a capital companion, when only good spirits and a strong head unadorned with brain-sauce were called for.

In 1808, or 1809, Blessington—then mere Mountjoy—fell in with a very charming and well-favoured lady named Brown, but there were "some difficulties in the way of the resolution he had formed of marrying the lady, but the obstacles were removed." The obstacle was the mere trifle of her already being possessed of if not blessed with a husband, Major Brown, who, however, discreetly and considerately departed this life in 1812, thus enabling Blessington to legalise the lady's position in his establishment, the outcome of his connection with her having already been that she had borne him two children, Charles John and Emilie Rosalie. This lady subsequently presented him with two further pledges of her fond affection, Lady Harriet Anne Frances Gardiner, born in 1812, and Luke Wellington, afterwards by courtesy Viscount Mountjoy, born in 1814. On the 9th of September of this same year she died.

Blessington was gifted with a penchant for losing his heart to ladies possessed of "obstacles" in the way of his complete happiness, for, as has been noted, he was in 1816 *vice* Jenkins befriending Marguerite Farmer. Again fortune smiled on his desires, Farmer dying of injuries received during a drunken frolic in October 1817. On 16th February of the following year his widow became Lady Blessington, she then being in her twenty-ninth, he in his thirty-seventh, year.

Her beauty had ripened into something near

akin to perfection, a bright and radiant spirit
shining through the physical tenement. Hers
was a vivid, compelling loveliness, supported by
a vivacious good humour. Her figure, though
somewhat tending toward over-fullness, was
moulded on exquisite lines and of almost perfect
proportions; her movements still graceful and
free, as they had been when she was a child;
her face—now pensively lovely, now suddenly
illuminated with a joyous fancy that first expressed itself in her sparkling eyes; pouting lips;
a clear, sweet-toned voice; the merriest of merry
laughs. In sober truth, a very fascinating woman.

This wild Irish girl, for certainly she had been a
leetle wild, had climbed high up the social ladder.
Without any other fortune than her face and her
winsome ways she had won a peer for her lord,
who if not highly endowed with ability possessed
fortune in abundance, which for the purposes of
her contentment was even more to be desired.

The fond pair paid a visit to my lord's estate
in County Tyrone, and also to Dublin, where the
appearance of my lady created no small stir.
From the first day of their marriage Blessington
exhibited a sumptuous extravagance in providing luxuries for Lady Blessington, who herself
records:—"The only complaint I ever have to
make of his taste, is its too great splendour; a
proof of which he gave me when I went to
Mountjoy Forest on my marriage, and found my
private sitting-room hung with crimson Genoa
silk velvet, trimmed with gold bullion fringe, and
all the furniture of equal richness—a richness that

was only suited to a state-room in a palace," or to any other room seldom used or seen.

The wilds of Ireland, however, were not a fitting stage for one so ambitious to charm as was Lady Blessington, so after a short sojourn in Tyrone she and her husband returned to London, where they took up their residence at 10 St James' Square, a house that had been dignified by the occupancy of Chatham and was to be by that of Gladstone.

Lady Blessington was as blest as was to be the Duke of Leeds' bride, of whom the rhyme ran :—

> " She shall have all that's fine and fair,
>   And the best of silk and satin shall wear ;
>   And ride in a coach to take the air,
>   And have a house in St James' Square."

The mansion was fitted and furnished in a style that only great wealth could afford or ill taste admire.

Lady Blessington with her " gorgeous charms " set the one-half of London society raving about her beauty and her extravagance ; the other half avoided the company of a lady with so speckled a past.

There were at that time two great *salons* in London : the one at Holland House to which wit, beauty and respectability resorted ; the second being at Lady Blessington's house, to which only wit and beauty were attracted. Among the constant visitors to the latter may be named Canning, Castlereagh, who lived a few doors off ; Brougham, Jekyll, Rogers, Moore,

Kemble, Mathews the elder, Lawrence, Wilkie. Moore records a visit paid by him in May 1822, accompanied by Washington Irving. He speaks of Lady Blessington as growing "very absurd."

"I have felt very melancholy and ill all this day," she said.

"Why is that?" Moore asked, doubtless with becoming sympathy in his voice and manner.

"Don't you know?"

"No."

"It is the anniversary of my poor Napoleon's death."

Joseph Jekyll, who was well known in society as a wit and teller of good stories and to his family as a writer of capital letters, was born in 1754, dying in 1837. It is quite startling to find him writing casually in 1829 of having talked with "Dr" Goldsmith; how close this brings long past times; there are those alive who met D'Orsay, who in turn knew Jekyll, who talked with Goldsmith. Jerdan speaks of Jekyll as having "a somewhat Voltaire-like countenance, and a flexible person and agreeable voice."

He was a great hand at dining-out, though it distressed him to meet other old folk, whom he unkindly dubbed "Methusalems."

In November 1821, he writes : "London still dreary enough; but I have dinners with judges and lawyers — nay, yesterday with the divine bit of blue, Lady Blessington and her comical Earl. I made love and Mathews (the elder) was invited to make faces."

c

And in the February of the succeeding year, he records another visit to St James' Square :—

"London is by no means yet a desert. Lately we had a grand dinner at Lord Blessington's, who has transmogrified Sir T. Heathcote's ground floor into a vast apartment, and bedizened it with black and gold like an enormous coffin. We had the Speaker, Lord Thanet, Sir T. Lawrence . . . ." etc.

In June 1822 we find Blessington in quite unexpected company and engaged upon matters that would scarcely have seemed likely to appeal to him. On the first of that month a meeting was held of the British and Foreign Philanthropic Society, of which the object was "to carry into effect measures for the permanent relief of the labouring classes, by communities for mutual interest and co-operation, in which, by means of education, example and employment, they will be gradually withdrawn from the evils induced by ignorance, bad habits, poverty and want of employment." Robert Owen was the moving spirit of the Society, and the membership was highly distinguished, including among other unforgotten names those of Brougham, John Galt and Sir James Graham. At a meeting at Freemasons' Hall, Blessington was entrusted with the reading of a report by the committee, in which it was recommended that communities should be established on Owen's wildly visionary plan. The meeting was enthusiastic, much money was promised, and—history does not record anything further of the Society.

III

In France—a youthful son of Mars ; in England —Venus at her zenith.

D'Orsay paid his first visit to London in 1821, as the guest of the Duc de Guiche, to whom his sister, Ida, was married. De Guiche, son of the Duc de Grammont, had been one of the many "emigrants" of high family who had sought and had found in England shelter from the tempest of the Revolution, and had shown his gratitude for hospitality received by serving in the 10th Hussars during the Peninsular War.

Landor, writing some twenty years later, says : " The Duc de Guiche is the handsomest man I ever saw. What poor animals other men seem in the presence of him and D'Orsay. He is also full of fun, of anecdote, of spirit and of information."

Gronow describes him as speaking English perfectly, and as "quiet in manner, and a most chivalrous, high-minded and honourable man. His complexion was very dark, with crisp black hair curling close to his small, well - shaped head. His features were regular and somewhat aquiline ; his eyes, large, dark and beautiful ; and his manner, voice, and smile were considered by the fair sex to be perfectly irresistible " ; concluding, "the most perfect gentleman I ever met with in any country."

So we may take it that D'Orsay did not feel that he was visiting a land with which he had not any tie of sympathy.

His sister Ida was a year older than himself, or, to put it more gallantly, a year less young, and bore to him a strong likeness in appearance but not in disposition—fortunately for her husband. Her good looks were supported by good sense.

William Archer Shee describes the Duchesse de Guiche as "a blonde, with blue eyes, fair hair, a majestic figure, an exquisite complexion . . ."

In those golden days the adornment of a handsome person with ultra-fashionable clothes did not qualify a man as a dandy. Much more was demanded. It was, therefore, no small feather in D'Orsay's cap that he came to London an unknown young man, was seen, and by his very rivals at once acknowledged as a conqueror. His youth, his handsome face, his debonairness, his wit, were irresistible. Everywhere, even at Holland House, he made a good impression. He rode in Hyde Park perfectly "turned out," the admired of those who were accustomed to receive, not to give, admiration. At a ball at the French Embassy where all the lights of fashionable society shone in a brilliant galaxy, he was a centre of attraction "with his usual escort of dandies."

At the Blessingtons' he was a favoured guest. Gronow, discreetly naming no names, writes of the "unfortunate circumstances which entangled the Count as with a fatal web from early youth";

St James's Square in 1812

[To face page 26

surely a poorly prosaic way of describing the romantic love of a young man for a beautiful woman only twelve years his senior?

As Grantley Berkeley puts it: "The young Count made a most favourable impression where-ever he appeared; but nowhere did it pierce so deep or so lasting as in the heart of his charming hostess of the magnificent *conversaziones, soirées,* dinners, balls, breakfasts and suppers, that followed each other in rapid succession in that brilliant mansion in St James' Square."

Grantley Berkeley also says: "At his first visit to England, he was pre-eminently hand-some; and, as he dressed fashionably, was thoroughly accomplished, and gifted with superior intelligence, he became a favourite with both sexes. He had the reputation of being a lady-killer . . . and his pure classical features, his accomplishments, and irreproachable get-up, were sure to be the centre of attraction, whether in the Park or dining-room."

Then of later times: "He used to ride pretty well to hounds, and joined the hunting men at Melton; but his style was rather that of the riding-school than of the hunting-field. . . .

"In dress he was more to the front; indeed, the name of D'Orsay was attached by tailors to any kind of raiment, till Vestris tried to turn the Count into ridicule. Application was made to his tailor for a coat made exactly after the Count's pattern. The man sent notice of it to his patron, asking whether he should supply the order, and the answer being in the affirmative, the garment was made and sent home. No doubt D'Orsay imagined that some enthusiastic admirer had in this way sought to testify his appreciation ; but, on going to the Olympic Theatre to witness a new piece, he had the gratification of seeing his coat worn by Liston as a burlesque of himself." This "take-off" did not please D'Orsay, who withdrew his patronage from the Olympic and appeared no more in the green-room which he had been wont to frequent. But the town, which had caught wind of the joke, was delighted, and roared with merriment.

Is there a hidden reference to D'Orsay's visit and possibly even to Lady Blessington in these lines from " Don Juan " ?

"No marvel then he was a favourite ;
  A full-grown Cupid, very much admired ;
A little spoilt, but by no means so quite ;
  At least he kept his vanity retired.
Such was his tact, he could alike delight
  The chaste, and those who are not so much inspired.
The Duchess of Fitz-Fulke, who loved ' tracasserie,'
  Began to treat him with some small ' agacerie.'

" She was a fine and somewhat full-blown blonde,
  Desirable, distinguished, celebrated
For several winters in the grand grand monde.
  I'd rather not say what might be related
Of her exploits, for this were ticklish ground. . . . '

At a later date we find Byron describing the Count to Tom Moore as one " who has all the air of a cupidon déchaîné, and is one of the few specimens I have ever seen of our ideal of a Frenchman before the Revolution."

Also at that later date (1823), when he met D'Orsay at Genoa with the Blessingtons, Byron was lent by Blessington a journal which the Count had written during this first visit of his to London. When returning it, he writes, on 5th April :—

" MY DEAR LORD,—How is your gout ? or rather how are you ? I return the Count d'Orsay's journal, which is a very extraordinary production, and of a most melancholy truth in all that regards high life in England. I know, or knew personally, most of the personages and societies which he describes ; and after reading his remarks, have the sensation fresh upon me as if I had seen them yesterday. I would, however, plead in behalf of some few exceptions, which I will mention by and bye. The most singular thing is, *how* he should have penetrated *not* the *facts*, but the *mystery* of English *ennui*. at two-and-twenty.* I was about the same age when I made the same discovery, in almost precisely the same circles—for there is scarcely a person whom I did not see nightly or daily, and was acquainted more or less intimately with most of them—but I never could have discovered it so well, *Il faut être Français* to effect this. But he ought also to have seen the country during the hunting season, with ' a select party of distinguished guests,' as the papers term it. He ought to have seen the gentlemen after dinner (on the hunting days), and the soirée ensuing thereupon—and the women looking as if they had hunted, or rather been hunted ; and I could have wished that he had been at a dinner in town, which I recollect at Lord

* D'Orsay was but twenty at the time of his first appearance in London.

Cowper's—small, but select, and composed of the most amusing people. . . . Altogether, your friend's journal is a very formidable production. Alas! our dearly-beloved countrymen have only discovered that they are tired, and not that they are tiresome; and I suspect that the communication of the latter unpleasant verity will not be better received than truths usually are. I have read the whole with great attention and instruction—I am too good a patriot to say *pleasure*—at least I won't say so, whatever I may think. . . . I beg that you will thank the young philosopher. . . ."

A few days later—how pleasing it is to find one great writer openly admiring another and a younger!—Byron writes to D'Orsay himself:—

"My Dear Count d'Orsay (if you will permit me to address you so familiarly)—you should be content with writing in your own language, like Grammont, and succeeding in London as nobody has succeeded since the days of Charles the Second, and the records of Antonio Hamilton, without deviating into our barbarous language — which you understand and write, however, much better than it deserves. 'My approbation,' as you are pleased to term it, was very sincere, but perhaps not very impartial; for, though I love my country, I do not love my countrymen—at least, such as they now are. And besides the seduction of talent and wit in your work, I fear that to me there was the attraction of vengeance. I have *seen* and *felt* much of what you have described so well . . .

the portraits are so like that I cannot but admire
the painter no less than his performance. But
I am sorry for you ; for if you are so well acquainted with life at your age, what will become
of you when the illusion is still more dissipated ? "

It is much to be regretted that this vivacious
journal has never seen the light of publicity ;
there must have been considerable interest in a
piece of writing which so greatly attracted and
excited the admiration of Byron ; but even more
important, its pages would have helped to the
understanding of D'Orsay and have brought us
closer to him in these his young days. Further,
a view of English society at that date by a
candid Frenchman must have been highly entertaining. D'Orsay, apparently having changed
his mind with regard to persons and things, or
fearing that the publication of so scathing an
indictment might savour of ingratitude toward
those who had entertained him with kindness,
consigned to the flames this " very formidable production " of his ebullient days of youth. Another
account is that it was destroyed by his sister.

In 1822 D'Orsay tore himself away from the
enchantments of London and bade farewell to
the beautiful enchantress of St James' Square.

IV

In November 1822, D'Orsay again met Lady Blessington.

Apparently it was at Blessington's express desire that the house in St James' Square was shut up; its glories were dimmed with holland sheetings; the mirrors that had reflected so much of youth and love and beauty were covered; the windows that had so often shone with hospitable lights were shuttered and barred. On 25th August a start was made on a Continental tour. Blessington was satiated with the turmoil of pleasures that London afforded, satiety held him in its bitter grasp. He had exhausted the wild joys of the life of a man about town; he was still thirsty for enjoyment, but the accustomed draughts no longer quenched his thirst. It was bluntly said by one that he was "prematurely impaired in mental energies." Whether that were or were not the case, judging by his conduct during the remainder of his life he must have lost all sense of honour and of social decency.

To the party of two a third member was added in the person of Lady Blessington's youngest sister, Mary Anne Power, a woman pretty in a less full-blown style than her sister, which caused her to be likened to a primrose set beside a peach blossom. Lady Blessington, who for herself preferred Marguerite to Margaret, renamed her sister Marianne. In 1831 Marianne married the Comte de St Marsault, but the union was disastrously unhappy. The Comte was an aged gentleman of ancient lineage, and his wintriness blighted the poor primrose.

The tourists travelled in great style by Dover, Calais, Rouen, St Germain-en-Laye, and so on to Paris. At St Germain Lady Blessington's thoughts naturally turned toward the unhallowed fortunes of the La Pompadour and du Barry. She pondered over the curious fact that decency does in social estimation take from vice half its sting, and over the coarseness displayed by Louis XV. in choosing his mistresses from outside the ranks of the ladies of his Court, rendering the refinement of Louis XIV. virtuous by contrast. She very truly says—and what better judgé could we wish for upon such a point than she?—" A true morality would be disposed to consider the courtly splendour attached to the loves of Louis XIV. as the more demoralising example of the two, from being the less disgusting."

In Paris they halted for some days, meeting among other distinguished men with the volatile Tom Moore, whom Lady Blessington hits off with the singular felicity and simplicity of language that distinguishes her literary style. She found him to be of "a happy temperament, that conveys the idea of having never lived out of sunshine, and his conversation reminds one of the evolutions of some bird of gorgeous plumage, each varied hue of which becomes visible as he carelessly sports in the air."

Lady Blessington's birthday, September 1st, was celebrated during this visit to Paris, and she tells us that after a woman has passed the age of thirty the recurrence of birthdays is not a matter for congratulation, concluding with the striking remark: "Youth is like health, we never value the possession of either until they have begun to decline."

From Paris they went on to Switzerland. Their travelling equipage not unnaturally aroused the wonderment of the onlookers who assembled to witness their departure. Travelling carriages and a baggage wagon—a *fourgon*—piled high with imperials and packages of all sizes; the courier, as important in his mien as a commander of an army corps, bustling here, bustling there; lady's maid busily packing; valets and footmen staggering and grumbling under heavy trunks. Lady Blessington heard a Frenchman under her window exclaim: "How strange those English are! One would suppose that instead of a single family, a regiment at least were about to move!"

Move at last the regiment did, though not without dire struggling. They are off! Amid a tornado of expostulations and exhortations; off along the straight, dusty roads to Switzerland. Further we need not accompany them. For us the centre of interest lies at Valence, on the Rhone, where D'Orsay was with his regiment under orders to march with the Duc d'Angoulême over the Pyrenees. But to war's alarms D'Orsay was now deaf. He heard above the din of trumpet and of drum the call of love, and answered to it. He resigned his commission. For at the hotel where was established the regimental mess the Blessingtons arrived on November 15th; the romance of love eclipsed the romance of war.

From this point onward there can be little doubt as to D'Orsay's position as regards Lady Blessington, but as concerns Blessington everything grows more and more extraordinary, and more and more discreditable to the blind or easy-going husband. Charles Greville says that Blessington was really fond of the fascinating young Frenchman. He looked on him as a charming, happy comrade. It was at his persuasion that D'Orsay threw up his commission, Blessington making "a formal promise to the Count's family that he should be provided for." At any rate such provision was made later on. Greville adds that D'Orsay's early connection with Lady Blessington was a mystery; certainly it was so as far as concerns the behaviour of the lady's husband. D'Orsay's conduct is explicable in two ways: either infatuation for a beautiful woman blinded him to his real interests and rendered him unable to count the cost of the course he now decided to pursue, or he preferred to that of the soldier the *dolce far niente* life of a dependent loafer. Possibly, however, the two motives mingled.

The company was now complete and each member of it apparently entirely content. They moved on to Orange, and on November 20th reached Avignon, at which place a considerable stay was made. Avignon! Petrarch and Laura! Lady Blessington and Count d'Orsay! Glory almost overwhelming for any one town. The battlemented walls; the ancient bridge; the swift stream of the Rhone; the storied palace of the Pope; and the famous fountain of Vaucluse, given to fame by Petrarch; a proper setting for the love of Alfred and of Marguerite.

They stayed at the *Hôtel de l'Europe*, a comfortable hostelry, an inn which many years before had been the scene of an incident which formed the groundwork of the comedy of *The Deaf Lover*. It was now the scene of incidents which might well have supplied the materials for a comedy of *The Blind Husband: or, There are None so Short-sighted as those who Won't See!*"

There was gaiety and society at Avignon, much social coming and going, dinners, dances, receptions and routs. The Duc and Duchesse de Caderousse Grammont, who resided in a château close to the town, were doubtless delighted to see their young connection the Count, and to welcome his friends. Lady Blessington enjoyed herself immensely, and it is interesting to know that her refined taste was charmed by the decorum of French dancing :—

"The waltz in France," she writes, "loses its objectionable familiarity by the manner in which it is performed. The gentleman does not clasp his fair partner round the waist with a freedom repugnant to the modesty and destructive to the *ceinture* of the lady ; but so arranges it, that he assists her movements, without incommoding her delicacy or her drapery.   In short, they manage these matters better in France than with us ;* and though no advocate for this exotic dance, I must admit that, executed as I have seen it, it could not offend the most fastidious eye."

Lady Blessington was, as we know, an authority upon "objectionable familiarity."   What would this fastidious dame have thought of the shocking indelicacy of modern ball-room romps ?   Would "kitchen" Lancers have appealed favourably to her ?   Would her approbation have honoured the graceful cake-walk ?   But we must not linger over such nice inquiries ; we must not lose ourselves in the maze of might-have-beens, but must move on to fact, Southward ho !   To Italy, the land of Love and Olives.

* *Cf.* Sterne, *A Sentimental Journey*, ch. i. l. i.

V

GENOA was reached on the last day of March
1823, and Lady Blessington, as also doubtless
D'Orsay, because of the sweet sympathy between
two hearts that beat as one, was enraptured with
the beautiful situation of the town, in her Journal
breaking forth into descriptive matter which must
be the envy of every conscientious journalist.
Their entrance was made by night, and they
found lodging at the *Alberga del la Villa*, a
house situated upon the sea front, bedecked with
marble balconies and the rooms adorned with a
plenitude of gilding that brought comfort to the
simple heart of Lady Blessington. But it was
not by matters so material as its beauties or the
comforts of its inns that her soul was really
touched. To be in Genoa was to be in the same
place as Byron, of whom the very morrow might
bring the sight. The only fly in the honey
was that the poet might still be fat, as, alack,
Tom Moore had reported him to be when at
Venice. An imperfect peer is sad enough ; but
an obese poet—Oh, fie !

On April first, auspicious date, the fair
inspirer of poems met with the writer of them,
the vision being not entrancing but disappointing
to the eager lady. What it was to the poet we

do not know, though there are, indeed, quite firm
grounds for surmising that Byron was not
entirely pleased by the invasion of the privacy
which he so jealously guarded, by the intrusion
upon his retirement of the Blessingtons even
when accompanied by D'Orsay.

Ingenuity was practised in order to secure
admission. The day selected for the drive out to
Albano was rainy, a circumstance which it was
calculated would compel even the most cur-
mudgeonly of poets to offer hospitality and
shelter. The event proved the soundness of the
calculation. The carriage drew up to the gates
of the *Casa Saluzzo;* the two gentlemen alighted,
sent in their names, were admitted, were cordially
welcomed. Outside in the downpour sat the two
pretty ladies. We know not what emotion, if
any, agitated Marianne Power; but who can
doubt that painful anxiety and doubt fluttered in
the bosom of her sister? Would Byron, or would
Byron not? To be admitted or not to be
admitted? Of what count were all the charms
of Genoa, what weighed all the joys of illicit love,
if she could not gain admission to the presence of
the poet whose conversation—and her own—she
was destined to record?

Slowly the minutes passed. Then at last
came relief. Byron had learned that the ladies
were at his gates; breathless, hatless, he ran
out.

"You must have thought me," he gasped,
"quite as ill-bred and *sauvage* as fame reports in
having permitted your ladyship to remain a

D

quarter of an hour at my door : but my old friend
Lord Blessington is to blame, for I only heard a
minute ago that it was so highly honoured. I
shall not think you do not pardon (*sic*) this
apparent rudeness, unless you enter my abode—
which I entreat you will do."

So the lady reports his speech, the which is
precisely the manner in which Byron would have
expressed himself—more or less.

Lady Blessington was quite easily mollified,
granting the pardon so gracefully sought, accepting his assisting hand, and, crossing the courtyard,
passed into the vestibule. Before them bowed
the uniformed *chasseur* and other obsequious attendants, all showing in their faces the surprise
they felt at their master displaying so much
cordiality in his reception of the visitors.

The whole account in her Journal gives
promise of the eminence to which Lady Blessington afterward attained as a writer of fiction.

Lady Blessington was disappointed in Byron
as Oscar Wilde was by the Atlantic and Mr
Bernard Shaw is by the world. He did not
reach the ideal she had framed of the author of
Childe Harold and *Manfred*. He was a jovial,
vivacious, even flippant man of the world. His
brow should have been gloomy with sardonic
melancholy, and his eyes shadowed by a hidden
grief which not even love or the loveliness of
Lady Blessington could assuage. But, alas, for
the evanescence of ideals!

Of this meeting we also have Byron's version.
He writes to Moore :—

LORD BYRON

(*By D'Orsay*)

[TO FACE PAGE 50

"Miladi seems highly literary, to which and your honour's acquaintance with the family, I attribute the pleasure of having seen them. She is also very pretty, even in a morning,—a species of beauty on which the sun of Italy does not shine so frequently as the chandelier. Certainly English women wear better than their Continental neighbours of the same sex."

Accounts differ as to whether Byron did or did not extend familiar friendship to the Blessingtons; it really does not much matter—if at all. But it is of importance to know that he fell before the charms of the irresistible D'Orsay. Indeed so blinded was he with admiration that he not only discovered the young Frenchman to be "clever, original, unpretending," but also stated that "he affected to be nothing that he was not." We fancy D'Orsay would not have counted an accusation of modesty as a compliment. In such a man, properly conscious of his gifts, modesty can only be a mockery. Mock modesty is to the true what mock is to real turtle—an insolent imitation. D'Orsay was above all things candid, when there existed no valid reason for being otherwise.

While at Genoa D'Orsay drew Byron's portrait, which afterward formed the frontispiece to Lady Blessington's *Conversations of Lord Byron*, which is quite the most realistic and skilful of her ladyship's works of fiction. The poet gave the painter a ring, a souvenir not to be worn for it was too large. It was made of lava, "and so far adapted to the fire of his years and character," so Byron wrote to Lady Blessington, through whose hand he conveyed the gift, perchance deeming that by so doing he would enhance its value.

Byron's yacht, the *Bolivar*, was purchased by Blessington for £300, having cost many times that sum. The vessel was fitted in the most sumptuous manner; soft cushions, alluring couches, marble baths, every extravagance that the heart of a woman could conceive or the purse of man pay for; suitable surroundings for our modern Antony and Cleopatra.

VI

"THE Pilgrims from St James' Square" travelled onward through Florence to Rome, from which latter city they were driven in haste by the heat and the fear of malaria; so to Naples where they arrived on July 17th. It was from the hill above the *Campo Santo* that they gained their first view of the town where they were to spend so many happy hours. On the brow of the eminence the postilions pulled up the horses, so that the travellers might at their leisure survey the wonderful panorama; the towers, the steeples, the domes, the palaces, the multitude of gardens, the blue waters of the famous Bay; Vesuvius outlined against the spotless sky; from behind the Isle of Capri the sun sending up broad shafts of light; directly below them the high walls and the solemn cedars of the city of the dead.

At the hotel *Gran Bretagna*, facing the sea, they secured comfortable quarters commanding a fine view over the Bay, which enchanted Lady Blessington. But it was quickly decided that a less noisy abode was desirable, and after a prolonged house-hunting the Palazzo Belvedere at Vomero was engaged. Before they could move into it English comforts had to be superimposed upon Italian magnificence, much to the amazement of the Prince and Princess Belvedere, who

had not found their home lacking in anything
material. Blessington must have been born
with the bump of extravagance highly developed,
and Lady Blessington did not do anything to
depress it. The gardens of the *Palazzo* were
superb and delightful the views they commanded.
So in these luxurious surroundings the toil-worn
travellers settled down to contentment—though
the heat was intense.

Of the rooms we may note that the *salon*
was a spacious apartment, of which the four
corners were turned into so many independent
territories, of which one was occupied by Lady
Blessington's paper-strewn table, and another
by D'Orsay's, artistically untidy ; the others were
allotted to Marianne Power and to young Charles
Mathews. Blessington had his own private
sanctum, in which he busied himself with literary
and artistic enterprises, all of which were still-
born, except a novel, concerning which Jekyll
gives this advice : " Don't read Lord Blessington's
Reginald de Vavasour . . . duller than death."

How charming a morning spent in that *salon*
in that charming company : the Lady of the
House, romantic and tender ; D'Orsay, debonair
and gracious ; Marianne, pretty, never in the
way, never out of it when her company was
wanted ; and gay, young Charles Mathews
intent upon his drawings. To them enter, upon
occasion fitting or otherwise, the Lord of the
House, too full of his own affairs to heed the
affair that was going on before his eyes, or
heedless of it, who can say which ; now bestow-

ing a caress upon his adoring wife, now casting a
heavy jest to his young *protégé*, the Count; now
summoning Mathews to come into his room and
discuss the plans for the superb home that he was
going to build in Ireland, but which remained a
castle in the air.

Charles James Mathews, who was born December 26th, 1803, was in his early years destined
for the Church, but his exuberant high spirits
scarcely foreshadowed success in that walk of
life. Having evinced a decided taste for archi-
tecture, he was articled to Augustus Pugin,
whose office he entered in 1819. Charles James
was a lively lad, quick of wit and ready of
tongue, a well-read young fellow, too. In
August, 1823, the elder Mathews received a
letter from Blessington, who had returned from
Italy and with whom he had long been intimately
acquainted, expressing his intention to build a
house at Mountjoy Forest and to give the
younger Mathews "an opportunity of making his
début as an architect." So off to the North of
Ireland went Charles James, and for a couple of
months lived a very jolly life with his "noble
patron." The plans for the new house were ap-
proved, but it was considered necessary to consult
Lady Blessington before any final decisions were
arrived at, and, eventually, the whole scheme
was shelved. Young Mathews was invited by
Blessington to accompany him on his return to
Italy, and—says Mathews—"on the twenty-first
of September, 1823, eyes were wiped and handkerchiefs waved, as, comfortably ensconced in the

well-laden travelling carriage, four post-horses rattled us away from St James' Square."

So it will be seen that kindly Blessington left Marguerite and Alfred to take care of each other this summer time, with Marianne to play gooseberry. Expeditions here, there and everywhere, were the order of the day; drives along the coast, or in the evening down into Naples, to the Chiaja thronged with carriages. There were many English then resident in Naples, among them Sir William Gell, whom D'Orsay once described as "Le brave Gell, protecteur-général des *humbugs*." He was evidently a bit of a "character"; a man of learning, withal, who wrote of the topography of Troy and the antiquities of Ithaca; chamberlain to the eccentric Queen Caroline, in whose favour he gave his evidence; an authority on Pompeii—and an amiable man. Mathews speaks of him as "Dear, old, kind, gay Sir William Gell, who, while wheeling himself about the room in his chair, for he was unable to walk a step without help, alternately kept his friends on the broad grin with his whimsical sallies" and talked archæological "shop"; "his hand was as big as a leg of mutton and covered with chalkstones"; nevertheless he could draw with admirable precision.

Greville tells of him, some years later, as living in "his eggshell of a house and pretty garden, which he planted himself ten years ago, and calls it the Boschetto Gellio." Moore speaks of him as "still a coxcomb, but rather amusing."

He was a man of sound humour; he could

make fun out of his own misfortunes, as in this letter written from Rome in 1824 : " I am sitting in my garden, under the shade of my own vines and figs, my dear Lady Blessington, where I have been looking at the people gathering the grapes, which are to produce six barrels of what I suspect will prove very bad wine ; and all this sounds very well, till I tell you that I am positively sitting in a wheelbarrow, which I found the only means of conveying my crazy person into the garden. Don't laugh, Miss Power."

He was not always respectful to his royal mistress, for he accuses her of being capable of saying, "O trumpery ! O Moses !"

Lady Blessington was indeed fortunate in the guides who chaperoned her on her visits to the many interesting places around Naples ; Uwins, the painter, escorted her to picture-galleries and museums ; so did Westmacott, the sculptor ; Herschel, afterward Sir John, accompanied her to the Observatory ; Sir William Gell was her cicerone at Pompeii, and to D'Orsay fell the honour of everywhere being by her side.

Pompeii inspired Lady Blessington to verse—

"Lonely city of the dead !
Body whence the soul has fled,
Leaving still upon thy face
Such a mild and pensive grace
As the lately dead display,
While yet stamped upon frail clay,
Rests the impress of the mind,
That the fragile earth refined."

The house-party was once again complete when Blessington and Mathews arrived in November.

Young Mathews fancied he had dropped into Paradise, and gives a glowing description of his environment: "The Palazzo Belvedere, situated about a mile and a half from the town on the heights of Vomero, overlooking the city, and the beautiful turquoise-coloured bay dotted with latine sails, with Vesuvius on the left, the island of Capri on the right, and the lovely coast of Sorrento stretched out in front, presented an enchanting scene. The house was the perfection of an Italian palace, with its exquisite frescoes, marble arcades, and succession of terraces one beneath the other, adorned with hanging groves of orange-trees and pomegranates, shaking their odours among festoons of vines and luxuriant creepers, affording agreeable shade from the noontide sun, made brighter by the brilliant parterres of glowing flowers, while refreshing fountains plashed in every direction among statues and vases innumerable."

Among the company Mathews found one of about his own age, with whom he struck up a firm friendship; D'Orsay was naturally a fascinating companion and exemplar for any young man of parts. Enthusiasm glows in the following description: "Count d'Orsay . . . I have no hesitation in asserting was the *beau-ideal* of manly dignity and grace. He had not yet assumed the marked peculiarities of dress and deportment which the sophistications of London life subsequently developed. He was the model of all that could be conceived of noble demeanour and youthful candour; handsome beyond all question; accomplished to the last degree; highly educated, and of great literary acquirements; with a gaiety of heart and cheerfulness of mind that spread happiness on all around him. His conversation was brilliant and engaging, as well as clever and instructive. He was moreover the best fencer, dancer, swimmer, runner, dresser; the best shot, the best horseman, the best draughtsman of his age." There are some touches of exaggeration here, but it is valuable as the impression made upon a shrewd youth of the world.

He notes, too, that D'Orsay spoke English in the prettiest manner; maybe with a touch of Marguerite's brogue.

Mathews has given us a description of the routine of life at the Palazzo Belvedere :— "In the morning we generally rise from our beds, couches, floors, or whatever we happen to have been reposing upon the night before, and those who have morning gowns or slippers put them on as soon as they are up. We then commence the ceremony of washing, which is longer or shorter in its duration, according to the taste of the persons who use it. You will be glad to know that from the moment Lady Blessington awakes she takes exactly one hour and a half to the time she makes her appearance, when we usually breakfast; this prescience is remarkably agreeable, as one can always calculate thus upon the probable time of our breakfasting; there is sometimes a difference of five or six minutes, but seldom more. This meal taking place latish in the day, I always have a premature breakfast in my own room the instant I am up, which prevents my feeling that hunger so natural to the human frame from fasting. After our collation, if it be fine we set off to see sights, walks, palaces, monasteries, views, galleries of pictures, antiquities, *and all that sort of thing;* if rainy, we set to our drawing, writing, reading, billiards, fencing, and *everything in the world.* . . . In the evening each person arranges himself (and herself) at his table and follows his own concerns till about ten o'clock, when we sometimes play whist, sometimes talk, and are always delightful! About half-past eleven we retire with our flat candlesticks in our hands. . . . At dinner Lady B. takes the head of the table, Lord B. on her left, Count d'Orsay on her right, and I at the bottom. We have generally for the first service a joint and five *entrées;* for the second, a *rôti* and five *entrées,* including sweet things. The name of our present cook is Raffelle, and a very good one when he likes."

A heated but brief quarrel between D'Orsay and Mathews gives us a glimpse of the former's hot temper. The two had become constant comrades, fencing, shooting, swimming, riding, drawing together.

Blessington had formed the habit of boring the party by insisting on their accompanying him on sailing trips aboard the *Bolivar,* his purchase from Byron, which expeditions had more than once culminated in their being becalmed for hours and overwhelmed with heat and *ennui.* One sultry morning when Blessington suggested a sail, they with one consent began to make excuses, good and bad : the ladies were afraid of the sun ; D'Orsay said a blunt "No," and Mathews was anxious to complete a sketch. To which last Lord Blessington remarked—

"As you please. I only hope you will really carry out your intention ; for even your friend Count d'Orsay says that you carry your sketch-book with you everywhere, but that you never bring back anything in it."

Possibly there was an element of truth in the criticism ; at any rate it struck home.

It was apparently a somewhat sulky party that went a-driving that afternoon ; two charming women and two ill-humoured young men. Suddenly, without any further provocation, Mathews burst out—

"I have to thank you, Count d'Orsay, for the high character you have given me to Lord Blessington, with regard to my diligence."

"Comment ?" responded D'Orsay.

"I should have been more gratified had you mentioned to me, instead of to his lordship, anything you might have—"

"Vous êtes un mauvais blagueur, par Dieu, la plus grande bête et blagueur que j'ai jamais rencontré, et la première fois que vous me parlez comme ça, je vous casserai la tête et je vous jetterai par la fenêtre."

Indubitably ill-temper, of which we know not the cause, had made the Count forget his manners; Mathews rightly kept silent, reserving the continuation of the quarrel for a future and more proper occasion, and Lady Blessington aided him by the rebuke—

"Count d'Orsay, I beg you to remember I am present, and that such language is not exactly what I should have expected before me."

But the fiery Frenchman was not to be suppressed and answered hotly.

In the evening Mathews received a note from D'Orsay, repeating the offence in almost more offensive terms. Of course, a duel was the order of the day; Mathews wrote demanding satisfaction or an apology; of which former he was promptly promised all he might desire to have. Mathews found his friend Madden willing to act as his second, but Blessington very naturally, as host of both the parties, refused to act for the Count. But Madden was a diplomatist, and despatched to D'Orsay what his principal terms a "very coolly written" letter, which called forth the following:—

"MON CHER MR MADDEN,—Je suis très loin d'être fâché que Mr Mathews vous ait choisi pour son témoin, ma seule crainte eut été qu'il en choisît un autre.

"Je suis aussi très loin d'être offensé d'un de vos avis. Lorsque j'estime quelqu'un, son opinion est toujours bien reçue.

"L'affaire, comme vous savez, est très simple dans le principe. On me fit la question si Mathews avait dessiné à Caprée; je dis que non, mais qu'il emportoit toujours ses crayons et son album pour ne rien faire—que cela étoit dommage avec ses grandes dispositions. Lord Blessington n'as pas eu le courage de lui représenter sans y mêler mon nom, et Mathews a pris la chose avec moi sur un ton si haut que j'ai été obligé de la rabaisser, après lui avoir exprimé que ce n'étoit que par intérêt pour lui que j'avois fait cette re-présentation. Il à continué sur le même ton ; je lui dis alors que la première fois qu'il prendroit un ton semblable avec moi je le jetterois hors de la voiture et lui casserois la tête. Je vous répète mot pour mot cette altercation. La seule différence que j'ai fait entre lui et un autre, c'est que je n'ai fait que dire ce que j'aurois fait certainement vis-à-vis d'un autre qui prendroit ce ton avec moi. Si j'ai accompagné mon projet d'avenir de mots offen-sants et inconvenants, j'en suis aussi fâché pour lui que pour moi, car c'est me manquer à moi-même que d'user des mots trop violents.

"Pour votre observation sur la différence des rangs, elle est inutile, car jamais je n'attache d'importance au rang qui se trouve souvent com-promis par tant de bêtes. Je juge les personnes pour ce qu'elles sont, sans m'informer qui étoient leurs ancêtres, et si mon supérieur eut employé la même manière de me rapprocher qu'a pris Mathews, j'aurois sûrement fait ce que je n'ai fait que dire à Mathews, que j'aime beaucoup trop pour le rabaisser à ses propres yeux. Il seroit ridicule à moi de ne pas avouer que j'ai tort de lui avoir dit des paroles trop fortes, mais en même temps je ne veux pas nier mes paroles, c'est-à-dire, mon projet de voiture, etc. Si

Mathews veut satisfaction, je lui donnerai tant qu'il lui plaira, tout en lui sachant bon gré de vous avoir choisi pour son témoin.

"Cette affaire est aussi désagréable pour vous que pour nous tous, mais au moins elle n'altérera pas l'amitié de votre tout dévoué,

"CTE. D'ORSAY."

Upon receipt of which letter Madden advised Mathews to shake hands, which on meeting the Count the following morning he proceeded to do, the overture of peace being cordially received.

"J'espère, mon cher Mathews," said D'Orsay, "que vous êtes satisfait. Je suis bien fâché pour ce que je vous ai dit, mais j'étais en colère et—"

To which Mathews, interrupting—

"Mon cher Comte, n'en parlons plus, je vous en prie, je l'ai tout-à-fait oublié!"

But apparently Lady Blessington had something to say upon the affair, for later on Mathews found the Count with her, in tears, and a further apology followed.

Then the storm-clouds cleared away and all again was sunshine.

Madden who played the peacemaker, was Richard Robert of that name, born in 1798, and at that time studying medicine at Naples. In after years he was author of *The United Irishmen*, and of that curious book, *The Literary Life and Correspondence of the Countess of Blessington.* Mathews writes of him as "the witty, lively Dr Madden, at that time as full of spirits as of mental acquirements."

VII

HERE stands D'Orsay, *jeune premier*, tne nero
of this comedy *à trois*, with the limelight full
upon him; supported by Marguerite, Lady
Blessington, as leading lady, of whom Landor
said to Crabb Robinson :—"She was to Lord
Blessington the most devoted wife he ever
knew," which either speaks badly for the wives
known to Walter Savage or more probably
shows that he was as blind in the matter of the
lady's virtue as he was with regard to her age,
which in 1832 he declared to be about thirty.
Probably in both cases he was judging simply by
appearances, which in women are so apt to
deceive men, particularly elderly poets.

For what part shall we consider Lord
Blessington as cast? Villain or fool? We
incline to the latter : it takes a fairly astute man
to play the villain with success ; moreover, no
man smiles and smiles and is a villain without
motive for his villainy—at least not in real life.
To complete our company we have two light
comedians, Marianne Power, pretty and ever
ready with a smile, and Mathews, always ready
to provide amusing entertainment. For stage

E   65

crowd, diplomatists, antiquarians, artists, noblemen, servants and so forth :—

Sir William Gell, whom we have met, with
pleasure ; an Hon. R. Grosvenor, whom Lady
Blessington declared "the liveliest Englishman I
have ever seen," and considered that his gaiety
sat very gracefully upon him ; queens of beauty,
too, such as the Duchess di Forli, "with hair
dark as the raven's wing, and lustrous eyes of
nearly as deep a hue, and her lips as crimson as
the flower of the pomegranate" ; the Princess
Centolla, who "might furnish a faultless model
for a Hebe, she is so fair, so youthful, and so
exquisitely beautiful" ; an Hanoverian soldier of
fortune, who came down to fight in Sicily and
captured the heart and wealth of the Princess
Bultera and her title too ; the lively, diminutive,
aged Thomas James Mathias, writer of that
pungent satire upon authors, *Pursuits of Literature*, whose denial of his being the only begetter
of it did not meet with credence.   He was a man
with peculiarities, one of which was the frequent
use of the exclamation, "God bless my soul!"
Another was his singularly accurate memory for
dates connected with the eating of any special
dish.   It was fortunate for him that motor-cars
were not of his day, for he was extremely
nervous when crossing the street.   He appears
also to have been curiously simple.   One day
while dining in a café a shower of rain came
down heavily, and Sir William Gell remarked to
Mathias that it was raining cats and dogs.   On
the instant, as luck would have it, a dog ran in

at one door and a cat at the other. "God bless my soul," said Mathias, solemnly, "so it does! so it does! Who would have believed it!"

There was Sir William Drummond, scholar and diplomatist, minister - plenipotentiary to Naples, whose brilliant conversation was a mixture of pedantry illuminated by flashes of imagination; the Archbishop of Tarentum, a typical father of the Roman Church, "his face, peculiarly handsome, is sicklied o'er with the pale hue of thought; his eyes are of the darkest brown, but soft, and full of sensibility, like those of a woman. His hair is white as snow, and contrasts well with the black silk *calotte* that crowns the top of his head. His figure is atten-uated and bowed by age, and his limbs are small and delicate . . . ;" the astronomer Piazzi, dis-coverer of the planet Ceres; General the Duc di' Rocco Romano, "the very personification of a *preux chevalier;* brave in arms, and gentle and courteous in society"; Lord Dudley, eccentric as is easily pardoned in a peer with an income of £40,000, with his unfortunate habit of expressing aloud his opinion, good or bad, of those with whom he conversed; James Milligan, the anti-quary, to whom it was mere waste of time to submit a forgery as a genuine antique; Casimir de la Vigne, who recited his unpublished 'Columbus" at the *Palazzo.*

Fine company, of which but a few have been named; a liberal education in themselves to a young man on his way through a world where the proper study of mankind is man—and woman.

In junketings and journeyings the days sped by very merrily. Blessington himself was not fond of walking and was an enemy to sightseeing of all kinds, so did not often join in the expeditions. Moreover, he was not an early riser, usually breakfasting in bed, and we cannot imagine that his company was very greatly missed; four is company, five is a crowd. The expeditionary party, therefore, consisted of Lady Blessington and D'Orsay, Marianne Power and Mathews; to which various guests were added as occasion and convenience dictated.

The romantic beauty of the gardens of the Palazzo appealed to at any rate some of the members of the household. In the evening they would resort to the charming Pavilion at the end of the terrace, and there listen to the playing and singing of the servants, some of whom proved to be delectable masters of music. There was, too, an open-air theatre in the grounds; the stage of springy turf, the proscenium formed of trees and shrubs, the seats of marble, backed by hedges of trimmed box and ilex. This shady playhouse the company frequented in the heat of the day; fruits and iced drinks were served. A pleasant earthly paradise, wherein the tempting of Adam by Eve was highly civilised—in its externals.

There were dinners on board the *Bolivar*, in the cabin wherein, it is said, Byron wrote much of " Don Juan "; D'Orsay must have felt quite in his element there.

In March 1825, the *Palazzo Belvedere* was deserted for the *Villa Gallo* at Capo di Monte, a less palatial but more comfortable abode, also possessing grounds of great beauty.

It was not until February 1826 that our party left Naples, where they had so greatly enjoyed themselves, returning to Rome, where they remained for a few weeks, going thence in April to Florence and in December being once again in Genoa. In Florence it may be noted that the Blessingtons and D'Orsay met Landor, with whom they quickly came to be upon terms of friendship.

It was while on their first visit to Genoa, three years before this, that news had reached Blessington of the death at the age of ten of his son and heir, Lord Mountjoy. Of this unhappy event one of the results was that Blessington was able to make such disposition of his property as he considered right and proper, or at any rate to a certain and very considerable extent. Of this freedom he availed himself in a manner that proves either a lack of common understanding or actual inhumanity. Included in the arrangements he made was the marriage to D'Orsay of one of his daughters, this apparently in fulfilment of his promise to see to it that D'Orsay's future was provided for. Not content that the young Frenchman should be his wife's lover he decided to make him also his daughter's husband. Such a story told as fiction would be incredible.

Three months after his son's death, Blessington signed a codicil to his will, which ran thus :—

" Having had the misfortune to lose my beloved son, Luke Wellington, and having entered into engagements with Alfred, Comte d'Orsay that an alliance should take place between him and my daughter, which engagement has been sanctioned by Albert, Comte d'Orsay, general, etc., in the service of France. This is to declare and publish my desire to leave to the said Alfred d'Orsay my estates in the city and county of Dublin (subject, however, to the annuity of three thousand per annum, which sum is to include the settlement of one thousand per annum to my wife, Margaret, Countess of Blesinton (*sic*) . . .). I make also the said Alfred d'Orsay sole guardian of my son Charles John, and my sister, Harriet Gardiner, guardian of my daughters, until they, the daughters, arrive at the age of sixteen, at which age I consider they will be marriageable. . . . (Signed) BLESINTON."

In August (1823) this amazing plan was more securely fixed by the making of a will. By this document D'Orsay was appointed one of three executors, each of whom received £1000; to Lady Blessington was allotted £2000 British, per annum, and all her own jewels. Then we must quote in full :—" I give to my daughter, Harriet Anne Jane Frances, commonly called Lady Harriet, born at my house in Seymour Place, London, on or about the 3rd day of August 1812, all my estates in the county and city of Dublin, subject to the following charge. Provided she intermarry with my friend, and intended son-in-law, Alfred d'Orsay, I bequeath her the sum of ten thousand pounds only. I give to my daughter, Emily Rosalie Hamilton, generally called Lady Mary Gardiner, born in Manchester Square, on the 24th of June 1811, whom I now acknowledge and adopt as my daughter, the sum of twenty thousand pounds.

" In case the said Alfred d'Orsay intermarries with the said Emily, otherwise Mary Gardiner, I bequeath to her my estates in the county and city of Dublin. . . ." It did not matter upon which daughter the gallant and chivalrous D'Orsay fixed his fancy ; in either case he was to be well rewarded. D'Orsay knew that his future was assured.

In fact, D'Orsay was handsomely dowered! How joyous must have been the meeting between him and his sister at Pisa in 1826. Lady Blessington has left a pleasant picture of it in her Journal :—

" PISA.—Arrived here yesterday, and found the Duc and Duchesse de Guiche (Ida d'Orsay) with their beautiful children, established in the Casa Chiarabati, on the south side of the Lung' Arno. The Duchesse is one of the most striking-looking women I ever beheld ; and though in very delicate health, her beauty is unimpaired. Tall and slight, her figure is finely proportioned, and her air remarkably noble and graceful. Her features are regular, her complexion dazzlingly fair, her countenance full of intelligence, softened by a feminine sweetness that gives it a peculiar attraction, and her limbs are so small and symmetrical, as to furnish an instance of Byron's favourite hypothesis, that delicately formed hands and feet were infallible indications of noble birth. But had the Duchesse de Guiche no other charm than her hair, that would constitute an irresistible one. Never did I see such a profusion, nor of so beautiful a colour and texture. When to those exterior attractions are added manners graceful and dignified, conversation witty and full of intelligence, joined to extreme gentleness, it cannot be wondered at that the Duchesse de Guiche is considered one of the most lovely and fascinating women of her day. It is a pleasing picture to see this fair young creature, for she is still in the bloom of youth, surrounded by her three beautiful boys, and holding in her arms a female infant strongly resembling her. One forgets *la grande dame* occupying her tabouret at Court, 'the observed of all observers,' in the interest excited by a fond young mother in the domestic circle, thinking only of the dear objects around her."

Who better could appreciate this happy scene than Lady Blessington, with all her dear objects around her : her sister, her husband, her dear friend ?

One more Pisan scene is worth quoting :—

" *March.*—Mr Wilkie,* our celebrated painter, has come to spend a few days with us. He enjoys Italy very much, and his health is, I am happy to say, much improved. He was present, last evening, at a concert at the Duchesse de

* Sir David Wilkie.

Guiche's, where a delicate compliment was offered
to her, the musicians having surprised her with
an elegantly turned song, addressed to her, and
very well sung; copies of which were presented
to each of the party, printed on paper *couleur de
rose*, and richly embossed. This *galanterie*
originated with half a dozen of the most distinguished of the Pisans, and the effect was excellent,
owing to the poetic merit of the verses, the good
music to which they were wedded, and the un-
affected surprise of the fair object to whom they
were addressed. Mr Wilkie seemed very much
pleased at the scene, and much struck with the
courtly style of beauty of our hostess."

Summer faded into autumn, but surely not too
quickly for the ardent D'Orsay, who must have
longed to take to his arms his schoolgirl bride,
who was coming over from Dublin, where she
had spent her childhood in the care of her aunt.

It was a cruel thing to do, to fling this girl
not yet sixteen years of age into the arms of a
man entirely strange to her, who could not even be
likely to learn to love her consumed with passion
as he already was for another. What chance
had the child of happiness? As little as had
Marguerite Power when forced to marry Farmer.
Did Lady Blessington recall her first wedding-
day as she stood by and watched this sacrifice?
She could not speak; her tongue was tied; what
could it be to her if D'Orsay married? And
D'Orsay, what word of exculpation or excuse can
be said for him? Not one. Had he been free from

intrigue this marriage would have been a mere episode—as marriage then was and now so often is—in the life of a man of the world. The little schoolgirl must marry someone; why not D'Orsay? D'Orsay must have money, why not obtain it by this simple means? Even if he had desired to hold back, what excuse could he offer —to Blessington? There have been few scenes so grimly sardonic, not one more tragic.

On December 1st 1827, Count Albert d'Orsay, only son of General Count d'Orsay, was married to Lady Harriet Anne Frances Gardiner at the British Embassy at Naples. Never can nuptials have been bigger with ill-fortune, which was the only fruit they bore.

Some few months after the wedding Madden met the bride at Rome, and writes of her :—

"Lady Harriet was exceedingly girlish-looking, pale and rather inanimate in expression, silent and reserved; there was no appearance of familiarity with any one around her; no air or look of womanhood, no semblance of satisfaction in her new position were to be observed in her demeanour or deportment. She seldom or ever spoke, she was little noticed, she was looked on as a mere schoolgirl; I think her feelings were crushed, repressed, and her emotions driven inwards, by the sense of slight and indifference, and by the strangeness and coldness of everything around her; and she became indifferent, and strange and cold, and apparently devoid of all vivacity and interest in society, or in the company of any person in it."

Juliet mated with Lothario. Doubtless the latter was quite contented with his bargain, as indeed he had good cause to be. He had been paid a fine price for bending his neck to the yoke matrimonial, as is shown by the marriage settle ments to which act the parties were Lord Blessington, D'Orsay, Lady Harriet, the Duc de Guiche, Lieutenant-General and Ecuyer of His Royal Highness the Dauphin, and Robert Power, formerly Captain of the 2nd Regiment of Foot. The deed is specifically stated as being designed to make provision for D'Orsay and Lady Harriet, "then an infant of the age of fifteen years or thereabouts."

VIII

EARLY one night in December 1827, the Blessingtons, the D'Orsays and Marianne Power arrived
in Rome to find that the palace hired for their
accommodation was entirely unsuitable and in-
sufficient. House-hunting once again was the
order of the day, the outcome being the renting
of the two principal floors of the Palazzo Negroni
for six months at one hundred guineas per month.
Additional and doubtless unnecessary furniture
was hired at a further cost of twenty guineas. It
is quite amusing to hear of the domesticated
Lady Blessington undertaking the transformation
of countless yards of white muslin into window
curtains and to see to a dozen or so of eider-
down pillows being recased so that the hardness
of half-stuffed sofas might be softened. Her
account of the advantages of possessing a
fourgon must be given in her own words, which
could not be re-written without diminishing their
merit :—

   " Thence comes the patent brass bed, that
gives repose at night ; and the copious supply of
books, which ensure amusement during the day.
Thence emerges the modern invention of easy-
chairs and sofas to occupy the smallest space

when packed; *batteries de cuisine*, to enable
a cook to fulfil the arduous duties of his
métier; and, though last, not least, cases to
contain the delicate *chapeaux, toques, bérets;* and
bonnets of a Herbault, too fragile to bear the
less easy motion of leathern bandboxes crowning
imperials."

Doubtless the noble authoress found it impossible to write unadulterated Saxon after listening through so many hours to D'Orsay's gallant
but broken English.

At this time there were many English folk in
Rome, to accommodate whose insular fancies there
were English shops, including a confectionery
establishment, which contributed to the indiges-
tions of the British and the entertainment of the
Romans. It was the custom then for English
travellers at Rome to make a point of doing what
the Romans did not do; happily all that has been
changed for the better and to-day the Britisher
abroad, and equally his cousins from America,
behave themselves with consideration and becoming modesty, always.

Here, as at Naples, D'Orsay made a large and
interesting circle of friends. Among these was
to be numbered the French Ambassador, the Duc
de Laval-Montmorenci, an antique who afforded
much amusement. He is described as having
been a curious mixture of opposites; simple and
at the same time acute, well-bred and clownish,
ostentatious and prudent, witty and wise—the last
a very rare combination; an old-fashioned *beau*
in spite of his short memory and his deafness, his

short sight and his unfortunate stammer; a
capital hand at an anecdote, good - tempered,
good-humoured. One of his quaint peculiarities
was the habit of falling asleep during a conversation; then an awakening after a few minutes' nap
to exclaim :—"*Oui, oui, vous avez bien raison,
c'est clair : je vous fais mes compliments : c'est
impossible d'être plus juste.*"

"Middle Ages" Hallam was another friend
of these days, when also Walter Savage Landor
was met again.

The time was passed in a round of merry
makings by all save the silent child-wife.

Then in May their backs were turned upon
Rome, or as Lady Blessington has it—"We
leave the Eternal City—perhaps to see it *no more*.
This presentiment filled me with sadness when
I this evening from the Monte Pincio saw the
golden sun sink beneath his purple clouds, his
last beams tinging with a brilliant radiance the
angel on the fortress of St Angelo, and the glorious
dome of St Peter's."

Of all their friends the one with whom they
were most loath to part was Sir William Gell,
who when bidding farewell to Lady Blessington
said: "You have been visiting our friend
Drummond's grave to-day, and if you *ever* come
to Italy again, you will find me in mine."

He died some eight years later, on 4th April
1836. Of his last days Keppel Craven wrote an
account to Lady Blessington :—

"He never ceased, I don't say for an hour,
but an *instant*, to have a book open before him;

and though he sometimes could not fix his eyes
for two minutes at a time on its contents, he
nevertheless understood it, and could afterwards
talk of the work in a manner which proved, that
while his mental powers were awake, they were
as strong as ever—more especially his memory;
but the state he was in, caused much confusion
in his ideas of time and distance, of which he was
aware, and complained of."

The first Lord Lytton wrote of Gell: "I
never knew so popular or so petted a man as Sir
William Gell; every one seems to love him."

Gell was a capital letter-writer, as the following example will suffice to show. In April 1824,
he writes to Lady Blessington:

"I did really arrive at Rome . . . having experienced in the way every possible misfortune,
except being overturned or carried into the mountains. In short, I know nothing to equal my journey,
except the ninety-nine misfortunes of Pulicinella
in a Neapolitan puppet-show. I set out without
my cloak in an open carriage; my only hope of
getting warmer at St Agatha was destroyed by
an English family, who had got possession of the
only chimney. I had a dreadful headache, which,
by-the-bye, recollecting to have lost at your house
by eating an orange, I tried again with almost
immediate effect. Next morning one grey horse
fell ill at the moment of being put to the carriage,
and has continued so ever since, so that I have
had to buy another, which is so very (what they
call) good, that it is nearly as useless as the other,
so that I never go out without risking my neck.

When, at length, I got to Rome in a storm of sleet, I found a bill of an hundred and fifty dollars against me for protecting useless lemon-trees against the frost of the winter, which, added to the expense of the new horse and the old one have ever since caused the horrors of a gaol to interpose themselves between me and every enjoyment, and so much for the ugly side of the question."

Through Loretto, Ancona, Ravenna, Ferrara, Padua, the Blessingtons and company made their way to Venice, where they halted for several weeks, and where once again they forgathered with Landor. Then by Verona and Milan to Genoa, and in June 1828 they arrived in Paris.

IX

BACK again in Paris, which lay blistering under the hot summer sun. Rooms were secured at the *Hôtel de Terrace* in the Rue de Rivoli; noisy quarters, and Lady Blessington was not fond of noise.

"On entering Paris," says Lady Blessington, " I felt my impatience to see our dear friends then redouble; and, before we had despatched the dinner awaiting our arrival, the Duc and Duchesse de Guiche came to us. How warm was our greeting; how many questions to be asked and answered; how many congratulations and pleasant plans for the future to be formed. . . ." Doubtless D'Orsay was again congratulated on having married a fortune. . . . " The Duchesse was in radiant health and beauty, and the Duc looking, as he always does, more *distingué* than anyone else—the perfect *beau-idéal* of a nobleman. We soon quitted the *salle à manger;* for who could eat during the joy of a first meeting with those so valued? "

The attitude of D'Orsay's family throughout this strange affair is amazing. Can they have really understood the situation? Did they thank Blessington for having provided so munificently for their brother? Did they express their grati-

F

tude to Lady Blessington for the many favours she had shown to him? We can scarcely believe it so. But however all these things were, the evening passed pleasantly; the windows of the *salon* looked out over the garden of the Tuileries, over their scented orange-trees and formal walks.

The Comte and Comtesse d'Orsay were also in Paris, later on, and great must have been their satisfaction at seeing their son so well settled. Of a dinner at their house Lady Blessington—*la belle mère* of their son—says there was a "large family party. The only stranger was Sir Francis Burdett. A most agreeable dinner followed by a very pleasant evening." Did Countess Alfred enjoy it?

The next day Lady Blessington devoted to shopping, visiting among other high shrines of fashion Herbault's, where the latest things in caps, hats and turbans were tried and sentenced; then on to Mdlle. La Touche where *canezus* and *robes de matin* were selected. Three hundred and twenty francs were given for a crape hat and feathers, two hundred for a *chapeau à fleurs*, one hundred for a *negligé de matin*, and eighty-five for an evening cap of tulle trimmed with blonde and flowers.

The hotel was a mere stop-gap, and the Blessingtons settled down in a house belonging to the Marquis de Lillers, which had once been the residence of Marshal Ney; it was situated in the Rue de Bourbon, the principal rooms giving on the Seine and commanding a view over the Tuileries' gardens. The sumptuous scale of the

decorations is typified by those of the bathroom,
where the bath of marble was sunk in a tessel-
lated pavement, and over it swung an alabaster
lamp hanging from the beak of a dove, the ceiling being painted with Cupids and flowers; the
walls were panelled alternately with mirrors and
allegorical groups. Furniture, equally luxurious,
was hired — dark crimson carpets with golden
borders, crimson satin curtains also bordered in
gold, sofas and chairs upholstered in crimson
satin and richly gilded, gilt *consoles*, buhl cabinets,
a multitude of mirrors; a veritable orgy of gold
and glitter. But all else was surpassed by the
Blessington's *chambre à coucher* and her dressing-
room, which she found to be exquisite, at any
rate, to her taste: the silvered bedstead was supported on the backs of two large silver swans,
the recess in which it stood being lined with
white fluted silk, bordered with blue lace; pale
blue curtains, lined with white, closed in its
sanctity. There was a silvered sofa, rich coffers
for jewels and for lace, a pale blue carpet, a lamp
of silver . . . "a more tasteful or elegant suite
of apartments cannot be imagined!" For the
housing of beauty and virtue what more fitting
than silver, white and light blue? "Chastely
beautiful," so said its owner. Then, Heaven commend us to the unchaste.

Gaiety was the order of the day, as it ever
was when Lady Blessington and D'Orsay were in
command; drives in the Bois de Boulogne with
the Duchesse de Guiche; evenings at Madame
Crawford's, whom Lady Blessington describes as

gifted with "all the naïveté of a child. She possesses a quick perception of character and a freshness of feeling rarely found in a person of her
advanced age." Here is a truly touching family
group at a leave-taking breakfast : " It was touching to behold Madame Crawford kissing again
and again her grandchildren and great-grand-
children, the tears streaming down her cheeks,
and the venerable Duc de Grammont, scarcely less
moved, embracing his son and daughter-in-law,
and exhorting the latter to take care of her health,
while the dear little Ida, his grand-daughter, not
yet two years old, patted his cheek, and smiled
in his face." Doubtless Madame Crawford was
not a little proud of her gallant D'Orsay; we
wonder what opinion, if any, she formed of his
bride, and whether she congratulated her on
marrying the grandson of a king?

Among other places of interest to which expeditions were made none can have come
more closely home to the heart of Lady Blessington than D'Orsay, the fortified château of
the family with which she was now so closely
connected.

Two letters written by members of the party
to Landor are interesting, not only as showing
the terms of friendship between the writers and
the recipient. The first was from Blessington,
dated 14th July :—

"Oh! it is an age, my dear Landor, since
I thought of having determined to write.
My first idea was to defend *Vavaseur*,* but

* His unsuccessful three-volume novel.

the book was lent to one friend or another, and always out of the way when the pen was in hand. My second inclination was, to inquire after you and yours; but I knew that you were not fond of corresponding, so that sensation passed away. And now my third is to tell you that Lady B. has taken an apartment in the late residence of Marshal Ney, and wishes much that some whim, caprice, or other impelling power, should transform you across the Alps, and give her the pleasure of again seeing you. Here we have been nearly five weeks, and, unlike Italy and its suns, we have no remembrance of the former, but in the rolling of the thunder; and when we see the latter, we espy at the same time the threatening clouds on the horizon. To balance or assist such pleasure, we have an apartment *bien décoré* with *Jardin de Tuileries en face*, and our apartment being at the corner, we have the double advantage of all the *row*, from morn till night. Diligences and fiacres — coachmen cracking their whips, stallions neighing—carts with empty wine-barrels—all sorts of discordant music, and all sorts of cries, songs, and the jingling of bells. . . ."

The second letter is from D'Orsay, who dates his note 4th September, and writes from the Hôtel Ney :—

" J'ai reçu, mon cher M. Landor, votre lettre. Elle nous a fait le plus grand plaisir. Vous devriez être plus que convaincu que j'apprécirois particulièrement une lettre de vous, mais il paroit que notre intimité de Florence ne compte pour rien à vos yeux, si vous doutez du plaisir que vos nouvelles doivent produire dans notre intérieur. Sitôt que je recevrai les tableaux je ferai votre commission avec exactitude. Je desirerois bien que vous veniez à Paris, car nous avons de belles choses à vous montrer ; surtout en fait de tableaux. A propos de cela, je vous envoye ci joint le portrait du Prince Borghése que vous trouverez j'espère ressemblant. . . . Nous parlons et pensons souvent de vous, il est assez curieux que vous soyez en odeur de sainteté dans cette famille, car il me semble que ce n'est pas la chose dont nous vous piquiez particulièrement d'être. Lady B. et toutes nos dames vous envoye mille amitiés, et moi je ne fais que renouveller l'assurance de la sincérité de la mienne. Votre très affectionné, D'ORSAY."

Of a visit to the opera this is a pleasant reminiscence :—"Went to the Opera last night, where I saw the *début* of the new *danseuse* Taglioni. Hers is a totally new style of dancing ; graceful beyond all comparison, wonderful lightness, an absence of all violent effort, or at least of the appearance of it, and a modesty as new as it is delightful to witness in her art. . . . The Duc de Gazes, who came into the Duchesse de Guiche's box, was enthusiastic in his praises of Mademoiselle Taglioni, and said hers was the most poetical style of dancing he had even seen. Another observed that it was indeed the poetry of motion. I would describe it as the epic of dancing," a not very brilliant remark for a woman of reputed wit.

Henry Greville writing in 1832 says: "Taglioni is dancing at Covent Garden; it is impossible to conceive the perfection to which she has brought the art. She is an animated statue; her motions are the perfection of grace and decency, and her strength quite marvellous." And again in Paris, four years later, when she was still highly proper: "Her grace and *décence* are something that no one can imagine who has not seen her." The actor complains that nothing remains of his art by which posterity can judge him; but the dancer can, at any rate, leave behind a reputation for propriety—while on the stage.

A welcome visitor was Charles Kemble, who dined with the Blessingtons, and after dinner read to the party his daughter's, Fanny Kemble's play, *Francis the First*. "I remembered," says Lady Blessington, "those pleasant evenings when he used to read to us in London, hour after hour, until the timepiece warned us to give over. I remembered, too, John Kemble—'the great John Kemble,' as Lord Guildford used to call him—twice or thrice reading to us with Sir T(homas) Lawrence; and the tones of Charles Kemble's voice, and the expression of his face, forcibly reminded me of our departed friend."

In 1829 an event befell, which probably altered the course of D'Orsay's career, and which may be counted as a nice stroke of irony on the part of Fate, that past-mistress of the ironical.

The question of the repeal of the civil disabilities inflicted upon the Irish Catholics had grown to be a burning question, and Lord Rosslyn wrote anxiously to Paris, urging Blessington to go over to London to support in the House of Lords the Duke of Wellington's Catholic Emancipation Act. On July 15th, Blessington set out for England; "his going," wrote his wife, "at this moment, when he is far from well, is no little sacrifice of personal comfort; but never did he consider himself when a duty was to be performed. I wish the question was carried, and he safely back again." While in town he presided at the Covent Garden Theatrical Fund annual dinner. After an absence of only a few days he returned to Paris, apparently in improved health, and—indulgent husband that he was—laden with gifts for his lovely wife.

But disaster was at hand. While riding out in the heat he was seized with apoplexy in the Champs Elysées. He lingered, speechless, until half-past four on the following Monday morning when he breathed his last. Lady Blessington was stunned with grief by the sudden calamity.

The remains were conveyed to Dublin, where they were interred in Saint Thomas' Church, Marlborough Street.

What epitaph are we to write? What character to paint of this man, so well-beloved, yet possessing so little strength, so little self-restraint, such a pittance of ability? Landor wrote of him to Lady Blessington—

"DEAR LADY BLESSINGTON,—If I defer it
any longer, I know not how or when I shall
be able to fulfil so melancholy a duty. The
whole of this day I have spent in that torpid
depression, which you may feel without a great
calamity, and which others can never feel at
all. Every one that knows me, knows the
sentiments I bore towards that disinterested, and
upright, and kind-hearted man, than whom none
was ever dearer, or more delightful to his friends.
If to be condoled with by many, if to be esteemed
and beloved by all whom you have admitted to
your society is any comfort, that comfort at least
is yours. I know how inadequate it must be
at such a moment, but I know too that the
sentiment will survive when the bitterness of
sorrow shall have passed away."

And again he writes to her :
"Too well was I aware how great my pain
must be in reading your letter. So many hopes
are thrown away from us by this cruel and
unexpected blow. I cannot part with the one
of which the greatness and the justness of your
grief almost deprives me, that you will recover
your health and spirits. If they could return at
once, or very soon, you would be unworthy of
that love which the kindest and best of human
beings lavished on you. Longer life was not
necessary for him to estimate your affection for
him, and those graces of soul which your beauty
in its brightest day but faintly shadowed. He
told me that you were requisite to his happiness,

and that he could not live without you. Suppose that he had survived you, his departure in that case could not have been so easy as it was, unconscious of pain, of giving it, or of leaving it behind. I am comforted at the reflection that so gentle a heart received no affliction from the anguish and despair of those he loved."

Five years later Lady Blessington writes to Landor:—

"I have often wished that you would note down for me your reminiscences of your friendship, and the conversations it led to with my dear and ever-to-be-lamented husband; he who so valued and loved you, and who was so little understood by the common herd of mankind. We, who knew the nobleness, the generosity, and the refined delicacy of his nature, can render justice to his memory. . . ."

Amid all this sugar, it is quite refreshing to come across a little acid, and Cyrus Redding speaks out quite plainly of Lady Blessington. He says: "She was a fine woman; she had understood too well how to captivate the other sex. She had won hearts, never having had a heart to return. No one could be more bland and polished, when she pleased. She understood from no short practice, when it was politic to be amiable, and yet no one could be less amiable, bland and polished when her temper was roused, and her language being then well suited to the circumstances of the provocation, both in style and epithet. . . . The gentry of this country, of all political creeds, are frequently censured for their pride and exclusiveness ; but they may sometimes be proud and exclusive to no ill end. The higher ranks have their exceptions, as well as others, of which Lord Blessington himself was an instance. The dissipation of Lord Blessington's fortune, and the reception of Lady Blessington's favourite, the handsome youth, D'Orsay, into Lord Blessington's house, ran together, it has been said, before the finish of his education. Old Countess d'Orsay was scarcely able to do much for her son, owing to the narrowness of her income ; but no family could be more respectable than hers. Lord Blessington was a weak-minded creature, and his after-dinner conversations, when the wine was in, became wretchedly maudlin."

However, exit Lord Blessington and end Act One of our tragi-comedy.

X

A SOLEMN UNDERTAKING

OUR hero henceforth will occupy the centre of
the stage, as a right-minded hero should do,
beside him the shadowy figure of his wife
gradually fading away into the background
until at last quite invisible, and that of the flam-
boyant personage of the widow of our hero's
dead patron. Truly ironical; while Blessington
lived and was an "obstacle" in the way of the
course of true love there had seemed to D'Orsay
to be no other way of settling his fortunes than
to marry one or other of Blessington's daughters,
he cared not which. Now that the obstacle had
been removed and the widow was free to be
openly wooed and won, the path he had chosen to
pursue appeared of those ways that had been open
to him to be the most stupid. The lady who had
been shackled was free; the lover who had been
free was now shackled. Fortune is a humorist
and her jokes are always at our expense, which
makes it difficult for us to laugh with her.

Lady Blessington was clever in the choice of
her physician, who prescribed company as a cure
for depression of spirits. So we read in her lady-
ship's Diary :—

"My old friends Mr and Mrs Mathews, and
their clever son have arrived in Paris, and dined
here yesterday. Mr Mathews is as entertaining

as ever, and his wife as amiable and *spirituelle*.
They are excellent as well as clever people,
and their society is very agreeable.   Charles
Mathews, the son, is full of talent, possesses
all his father's powers of imitation, and sings
comic songs of his own composition that
James Smith himself might be proud to have
written."

Old and young Mathews delighted with their
songs and recitations a party attended among
others by the Duc and Duchesse de Guiche
Madame Crawford and Count Walewski.

Later on we find Rogers and Luttrell calling
upon her, and the former chatting of Byron. Lady
Blessington mentions a lampoon which the great
had written on the little poet, and which Byron
had read to her and D'Orsay one day at Genoa.

" I thought you were one of Mr Rogers's
most intimate friends, and so all the world had
reason to think, after reading your dedication
of the *Giaour* to him."

"Yes," said Byron, with a laugh, "and it is
our friendship that gives me the privilege of
taking a liberty with him."

" If it is thus you evince your friendship, I
should be disposed to prefer your enmity."

"Oh!" said Byron, "you could never excite
this last sentiment in my heart, for you neither
say nor do spiteful things."

Of Luttrell, Lady Blessington held a high
opinion : " His conversation, like a limpid stream,
flows smoothly and brightly along, revealing the
depths beneath its current, now sparkling over

the objects it discloses or reflecting those by which it glides. He never talks for talking's sake ; but his mind is so well filled that, like a fountain which when stirred sends up from its bosom sparkling showers, his mind, when excited, sends forth thoughts no less bright than pro- found, revealing the treasures with which it is so richly stored. The conversation of Mr Luttrell makes me think, while that of many others only amuses me."

Luttrell, who was a natural son of Lord Car- hampton, was born about 1765, dying in 1851.

Charles Greville tells us of these two friends, they were "always bracketed together, intimate friends, seldom apart, and always hating, abusing, and ridiculing each other. Luttrell's *bons mots* and repartees were excellent, but he was less caustic, more good-natured, but in some respects less striking in conversation than his companion, who had more knowledge, more imagination, and though in a different way, as much wit."

An entry in Henry Greville's "Diary" is amusing, bearing in mind the above about Rogers and Byron :—

" *Thursday, October* 27 (1836).—Dined with Lady Williams, Lord Lyndhurst, and Rogers. The latter said Lord Byron was very affected, and his conversation rarely agreeable and a con- stant effort at wit. I said I supposed he knew a great deal and had read. He answered : ' If you believe Moore he has read everything. I don't believe he ever read at all !' Rogers hated Byron, and was absurd enough to be jealous of him."

Poets do not dwell together in unity.

Rogers even in his young days was known, by reason of his corpse-like appearance, as the Dead Dandy ; and later on a wag said to him : " Rogers, you're rich enough, why don't you keep your hearse ? "

This is a dinner-party that must have been interesting, Lord John Russell, Rogers, Luttrell, Thiers, Mignet, and Poulett Thomson ; Lady Blessington says :—

" Monsieur Thiers is a very remarkable person—quick, animated, and observant ; nothing escapes him, and his remarks are indicative of a mind of great power. I enjoy listening to his conversation, which is at once full of originality, yet free from the slightest shade of eccentricity.

" Monsieur Mignet, who is the inseparable friend of Monsieur Thiers, reminds me every time I see him of Byron, for there is a striking likeness in the countenance."

The following reads strangely, so much have our habits and manners changed since 1829 :—

" We dined at the Rocher de Cancale yesterday ; and Counts S——— and Valeski (Walewski) composed our party. The Rocher de Cancale is the Greenwich of Paris ; the oysters and various other kinds of fish served up *con gusto*, attracting people to it, as the white-bait draw visitors to Greenwich. Our dinner was excellent, and our party very agreeable.

" A *dîner de restaurant* is pleasant from its novelty. The guests seem less ceremonious and more gay ; the absence of the elegance that marks the dinner-table appointments in a *maison bien montée*, gives a homeliness and heartiness to the repast ; and even the attendance of two or three ill-dressed *garçons* hurrying about, instead of half-a-dozen sedate servants in rich liveries, marshalled by a solemn-looking *maître d'hôtel* and groom of the chambers, gives a zest to the dinner often wanted in more luxurious feasts."

Then what shall we say to this for a sleighing-party, save that we would that we also had been there ?

" The prettiest sight imaginable was a party of our friends in sledges. . . . Count A. d'Orsay's sledge presented the form of a dragon, and the accoutrements and horse were beautiful ; the harness was of red morocco, embroidered in gold. . . . The dragon of Comte A. d'Orsay looked strangely fantastic at night. In the mouth, as well as the eyes, was a brilliant red light ; and to a tiger-skin covering, that nearly concealed the cream-coloured horse, revealing only the white mane and tail, was attached a double line of silver-gilt bells, the jingle of which was very musical and cheerful."

Lady Blessington, the D'Orsays, and Marianne Power remained on for some considerable time in Paris after the death of Lord Blessington, the Revolution of 1830 providing them with some excitement. D'Orsay was always out and about, and though his brother-in-law de Guiche was a well-known legitimist and he himself a Bonapartist, the crowd was quite ready to greet the dandy with good-humoured shouts of " Vive

D'ORSAY
(1830)

[TO FACE PAGE 96

le Comte d'Orsay." Your crowd of *sans-culottes*
dearly loves a dandy.

Here is a quite pretty picture by Lady
Blessington :—

"*6th August.*—I walked with Comte d'O(rsay)
this evening into the Champs Elysées, and great
was the change effected there within the last few
days. It looks ruined and desolate, the ground
cut up by the pieces of cannon and troops as
well as the mobs that have made it a thorough-
fare, and many of the trees greatly injured, if
not destroyed.

" A crowd was assembled around a man who
was reading aloud for their edification a pro-
clamation nailed to one of the trees. We
paused for a moment to hear it, when some of
the persons, recognising my companion, shouted
aloud, ' *Vive le Comte d'Orsay! Vive le Comte
d'Orsay !*' and the cry being taken up by the
mass, the reader was deserted, the fickle multitude directing all their attention and enthusiasm
to the new-comer."

D'Orsay's love of the fine arts induced him
to make an effort to save the portrait of the
Dauphin by Lawrence which hung in the
Louvre. To achieve this he sent two of his
servants, Brement, formerly a drill-sergeant in
the Guards, and Charles, an ex-Hussar ; they
found the picture, torn to ribbons and the
fragments strewn upon the floor.

As another example of his epistolary style
we will quote this following from D'Orsay to
Landor, dated Paris, 22nd Août, 1830 :—

G

"Je viens de recevoir votre lettre du 10. Il falloit un aussi grand événement pour avoir de vos nouvelles. Le fait est que c'est dans ces grandes circonstances que les gens bien pensant se retrouvent. Vous donner des détails de tout l'héroïsme qui a été déployé dans ces journées mémorables, et difficiles il faudroit un Salluste pour rendre justice, et d'écrire cette plus belle page de l'histoire des temps modernes. On ne sait quoi admirer de plus, de la valeur dans l'action, ou de la modération après la victoire. Paris est tranquille comme la veille d'un jour de fête, it seroit injuste de dire comme le lendemain, car la réaction de la veille donne souvent une apparence *unsettled*, tandis qu'ici tout est digne et noble, le grand peuple sent sa puissance. Chaque homme se sent relevé à ses propres yeux, et croiroit manquer à sa nation en commettant le moindre excès. Vous, véritable philosophe, serait heureux de voir ce qu'a pu faire l'éducation en 40 années ; voir ce peuple après, ou à l'époque où La Fayette le commanda pour la première fois, est bien différent ; en 1790 — l'accouchement laborieux de la liberté eut des suites funestes, maintenant l'on peut dire que la mère et l'enfant se portent bien. Notre présent Roi est le premier citoyen de son pays, il sent bien que les Rois sont faits pour les peuples, et non les peuples pour les Rois. Si Charles Dix eut pensé de même s'il eut été moins Jésuite, nous aurions encore cette Race Capétienne. Ainsi comme il n'ya aucun moyen curatif connu pour guérir de cette maladie, il est encore très heureux qu'il ait donné l'excuse légale pour qu'on renvoye. . . . La Comtesse et Lady B. ont été d'un courage sublime, elles se portent bien. . . . Adieu, pour le moment. Votre très affectionné,

"D'Orsay."

Before leaving Paris for London we must quote from Madden a passage which proves conclusively that not every Irishman has a saving sense of humour. "Shortly before the death of Count d'Orsay's mother," he writes, "who entertained feelings of strong attachment for Lady Blessington, the former had spoken with great earnestness of her apprehensions for her son, on account of his tendency to extravagance, and of her desire that Lady Blessington would advise and counsel him, and do her utmost to counteract those propensities which had already been attended with embarrassments, and had occasioned her great fears for his welfare. The promise that was given on that occasion was often alluded to by Lady Blessington, and after her death, by Count d'Orsay."

Such a solemn undertaking must of course be carried out by an honourable woman, so when the Paris establishment was broken up by Lady Blessington, Count and Countess d'Orsay followed in her train, so that they might be near by to receive her counsel and advice.

XI

SEAMORE PLACE

THE London in which D'Orsay was destined to spend the majority of his remaining years, and of which he became so distinguished an ornament is far away from modern London, farther away from us, in fact, in manners, customs and appearance than it was from the metropolis of the England of Queen Elizabeth. Astounding is the change that has come about since the year 1830; the advent of steam and electricity, the stupendous increase of wealth, the extension of education if not of culture, wrought a revolution during the nineteenth century. The first half of that century has rightly been described as "cruel, unlovely, but abounding in vital force." London was then a city very dull to look upon, very dirty, very dismal; hackney coaches were the chief means of locomotion for those who could not afford to keep their own chariot, and were rumbling, lumbering, bumpy vehicles, whose drivers were dubbed jarvies. Fast young men were beginning to sport a cabriolet or cab; omnibuses were of the future. "Bobbies" had only come into being recently, taking the place of the watchmen and Bow Street runners, who hitherto had taken charge of the public morals. Debtors were treated worse than we now treat criminals;

10 St James's Square

[TO FACE PAGE 100

gaming-houses were in abundance, and to their proprietors profitable institutions. Drinking shops were open to any hour of the night, and drinking to excess was only gradually ceasing to be a gentlemanly, even a lordly, diversion ; clubs in our modern sense of the word were comparatively few, coffee - houses, chop-houses, and taverns occupying their place to some extent. Restaurants and fashionable hotels were not, and ladies dined at home when their husbands disported themselves abroad. Prize-fighting was in its heyday ; duelling was the fashion.

To this London, which, however, was not so dull as it looked, D'Orsay came in November 1830, taking up his residence with Lady Blessington and his wife in St James' Square. But Lady Blessington soon found that her jointure of £2000 a year could not by any stretching meet the expenses of such an establishment, and that a removal to cheaper quarters was compulsory. D'Orsay and his wife took furnished lodgings in Curzon Street, but later on joined Lady Blessington in the house in Seamore Place, which she had rented from Lord Mountford and furnished with an extravagance worthy of an ill-educated millionaire. As for example, let us take a peep into the library — Lady Blessington was very literary— which looked out upon Hyde Park ; the ceiling was arched and from it hung a lamp of splendour ; there were enamelled tables crowded with costly trinkets and knick-knacks ; the walls were lined with a medley of mirrors and book-cases, with as chief adornment Lawrence's delightful portrait of the mistress of the house, now in the Wallace Collection. The dining-room was octagonal, and environed by mirrors ; it was an age of mirrors and cut glass.

Joseph Jekyll writes on June 20th, 1831 : "*Nostra senora*, of Blessington, has a house of *bijoux* in Seymour (*sic*) Place. Le Comte d'Orsay, an Antinous of beauty and an exquisite of Paris, married the rich daughter of Lord Blessington, and they live here with *la belle mère*." And on 18th July :—"The Countess of Blessington gave a dinner to us on Friday. Lord Wilton, General Phipps, Le Comte d'Orsay, and myself—*Cuisine de Paris exquise.* The pretty melancholy Comtesse glided in for a few minutes, and then left us to nurse her influenza. The Misses Berry tell me they have dined with the Speaker and wife, who have thrown my Blessington overboard.* The English at Naples called my friend the Countess of Cursington."

In January of the next year Jekyll was again present at a dinner in Seamore Place, other guests being George Colman, James Smith, Rogers and Campbell; "There was wit, fun, epigram, and raillery enough to supply fifty county members for a twelvemonth. *Miladi* has doffed her widow's weeds, and was almost in pristine beauty. Her house is a *bijou*, or, as Sir W. Curtis' lady said, 'a perfect bougie.'"

At Seamore Place Lady Blessington, with

D'Orsay as ally and master of the ceremonies, gathered around her many of the most interesting and distinguished men of the time—statesmen, soldiers, writers, painters, musicians, actors, and many gay butterflies of fashion.

But the triple alliance was soon reduced to a dual, Lady Harriet leaving Seamore Place, her husband and her stepmother—who doubtless had given her much good counsel and advice—in August, 1831. It was not, however, until February, 1838, that a formal deed of separation was executed. This diminution of the number of the household in nowise damped the gaiety of the two who were left behind, indeed the presence of the child-wife must often have been a wet-blanket. As far as D'Orsay was concerned, she had fulfilled her fate by supplying him with an income, which he speedily overspent and frittered away. It is surely a blot upon our social economy that such a man should have been driven to such a course in order to secure the means of living. There ought to be a young-age pension for dandies, and their debts ought to be paid by the State, thus leaving them free to do their duty without harassing cares as to ways and means. A dandy of the first water is a public benefactor and as such should be subsidised.

Nathaniel Parker Willis, an American journalist and verse writer, who wrote much that is now little read, has given accounts of various visits paid by him to Lady Blessington and D'Orsay, to the mistress and to her master, at Seamore Place, and, as was the case with others who went there, apparently accepted the Count's constant presence as quite natural. In truth, why should he not frequent the house of his adorable stepmother-in-law? Even when he was not chaperoned by his wife?

On the occasion of his first call Willis found Lady Blessington reclining on a yellow satin sofa, book in hand, her bejewelled fingers blazing with diamonds. He tells us that he judged her lady-ship to be on the sunny side of thirty, being more than ten years out in his surmise, which proves that either the lady was extremely well preserved or the visitor too dazzled by her beauty or her diamonds to be in full possession of his powers of observation. But then, what man could be so ungallant as to guess any pretty woman's age at more than thirty?

She was dressed in blue satin, which against the yellow of the couch must have produced an hysterically Whistlerian fantasia. Willis describes her features as regular and her mouth as expres-sive of unsuspecting good-humour; her voice now sad, now merry, and always melodious.

To them enter D'Orsay in all his splendour, to whom the fascinated Willis was presented.

Thereon followed tea and polite conversation, the talk very naturally turning upon America and the Americans, Lady Blessington being anxious to learn in what esteem such writers as the young Disraeli and Bulwer were held in the States.

"If you will come to-morrow night," she said, "you will see Bulwer. I am delighted that he is

popular in America. He is envied and abused—
for nothing, I believe, except for the superiority
of his genius, and the brilliant literary success it
commands ; and knowing this, he chooses to
assume a pride which is only the armour of a
sensitive mind afraid of a wound. He is to his
friends the most frank and noble creature in the
world, and open to boyishness with those whom
he thinks understand and value him. He has a
brother, Henry,* who is also very clever in a
different vein, and is just now publishing a book
on the present condition of France.† Do they
like the D'Israelis in America ? "

Willis replied that the *Curiosities of Literature, Vivian Grey* and *Contarini Fleming* were
much appreciated.

To which Lady Blessington graciously responded :

" I am pleased at that, for I like them both.
D'Israeli the elder came here with his son the
other night. It would have delighted you to see
the old man's pride in him, and the son's respect
and affection for his father. D'Israeli the elder
lives in the country, about twenty miles from
town ; seldom comes up to London, and leads a
life of learned leisure, each day hoarding up and
dispensing forth treasures of literature. He is
courtly, yet urbane, and impresses one at once
with confidence in his goodness. In his manners,
D'Israeli the younger is quite his own character
of 'Vivian Grey'; full of genius and eloquence,

---

* Created Baron Dalling and Bulwer in 1871.
† *France, Social, Literary and Political.*

with extreme good-nature, and a perfect frankness of character."

After some further desultory chat, Willis asked Lady Blessington if she knew many Americans, to which the reply was—

"Not in London, but a great many abroad. I was with Lord Blessington in his yacht at Naples when the American fleet was lying there . . . and we were constantly on board your ships. I knew Commodore Creighton and Captain Deacon extremely well, and liked them particularly. They were with us frequently of an evening on board the yacht or the frigate, and I remember very well the bands playing always 'God save the King' as we went up the side. Count d'Orsay here, who spoke very little English at the time, had a great passion for 'Yankee Doodle,' and it was always played at his request."

Thereupon D'Orsay, in his pleasant, broken English, inquired after several of the officers, who, however, it turned out were not known to Willis. The conversation afterward turned upon Byron, and Willis asked Lady Blessington if she knew the Countess Guiccioli.

"Yes, very well. We were at Genoa when they were living there, but we never saw her. It was at Rome, in 1828, that I first knew her, having formed her acquaintance at Count Funchal's, the Portuguese Ambassador."

In the evening Willis availed himself of the invitation he had received, finding Lady Blessington now in the drawing-room, with some half dozen or so of men in attendance. Among these was James Smith, an intimate of D'Orsay's, in whose gaiety and *savoir-faire* he delighted. A pleasant story is this of later days, when Smith met the Countess Guiccioli at Gore House. After dinner these two chatted confidentially for the remainder of the evening, chiefly of their reminiscences of Byron, Leigh Hunt and Shelley. D'Orsay saw Smith home to his residence in Craven Street, and as he parted with him, asked—

"What was all that Madame Guiccioli was saying to you just now?"

"She was telling me her apartments are in the Rue de Rivoli, and that if I visited the French capital she hoped I would not forget her address."

"What! It took all that time to say that? Ah! Smeeth, you old humbug! That won't do!"

James Smith, who, with his brother Horace, was the author of the *Rejected Addresses*, was born in 1775.* He was a wit in talk and in prose as well as on paper and in verse. Here are some lines he addressed to Lady Blessington when she moved westward to Gore House—

> "You who erst, in festive legions,
>   Sought in *May Fair, Seamore* Place,
> Henceforth in more westward regions
>   Seek its ornament and grace.
>
> Would you *see more* taste and splendour,
>   Mark the notice I rehearse—
> Now at Kensington attend her—
>   Farther on, you *may fare* worse."

* He died in 1839.

Gout and rheumatism afflicted him sorely in his latter years, though his face retained its hale good looks. At Seamore Place—and on similar occasions—he was compelled to move about with the aid of a crutch, or in a wheel-chair, which he could manœuvre himself, his feet sometimes encased in india-rubber shoes. Despite his infirmities his smile was always bright and his tongue ready with a witticism.

When Jekyll asked him why he had never married, the response came in verse—

> " Should I seek Hymen's tie?
> As a poet I die,
> Ye Benedicts mourn my distresses.
> For what little fame
> Is annexed to my name,
> Is derived from *Rejected Addresses.*"

But we must return to the drawing-room in Seamore Place.

On the other side of the hostess, busily discussing a speech of Dan O'Connell, stood a dapper little man, rather languid in appearance, but with winning, prepossessing manners, and a playful, ready tongue; Henry Bulwer. There were others, such as a German prince and a French duke and a famous traveller. And—there was D'Orsay, a host in himself in both senses of the word, the best-looking, best-dressed, most fortunate man in the room; yet despite it all—there he sat in a careless attitude upon an ottoman.

It was nearly twelve o'clock, the witching hour, before Mr Lytton Bulwer (" Pelham ") was announced, who ran gaily up to his hostess, and was greeted with a cordial chorus of " How d'ye, Bulwer?" Gay, quick, partly satirical, his conversation was fresh and buoyant. A dandy, too!

Toward three o'clock i' the morn James Smith made a move and Willis his exit.

In June 1834, Willis dined at Seamore Place, the hour appointed being the then unusually late one of eight o'clock. Again the company, who were awaiting the arrival of Tom Moore, was of mingled nationalities—a Russian count, an Italian banker, an English peer, Willis an American, and for host and hostess, a French count and an Irish peeress. Lady Blessington took the lead—so says Willis, and he should know for he was there, lucky dog—in the war of witty words that waged round the dinner-table, and we may be sure that D'Orsay was not among the hindmost.

The talk was turned by Moore upon duelling—

"They may say what they will of duelling; it is the great preserver of the decencies of society. The old school, which made a man responsible for his words, was the better. I must confess I think so." He then told an amusing story of an Irishman—of all men on earth!—who "refused a challenge on account of the illness of his daughter,' and one of the Dublin wits made a good epigram on the two—

> "Some men, with a horror of slaughter,
>   Improve on the Scripture command;
> And 'honour their'—wife and their daughter—
>   'That their days may be long in the land.'"

The " two " being the gentleman above referred to, and O'Connell, who had pleaded his wife's illness as an excuse upon a similar occasion.

"The great period of Ireland's glory," continued Moore, "was between '82 and '98, and it was a time when a man almost lived with a pistol in his hand. Grattan's dying advice to his son was: 'Be always ready with the pistol!' He himself never hesitated a minute."

This we must take as a mere spark from the coruscations of brilliancy that fell from the lips of the beautiful hostess and her clever guests, from whom she had the art of drawing their best.

Coffee was served in the drawing-room. Moore was persuaded to sing. Singing always to his own accompaniment and in a fashion that more nearly approached to recitation than to ordinary singing, Moore was possessed of peculiar gifts in the arousing of the emotions of his hearers, and accounted any performance a failure that did not receive the award of tears. On this occasion, after two or three songs chosen by Lady Blessington, his fingers wandered apparently aimlessly over the keys for a while, and then with poignant pathos he sang—

"When first I met thee, warm and young,
    There shone such truth about thee,
And on thy lip such promise hung,
    I did not dare to doubt thee.
I saw thee change, yet still relied,
    Still clung with hope the fonder,
And thought, though false to all beside,
    From me thou could'st not wander.

But go, deceiver ! go—
The heart, whose hopes could make it
Trust one so false, so low,
Deserves that thou should'st break it."

Then when the last note had died away, he said " Good-night " to his hostess, and before the silence was otherwise broken—was gone.

Dizzy was party to a famous duel which did not come off, consequent on fiery language used by O'Connell, who courteously rated him thus : " He is the most degraded of his species and his kind, and England is degraded in tolerating and having on the face of her society a miscreant of his abominable, foul and atrocious nature. His name shows that he is by descent a Jew. They were once the chosen people of God. There were miscreants amongst them, however, also, and it must certainly have been from one of these that Disraeli descended. He possesses just the qualities of the impenitent thief that died upon the cross, whose name I verily believe must have been Disraeli."

Dizzy put himself in D'Orsay's hands, but the latter thought that it would scarcely be becoming for a foreigner to be mixed up in a political duel, though he consented to " stage-manage " the affair, which never came off, owing to O'Connell's oath never again to fight a duel.

D'Orsay was exceedingly ingenious in drawing out the peculiarities of any eccentric with whom he came in contact, among his principal butts being M. Julien le Jeune de Paris, as he dubbed himself; he had played his small part in the French Revolution and had been employed by Robespierre. This queer old gentleman had perpetrated a considerable quantity of fearful poetry, portions of which it was his delight to recite. These effusions he called "*Mes Chagrins*," and carried about with him written out upon sheets of foolscap, which peeped out modestly from the breast-pocket of his coat. It was D'Orsay's delight when M. Julien visited Seamore Place to induce him to recite a "*Chagrin*," the doing of which reduced the old man to tears of sorrow and the listeners to tears of laughter. One evening a large party was assembled, among whom were M. Julien, James Smith, Madden, and Dr Quin, a physician whom young Mathews describes as "The ever genial Dr Quin . . . inexhaustible flow of fun and good-humour." D'Orsay gravely begged Julien to oblige the company, and overcame his assumed reluctance, by the appeal—

"N'est ce pas Madden vous n'avez jamais entendu les Chagrins politiques de notre cher ami, Monsieur Julien ? "

"Jamais," Madden stammered out, stifling a laugh.

"Allons, mon ami," D'Orsay continued, turning again to his victim, "ce pauvre Madden a bien besoin d'entendre vos Chagrins politiques— il a les siens aussi—il a souffert—lui—il a des sympathies pour les blessés, il faut lui donner ce triste plaisir—n'est ce pas, Madden ? "

"Oui," gurgled Madden.

Then the funereal fun began. Julien planted

himself at the upper end of the room, near to a table upon which some wax candles were burning, and drew forth his "*Chagrins*" from his breast. Lady Blessington seated herself at his left hand, gazing solicitously into his face; at his other hand stood D'Orsay, ever and anon pressing his handkerchief to his eyes, and turning at one of the saddest moments to Madden, and whispering, "Pleurez donc!"

Quin, looking amazingly youthful, made his appearance during a particularly melting "*Chagrin*," wherein the author, supposed to be in chase of capricious happiness, exclaimed :—

> "Le bonheur! le voilà!
> Ici! Ici! La! La!
> En haut, en bas! En bas!"

The doctor entered into the spirit of the affair, and whenever D'Orsay acclaimed any passage, would chime in with "Magnifique!" "Superbe!" "Vraiment beau!"

The recital ended as usual in a flood of tears. But D'Orsay was not yet contented, but must be further plaguing the tearful old gentleman. He whispered mysteriously to him, drawing his attention to Quin and James Smith.

"Ah! Que c'est touchant!" exclaimed Julien. "Ah! mon Dieu! Ce tendre amour filial comme c'est beau! comme c'est touchant!"

Then D'Orsay went up to Quin, and to his amazement said—

"Allez, mon ami, embrassez votre père! Embrassez le, mon pauvre enfant," then added,

H

pointing to Smith, who was holding out his arms, "C'est toujours comme ça, toujours comme ça, ce pauvre garçon—avant le monde il a honte d'embrasser son père."

Quin took the cue; jumped from his chair, and flung himself violently in Smith's arms, nearly upsetting the gouty old gentleman. Locked in each other's arms, they exclaimed— "Oh, fortunate meeting! Oh, happy reconciliation! Oh, fond father! Oh, affectionate son!" while D'Orsay stood beside them overwhelmed with emotion, Julien equally and really affected, sobbing, gasping, and exclaiming—

"Ah! Mon Dieu! Que c'est touchant! Pauvre jeune homme! Pauvre père!"

Lord William Pitt Lennox first met Louis Napoleon at Seamore Place, also the Countess Guiccioli :—

"My first acquaintance with Napoleon," he says, "was at an evening party at the Countess of Blessington's, in Seymour Place. On arriving there my attention was attracted to two individuals, whom I had never previously seen. The one was a lady, who appeared to have numbered nearly forty years, with the most luxuriant gold-coloured hair, blue eyes and fresh complexion, that I ever saw. The other a gentleman, who, from the deference paid him, was evidently a distinguished foreigner. Before I had time to ascertain the name of the latter, a friend remarked: 'How handsome the Guiccioli is looking this evening!'

"'Splendidly,' I replied, as the idea flashed across my mind that the *incognita* must be

SEAMORE PLACE

[TO FACE PAGE 114

Byron's 'fair-haired daughter of Italia,' Teresa Gamba, Countess Guiccioli. 'Do you know Madame Guiccioli?' I asked.

"'Yes,' responded my companion; 'I met her at Venice, and shall be delighted to present you. . . .'

"While conversing with the Guiccioli, Count d'Orsay approached us, and, apologising for his intrusion, said that Prince Louis Napoleon was anxious to be introduced to me, with a view to thanking me for my kind advice. Accordingly, I took leave of madame, but not before I had received her permission to call upon her at Sablonière's Hotel, in what the ordinary frequenters of Leicester Square call '*le plus beau quartier de Londres.*'"

The advice referred to had come in a round-about way to Louis Napoleon, and had reference to the projected duel with Léon.*

* See page 202.

XII

WHAT manner of man was D'Orsay at this period of his life, when he was treading so gaily the primrose way of pleasure as a man about London town? What were his claims to the reputation he gained as a dandy and a wit? How did he appear to his contemporaries.

That he was generally liked and by many looked on with something approaching to affection there is ample evidence to prove. Was ever a social sinner so beloved? Was dandy ever so trusted?

He was strikingly handsome in face and figure, of that his portraits assure us. One enthusiast tells us: "He was incomparably the handsomest man of his time . . . uniting to a figure scarcely inferior in the perfection of its form to that of Apollo, a head and face that blended the grace and dignity of the Antinous with the beaming intellect of the younger Bacchus, and the almost feminine softness and beauty of the Ganymede."

He was an adept in the mysteries of the toilet, as careful of his complexion as a professional *belle;* revelling in perfumed baths; equipped with an enormous dressing-case fitted in gold, as became the prince of dandies, which he carried everywhere, though it took two men to lift it.

As to clothes, he led the fashion by the nose,

and led it whithersoever he wished. He indulged
in extravagances, which he knew his reputation
and his figure could carry off, and then laughed
to see his satellites and toadies making themselves
ridiculous by adopting them. His tailor, Herr
Stultz, is reported to have proudly described
himself as "Tailor to M. le Comte d'Orsay," full
well knowing that the recommendation of mere
royalty could carry no such weight. Where
D'Orsay led the way all men of fashion must
follow. Indeed, it was said that D'Orsay was
fully aware of the value of his patronage, and that
he expected his tailors to express substantial
gratitude for it. When clothes arrived at Seamore Place, in the most mysterious manner banknotes had found their way into their pockets. Once
when this accident had not happened, D'Orsay
bade his valet return the garment with the message
that "the lining of the pockets had been forgotten."

The ordinary man, as regards his costume,
takes care about the main points and permits
the details to take care of themselves. Not so
your true dandy. Thus we find D'Orsay writing
to Banker Moritz Feist at Frankfort: "Will you
send me a dozen pair of gloves colour 'feuille-
morte,' such as they have on sale at the Tyrolean
glove shops? They ought to fit your hand (that's
a compliment!), and (this is a fib!) I'll send along
the cash."

D'Orsay was sometimes quite unkind when
friends spoke to him on the subject of some new
garment he was sporting.

Gronow meeting D'Orsay one day arrayed in

a vest of supreme originality, exclaimed : " My dear Count, you really must give me that waistcoat."

"Wiz pleasure, Nogrow,"—the Count's comical misrendering of Gronow's name—" but what shall you do wiz him ? Aha! he shall make you an dressing-gown."

What the Count could carry off would have extinguished the less-distinguished Gronow.

In Hyde Park, at the happy hour when all " the world " assembled there, some driving, some riding, some strolling, some leaning on the railings and quizzing the passers-by, D'Orsay was to be seen in all his glory. An afternoon lounge in the Park was as delightful then as it is nowadays.

To quote Patmore :—

" See! what is this vision of the age of chivalry, that comes careering towards us on horseback, in the form of a stately cavalier, than whom nothing has been witnessed in modern times more noble in air and bearing, more splendid in person, more *distingué* in dress, more consummate in equestrian skill, more radiant in intellectual expression, and altogether more worthy and fitting to represent one of those knights of the olden time, who warred for truth and beauty, beneath the banner of Cœur de Lion. It is Count D'Orsay."

This language is as dazzling as the vision itself must have been !

Writing of various fashions in horsemanship, Sidney says :—

" As late as 1835 it was the fashion for the swells or dandies of the period—Count d'Orsay, the Earl of Chesterfield, and their imitators—to tittup along the streets and in the Park with their toes just touching the stirrups, which hung three inches lower than in the hunting-field."

Abraham Hayward rode in the Park with D'Orsay in March 1838, "to the admiration of all beholders, for every eye is sure to be fixed upon him, and the whole world was out, so that I began to tremble for my character."

Here is another contemporary account, which deals rather with the outer habit than with knight-like man :—

"From the colour and tie of the kerchief which adorned his neck, to the spurs ornamenting the heels of his patent boots, he was the original for countless copyists, particularly and collectively. The hue and cut of his many faultless coats, the turn of his closely-fitting inexpressibles, the shade of his gloves, the knot of his scarf, were studied by the motley multitude with greater interest and avidity than objects more profitable and worthy of their regard, perchance, could possibly hope to obtain. Nor did the beard that flourished luxuriantly upon the delicate and nicely-chiselled features of the Marquis (Count) escape the universal imitation. Those who could not cultivate their scanty crops into the desirable arrangement, had recourse to art and stratagem to supply the natural deficiency."

D'Orsay was indeed the Prince of the Dandies, it might be more truthfully said, the Tyrant. What he did and wore, they must do and wear; the cut of his coat and the cut of his hair, the arrangement of his tie—the Prince could do no wrong. Of this sincere form of flattery a comical tale is told. Riding back to town one day, as usual capitally mounted, D'Orsay was overtaken by a downpour of rain. The groom, who usually carried an overcoat for his master, had this day forgotten to bring it. D'Orsay was equal to this as to most occasions. He spied a sailor who wore a long, heavy waistcoat which kept him snug.

" Hullo, friend," called out D'Orsay, pulling up, "would you like to go into that inn and drink to my health until the rain's over?"

The sailor was naturally enough somewhat surprised, and asked D'Orsay why he was chaffing him.

"I'm not," said D'Orsay, dismounting and going into the inn, followed by the sailor, "but I want your vest, sell it me."

He took out and offered the poor devil ten guineas, assuring him at the same time that he "could buy another after the rain was over."

D'Orsay put on the vest over his coat, buttoned it from top to bottom, remounted and rode on to town.

The rain passed over, the sun came out again, and as it was the proper hour to show himself in Hyde Park, D'Orsay showed himself.

"How original! How charming! How delicious!" cried the elegant dandies, astonished by D'Orsay's new garment, " only a D'Orsay could have thought of such a creation!"

The next day dandies similarly enveloped were " the thing," and thus the paletot was invented.

An anecdote is told, with what authority or want of it we do not know, by the Comtesse de

Basanville, bearing upon D'Orsay's good nature. One day out riding he stopped at an inn, took out a cigar, and was going to call out for a light, when a lad who came out of the tavern, offered him the match with which he had been going to light his own pipe. D'Orsay, who was struck by the boy's politeness and good looks, began to chat with him.

"From what country do you come?"

"From Wales, my lord."

"And you don't mind leaving your mountains for the smoky streets of London?"

"I'd go back without minding at all," answered the boy, "but poor folk can't do what they want, and God knows when I'll be going back to my old mother who's crying and waiting for me."

"You're ambitious then?"

"I want to get bread. I'm young and strong, and work's better paid in London than at home. That's why I've come."

"Well," said D'Orsay, "I'd like to help you make your fortune. Here's a guinea for your match. To-morrow, come to Hyde Park when the promenade is full; bring with you a box of matches, and when you see me with a lot of people round me, come up and offer me your ware."

Naturally enough the boy turned up at the right hour and the right place.

"Who'll buy my matches," he called out.

"Aha! It's you," said D'Orsay. "Give me one quick to light my cigar."

Another guinea—and the Count said carelessly to those grouped around him—

"Just imagine, that I couldn't smoke a cigar

which is not lit with one of this boy's matches—others seem to me horrible."

No sooner hinted than done; off went the matches and down came the guineas, and addresses even were given for delivery of a further supply.

Even if this story be not true, it is characteristic.

One other story of his power.

A certain peer quarrelled violently with him; result, a duel. It was pointed out to the unfortunate gentleman that if D'Orsay fought with him it would become the fashion to do so! When D'Orsay heard of his adversary's urgent reason for wishing not to meet him, he agreed readily that it was reasonable, and the affair was arranged. D'Orsay laughingly added: "It's lucky I'm a Frenchman and don't suffer from the dumps. If I cut my throat, to-morrow there'd be three hundred suicides in London, and for a time at any rate the race of dandies would disappear."

By Greville we are informed that D'Orsay was "tolerably well-informed," which surely must be the judgment of jealousy.

In manner and habits D'Orsay grew to be thoroughly English, no small feat, while retaining all the vivacity, *joie de vivre*, and "little arts" of the Frenchman. But he does not seem ever to have acquired a perfect English accent; Willis in 1835 says of him, he "still speaks the language with a very slight accent, but with a choice of words that shows him to be a man of uncommon tact and elegance of mind." The language and

the waistcoats of those dandy days were alike
flowery.

It is difficult to decide, the evidence being
scanty, whether or not D'Orsay was a wit of
eminence, or a mere humorist. Chorley the
musical critic, or rather the critic of music, said
that his wit "was more quaint than anything I
have heard from Frenchmen (there are touches
of like quality in Rabelais), more airy than the
brightest London wit of my time, those of Sydney
Smith and Mr Fonblanque not excepted." It was
a kindly wit, too, which counts for grace. It is
not unlikely that the broken English which he
knew well how to use to the best advantage
helped to add a sense of comicality to remarks
otherwise not particularly amusing ; just as Lamb
found his stammer of assistance.

A little wit carried off with a radiant manner
goes a long way, and we are inclined to believe
that D'Orsay on account of his good-humoured
chaff and laughing impertinences gained a reputation for a higher wit than he really possessed.
True wit raises only a smile, sometimes a rather
wry one ; humour forces us to break out into
laughter such as apparently usually accompanied
D'Orsay's sallies. The following is preserved for
us by Gronow, who held that D'Orsay's conversation was original and amusing, but "more humour
and à propos than actual wit." Tom Raikes,
whose face was badly marked by small-pox, for
some reason or other, wrote D'Orsay an anonymous letter, and sealed it, using something like the
top of a thimble for the purpose. D'Orsay found

out who was the writer of the epistle, and accosted him with—"Ha! ha! my good Raikes, the next time you write an anonymous letter, you must not seal it with your nose!"—looking at that pock-pitted organ. Which is more facetious than witty.

Here is another story of a somewhat similar character, kindly provided me by Mr Charles Brookfield:—"My father once met D'Orsay at breakfast. After the meal was over and the company were lounging about the fireplace, a singularly tactless gentleman of the name of Powell crept up behind the Count, and twitching suddenly a hair out of the back of his head exclaimed: 'Excuse me, Count, one solitary white hair!' D'Orsay contrived to conceal his annoyance, but bided his time. Very soon he found his chance and approaching Mr Powell he deliberately plucked a hair from his head, exclaiming, 'Parrdon, Pow-ail, one solitary *black* 'air.'"

Gronow also tells this. "Lord Allen, none the better for drink, was indulging in some rough rather than ready chaff at D'Orsay's expense. When John Bush came in, d'Orsay greeted him cordially, exclaiming: "*Voilà la différence entre une bonne bouche et une mauvais haleine.*"

D'Orsay, Lord William Pitt Lennox and "King" Allen were invited to dinner at the house of a Jewish millionaire, and the first-named promised to call for the other two.

"We shall be late," grumbled Allen. "You're never in time, D'Orsay."

"You shall see," answered D'Orsay, unruffled, and drove off at a fine pace.

Even though they arrived in time Allen was not appeased, and grumbled at everything and everybody, and the cup of his wrath hopelessly overflowed when he overheard one of the servants saying to another :

" The gents are come."

" Gents," snorted Allen. " Gents! What a wretched low fellow! It's worthy of a public-house! "

" I beg your pardon, Allen, it is quite correct. The man is a Jew. He means to say the Gentiles have arrived. Gent is the short for Gentile! "

Landor writes in June 1840 : " I sat at dinner (at Gore House) by Charles Forester, Lady Chesterfield's brother. In the last hunting season Lord Chesterfield, wanting to address a letter to him, and not knowing exactly where to find him, gave it to D'Orsay to direct it. He directed it— Charles Forester, one field before the hounds, Melton Mowbray. Lord Alvanley took it, and (he himself told me) gave it to him on the very spot." Landor goes on to speak of meeting a lady who accosted him with: " Sure, Landor, it is a beautiful book, your *Periwinkle and Asparagus !* "

But surely the most delightful thing D'Orsay ever said was on the occasion of a visit of him to Lady Blessington's publishers, whom he rated in high language.

" Count d'Orsay," said a solemn personage in a high, white neckcloth, " I would sooner lose Lady Blessington's patronage than submit to such personal abuse."

"There is nothing personal," retorted D'Orsay, suavely. " If you are Otley, then damn Saunders ; if you are Saunders, then damn Otley."

Edward Barrington de Fonblanque, nephew of Albany, records that D'Orsay was a capital *raconteur*, with an inexhaustible stock of stories, which he retailed "in a manner irresistibly droll." One of these anecdotes ran thus :—

Méhémet Ali asked of a Frenchman what was a republic.

The reply was—

"Si l'Egypte était une république, vous seriez le peuple et le peuple serait le Pacha."

Méhémet responded that he could not summon up "aucun goût, aucune sympathie, pour une république."

Madden says : "A mere report would be in vain, of the *bons mots* he uttered, without a faithful representation of his quiet, imperturbable manner —his arch look, the command of varied emphasis in his utterance, the anticipatory indications of coming drollery in the expression of his countenance—the power of making his *entourage* enter into his thoughts, and his success in prefacing his *jeux d'esprit* by significant glances and gestures, suggestive of ridiculous ideas."

To turn to another essential of the equipment of a complete dandy, D'Orsay was an accomplished *gourmet*. This gift must have added greatly to his usefulness in Lady Blessington's establishment, where doubtless he was master of the *menus*. Other folk also availed themselves of his skill in this direction.

We quote from that staid depository of learning, *The Quarterly Review*, from an article published in 1835 and written by Abraham Hayward :—

"It seems allowed on all hands that a first-rate dinner in England is out of all comparison better than a dinner of the same class in any other country ; for we get the best cooks, as we get the best singers and dancers, by bidding highest for them, and we have cultivated certain national dishes to a point which makes them the envy of the world. In proof of this bold assertion, which is backed, moreover, by the unqualified admission of Ude, we request attention to the *menu* of the dinner given in May last to Lord Chesterfield, on his quitting the office of Master of the Buckhounds, at the Clarendon. The party consisted of thirty ; the price was six guineas a head ; and the dinner was ordered by Comte d'Orsay, who stands without a rival amongst connoisseurs in this department of art :—

" ' PREMIER SERVICE.

" ' *Potages.*—Printanier : à la reine : *turtle (two tureens)*.

" ' Poissons. — Turbot (*lobster and Dutch sauces*) : saumon à la Tartare : rougets à la cardinal : friture de morue : *white-bait*.

" ' Relévés.—Filet de bœuf à la Napolitaine : dindon à la chipolate : timballe de macaroni : *haunch of venison*.

" ' Entrées. — Croquettes de volaille : petits pâtés aux huîtres : côtelettes d'agneau : purée de champignons : côtelettes d'agneau aux pointes d'asperges : fricandeau de veau à l'oseille : ris de veau piqué aux tomates : côtelettes de pigeons à la Dusselle : chartreuse de légumes aux faisans : filets de cannetons à la Bigarrade : boudins à la Richelieu : sauté de volaille aux truffes : pâté de mouton monté.

" ' Coté.—Bœuf rôti : jambon : salade.

" ' SECOND SERVICE.

" ' *Rots.*—Chapons, and quails, turkey poults, *green goose.*

" ' Entremets.—Asperges : haricots à la Française : mayonnaise d'homard : gelée Macédoine : aspic d'œufs de pluvier : Charlotte Russe : gelée au Marasquin : crême marbre : corbeille de pâtisserie : vol-au-vent de rhubarb : tourte d'abricots : corbeille de meringues : *dressed crab :* salade à la gélantine.—Champignons aux fines herbes.

" ' Relévés.—Soufflée à la vanille : Nesselrode pudding : Adelaide sandwiches : fondus. Pièces montées, etc., etc.'

" The reader will not fail to observe how well the English dishes—turtle, white-bait, and venison—relieve the French in this dinner ; and what a breadth, depth, solidity, and dignity they add to it. Green goose, also, may rank as English, the goose being held in little honour, with the exception of its liver, by the French ; but we think Comte d'Orsay did quite right in inserting it. . . . The moderation of the price must strike everyone."

The Clarendon Hotel was situated in Bond

Street and Albemarle Street, and with Mivart's in Brook Street shared the reputation of being the best hotel in town, holding the premier place for dining in luxury and elegance.

In the later Gore House days D'Orsay must have been sorely vexed, though he showed it not openly, at a mishap at a dinner given by Lady Blessington and himself. It is best told in the words of one who was present :—

"I well remember a dinner at Lady Blessington's, when an event occurred that proved how ready the *Cupidon déchaîné*, as Byron called him, was to extricate himself from any difficulty. The party consisted of ten, and out of them there were about six who enjoyed what is called a glass of wine, meaning a bottle. Before dinner the Count had alluded to some splendid Clicquot champagne and claret of celebrated vintage. While we were waiting to sit down, D'Orsay was more than once called out of the room, and a quick-sighted individual hinted to me that he feared some unpleasant visitors of the dun family were importunate for some 'small account.' Still, there was nothing on the light-hearted Frenchman's face to show that he was at all put out. Dinner was announced, and all promised to go well, as the soup and the fish were unexceptionable, when my quick-sighted friend, who was a great *gourmet*, remarked that he saw no champagne. 'Perhaps,' I replied, *sotto voce*, 'it is being kept in ice outside.' The sherry was handed round, and repeated looks passed between the hostess and the Count, and between the same and the head servant. The

I

entrées were handed round, and a thirsty soul, with rather bad tact, for he was too gentleman-like to be deficient in taste, asked in an under-tone for a glass of champagne. The servant looked confused; D'Orsay saw it, and exclaimed aloud : 'No champagne to-day; my Lady and I have a treat for you—a royal treat. You know that the Queen has lately patronised what is called the Balmoral brose, and here is some.' At this moment one of the servants entered with a large jug containing this Scotch delicacy, which, of course, following the example of our hostess, we all declared to be excellent. 'Far better than wine,' said the late Lord Pembroke, a sentiment, I need scarcely say, in which the rest did not agree. Balmoral brose did duty for champagne and claret, and the only wine upon that memorable occasion was sherry. Whether the butler was absent without leave, or the key of the cellar lost or mislaid, or, as was hinted by my neighbour at dinner, the wine merchant had been seized with a sudden fit of hard-heartedness, I know not. All I do know is, that a mixture of Highland whisky and honey was substituted for the foaming grape of eastern France."

"Foaming grape" is good! Not good, however, is the taste left by this anecdote; a party of well-to-do men dining with D'Orsay and Lady Blessington, and cracking jokes behind their backs at their impecuniosity.

D'Orsay was once dining with his brother dandy Disraeli, and was grieved by the undoubted fact that the dishes were served up distinctly cool.

But the climax was reached when tepid ices were brought forward.

"Thank Heaven!" exclaimed D'Orsay, "at last we have got something hot!"

As a matter of course the circumstances in which he was so ostentatiously living and his general reputation kept D'Orsay outside the houses of those who did not open their doors to everybody, though most male folk were pleased enough to visit him and Lady Blessington at Seamore Place, where of womankind, however, none except relatives and exotics were to be met with. But even a dandy must find occasionally a crumpled rose-leaf in his bed. But what counted this exclusion against the having been spoken of by young Ben Dizzy as "the most delightful of men and best of friends," and by Victor Prévost, Viscount d'Arlincourt, as "*le roi de la grâce et du goût*"?

It took much to disturb D'Orsay's serenity and peace of mind; he was one of those blessed beings, whom all we poor miserable sinners must envy, who did not own to a conscience. Certainly the being head over ears in debt did not cause him a moment's anxiety. He did not realise that money had any value; guineas to him were simply counters of which it was convenient to have a sufficient supply wherewith to pay gambling debts and to discharge the incidental ready-money expenditure of each day. As for other expenses, were not tradesmen honoured by his custom, were they not a race of slaves ordained to supply the necessities of noble men such as D'Orsay, was it not a scandal that they should dare to ask him to pay his bills? What pleasure is there in the bills we pay? D'Orsay never denied himself anything which he could obtain for love or by owing money. It has even been said of him—and what will not little men say of even the greatest?—that he was "unscrupulous and indelicate about money matters." How poor-spirited the creature who could ask such a man as D'Orsay to pay back the money he had lent him or to render their due to the tailors and such like whom he had honoured with his patronage! The spirit of a D'Orsay cannot be appreciated rightly save by one of kindred genius. Who that was worthy to be his friend would not feel honoured by a request from him for a loan, and injured by even a hint at repayment? Of what value is a rich friend if he will not be your banker?

D'Orsay's finances from now onward were in a state of hopeless chaos, from which the efforts of his friends signally failed to extricate him. Which failure, however, in the long run cannot have made any difference; to have hauled him out of his ocean of debt would only have landed him for a brief space upon dry land, whereon he would have gasped like a fish out of water; he was a born debtor. His marriage had replenished, or rather filled, his exchequer; then he proceeded with skill and rapidity to empty it. Why should not a colour-less wife contribute to the support of a resplendent husband? Yet, marvellous, almost incredible, there were carping and jealous spirits who boggled over this and other transactions of Count d'Orsay.

As for instance Patmore, commenting on D'Orsay's social difficulties, writes :—

"And yet it was in England, that Count d'Orsay while a mere boy, made the fatal mistake of marrying one beautiful woman, while he was, without daring to confess it even to himself, madly in love with another, still more beautiful, whom he could not marry—because, I say, under these circumstances, and discovering his fatal error when too late, he separated himself from his wife almost at the church door, he was, during the greatest part of his social career in England, cut off from the advantages of the more fastidious portion of female society, by the indignant fiat of its heads and leaders."

There are quite a wonderful number of blunders in the above meandering sentences.

True as it was that he was cut by "the more fastidious portion of female society," D'Orsay found consolation, sympathy and understanding—doubtless also advice and counsel—in the comradeship of Lady Blessington — and others. Grantley Berkeley tells us that D'Orsay "was as fickle as a French lover might be expected to be to a woman some years his senior." In which sneer there is a smack of insular envy. On the other hand Dickens, the exponent of the middle-class conscience, wrote of him as one "whose gentle heart even a world of fashion left unspoiled!" How can history be written with any approach to truth when contemporary evidence differs so widely ? Was D'Orsay a saint or a sinner ? Who dare say ?

Society gossiped evilly about him, as it will

do about anyone and everyone, telling tales that did not redound to his credit. The Duchesse de Dino retails this, under date February 20th, 1834:—

"A new and very ugly story is afloat concerning Count Alfred d'Orsay, which is as follows: Sir Willoughby Cotton, writing from Brighton at the same time to Count d'Orsay and to Lady Fitzroy Somerset, cross-directed the letters so that M. d'Orsay on opening the letter which he received, instead of seeing the mistake and stopping at the first line, which ran 'Dear Lady Fitzroy,' read it through and found, among other Brighton gossip, some pleasantries about Lady Tullemore and one of her lovers, and a sharp saying about himself. What did he do but go to the club, read out the letter before every one, and finally put it under cover and send it to Lord Tullemore! The result very nearly was a crop of duels. Lady Tullemore is very ill, and the guilty lover has fled to Paris. Friends intervened, however, and the thing was hushed up for the sake of the ladies, but M. d'Orsay cut (and cuts) an odious figure."

Such a story disgraces those who tell it, not him of whom it is told. D'Orsay guilty of hurting a woman's reputation, directly or indirectly? The idea is absurd! Of a man too who was a philanthropist and one of the founders of the Société de Bienfaisance in London!

XIII

WHAT have been the causes of the decline and fall in London of the *salon* as a social and sociable institution? It is a difficult question to answer. Our hostesses are as lovely, as charming, as cultured and as hospitable to-day as ever they were; our men as gallant and as fond of feminine society; where then lurked the seeds of decay?

A successful *salon* depended upon the brilliancy of the conversation of those who frequented it; a *salon* without wit would be as a pond without water, or a sky at night empty of stars. Conversation is a lost art. Talk we have in superabundance, also argument. But the light give and take, the prompt wit, the ready repartee, which form the mainstay of a conversation, are now all so rare that it would be impossible to gather together anything like a company of true masters and mistresses of conversation. The finest conversation to-day is heard among those who do not frequent the drawing-rooms of the leaders of fashion. Moreover, in those bygone days men of fashion were expected to be also men of wit and of culture; now-a-days men are rated at cheque-value not at brain-value, more's the pity. D'Orsay would be hopelessly at sea in London society to-day, not on account of his morals, but because he would not be able to

135

contribute his share of unconsidered and plati-
tudinous trifles at tea-fights, over-lengthy dinners
and over-crowded dances.

In the London of D'Orsay's prime the *salon*
was still a power for pleasure, and he and Lady
Blessington reigned over that which was perhaps
the most brilliant that our country has ever seen.
There were others. That at Holland House, for
example, where Lady Holland reigned supreme
and somewhat severe. To that select circle, from
which he was now, alas, excluded, D'Orsay had
been admitted when as a mere youth he first
visited London. Dining there one day, he was
honoured by a seat next his hostess, who apparently looked upon the young Frenchman as
sure to be awe-stricken by her presence. She did
not know her man. Time and again she allowed
her napkin to slip down to the floor, on each
occasion asking D'Orsay to recover it for her.
This exercise at last exhausted his patience, and
when the "accident" occurred again he startled
her haughtiness by saying, "*Ne ferais-je pas
mieux, madame, de m'asseoir sous la table, afin de
pouvoir vous passer la serviette plus rapidement ?*"

Lady Holland had been a wealthy Miss
Vassall, and deserted her first husband, Sir
Godfrey Webster, at the charming of Lord
Holland. The latter has been described as "the
last and the best of the Whigs of the old school,"
and was a man of highly cultivated mind, of
genial hospitality, of wit, and a master of the art
of conversation. Among the frequenters of the
Holland House circle were Tom Moore, Macaulay,

Lord John Russell, to mention three men of very different character. D'Orsay, in what is perchance a stray relic of that famous Journal of his, gives this picture of Lord Holland :—" It is impossible to know Lord Holland without feeling for him a strong sentiment of affection ; he has so much goodness of heart, that one forgets often the superior qualities of mind which distinguish him ; and it is difficult to conceive that a man so simple, so natural and so good, should be one of the most distinguished senators of our days." Lady Holland had not shown her best self to D'Orsay ; she was a despot, but benevolent in the use of her power and full of the milk of human kindness.

That D'Orsay was fully equipped to king it over a *salon* frequented by distinguished men is evident ; no less was Lady Blessington endowed with all the requisites to reign as queen. The gift of all gifts to a woman, beauty, was hers in a high degree. Willis thus describes her :—

" Her person is full, but preserves all the fineness of an admirable shape ; her foot is not pressed in a satin slipper for which a Cinderella might long be sought in vain ; and her complexion (an unusually fair skin, with very dark hair and eyebrows) is of even a girlish delicacy and freshness. Her dress, of blue satin . . . was cut low, and folded across her bosom, in a way to show to advantage the round and sculpture-like curve and whiteness of a pair of exquisite shoulders, while her hair, dressed close to her head, and parted simply on her forehead with a

rich *ferronier* of turquoise, enveloped in clear out-
line a head with which it would be difficult to find
a fault.   Her features are regular, and her mouth,
the most expressive of them, has a ripe fullness
and   freedom   of   play   peculiar   to   the   Irish
physiognomy, and expressive of the most un-
suspicious good-humour.   Add to all this, a voice
merry and sad by turns, but always musical, and
manners of the most unpretending elegance, yet
even more remarkable for their winning kindness,
and you have the prominent traits of one of the
most lovely and fascinating women I have ever
seen."

In these years her conversation was full of
frank spontaneity ; a smile always hovered round
her lips, and there was not mingled with her wit
any spite of malice.   She expressed herself with
felicity, though not in any studied manner, and
accompanied her words with expressive looks and
gestures.   Above all, she understood that conversation is a game of give and take, "one *bon
mot* followed another, without pause or effort, for
a minute or two, and then, while her wit and
humour were producing their desired effect, she
would take care, by an apt word or gesture,
provocative of mirth and communicativeness, to
draw out the persons who were best fitted to
shine in company, and leave no intelligence, however humble, without affording it an opportunity
and encouragement to make some display, even
in a single trite remark, a telling observation in
the course of conversation."

The evening at Seamore Place often began

with a dinner party; some of these it will be pleasant for us to attend, in a proper spirit.

Habitués not only dined there, but when so disposed dropped in of an evening at almost any hour. Tom Moore records in his memoirs that he did so on 17th December 1833 :—" Went to Lady Blessington's, having heard that she is at home most evenings. Found her gay rooms splendidly lighted up, and herself in a similar state of illumination, sitting 'alone in her glory,' reading. It was like the solitude of some princess confined in a fairy palace. After I had been a few minutes with her, however, D'Orsay made his appearance. Stayed about three-quarters of an hour conversing. . . ."

Then on 11th August of the following year he " Dined at Lady Blessington's: company, D'Orsay (as master of the house), John Ponsonby, Willis the American, Count Pahlen (whom I saw a good deal of when he was formerly in London, and liked), Fonblanque, the editor of *The Examiner*, and a foreigner, whose name I forget. Sat next to Fonblanque, and was glad of the opportunity of knowing him. A clever fellow certainly, and with great powers occasionally as a writer. Got on very well together."

That must have been a pleasant gathering : a witty hostess, a witty host, and several other wits, Fonblanque among them, of whom Lytton speaks enthusiastically to Lady Blessington : " What a combination to reconcile one to mankind, and *such* honour, *such* wisdom and *such* genius." Albany Fonblanque, as so many others have done, deserted law for journalism, achieving a high degree of success as editor of *The Examiner*. He was a master of sarcasm. Before Dickens set out on his first trip to America, in 1842, Fonblanque cuttingly said : " Why, aren't there disagreeable people enough to describe in Blackburn or Leeds ? "

In the same year (1834) Benjamin Disraeli was one of a distinguished company entertained one night in May :—" On Monday I dined with Lady Blessington, the Prince of Moskowa, Charles Lafitte, Lords Castlereagh, Elphinstone, and Allen, Mr Talbot, myself. . . ." Disraeli in his thirtieth year was a man after D'Orsay's heart, a fellow dandy and a brother wit. But there was a difference in kind : Disraeli was an amateur, D'Orsay a professional ; to the former dandyism was a pose, of his life a thing apart, it was the latter's whole existence ; dandyism with Disraeli was part of a means to an end, with D'Orsay it was the end itself. The useful Willis gives a description of Disraeli at somewhere about this date, but Madden casts a doubt upon his accuracy. It was a strange scene, like pages torn from *Vivian Grey*, and from what we learn from other sources the " atmosphere " at any rate is correct and typical :—

" Disraeli had arrived before me at Lady Blessington's," Willis writes, " and sat in the deep window, looking out upon Hyde Park, with the last rays of daylight reflected from the gorgeous gold flowers of an embroidered waist-coat. Patent leather pumps, a white stick, with a black cord and tassel, and a quantity of chains about his neck and pockets, served to make him, even in the dim light, rather a conspicuous object. Disraeli has one of the most remarkable faces I ever saw. He is lividly pale, and, but for the energy of his action and the strength of his lungs, would seem a victim to consumption. His eye is black as Erebus, and has the most mocking and lying-in-wait sort of expression conceivable. . . . His hair is as extraordinary as his taste in waistcoats. A thick heavy mass of jet-black ringlets falls over his left cheek almost to his collarless stock; while on the right it is parted and put away with the smooth carefulness of a girl, and shines most unctuously,

'With thy incomparable oil, Macassar.'

Disraeli was the only one at table who knew Beckford, and the style in which he gave a sketch of his habits and manners was worthy of himself. I might as well attempt to gather up the foam of the sea, as to convey an idea of the extraordinary language in which he clothed his description. There were, at least, five words in every sentence that must have been very much astonished at the use they were put to, and yet no others apparently could so well have conveyed his idea. He talked like a race-horse approaching the winning-post, every muscle in action, and the utmost energy of expression flung out in every burst. Victor Hugo and his extraordinary novels came next under discussion; and Disraeli, who was fired with his own eloquence, started off *apropos de bottes*, with a long story of empalement he had seen in Upper Egypt. It was as good, and perhaps as authentic, as the description of the chow-chow-tow in *Vivian Grey*. The circumstantiality of the account was equally horrible and amusing. Then followed the sufferer's history, with a score of murders and barbarities heaped together like Martin's feast of Belshazzar, with a mixture of horror and splendour that was unparalleled in my experience of improvisation. No mystic priest of the Corybantes could have worked himself up into a finer frenzy of language."

Willis himself seems to have been bitten with this fine frenzy.

Madden says that it was Disraeli's wont to be reserved and silent in company, but that when he was aroused "his command of language was truly wonderful, his power of sarcasm unsurpassed."

Disraeli apparently met D'Orsay for the first time in February 1832, at a *réunion* at Bulwer's house, and he describes him as "the famous Parisian dandy." They quickly struck up a friendship. It is easy to understand what a fascinating study D'Orsay must have offered to Disraeli. We hear of the latter, a few months after his marriage, entertaining Lyndhurst, Bulwer, and D'Orsay. And in the spring of 1835 there was a party at Lyndhurst's at 25 George Street, at which Disraeli and d'Orsay were present. One of the company was wearing a waistcoat of splendour exceptional even for those splendid days. Said Disraeli as he entered the room: "What a beautiful pattern! Where did you find it?" Then as the guests with one accord displayed their vests, the host exclaimed: "By the way, this brings to my mind a very curious suit I had about a waistcoat, in which I was counsel for a Jew, and won his case." And the story? It is lost! As hopelessly as the story of "Ould Grouse in the Gun-room."

After dinner some of the party went on to the Opera to hear *La Sonnambula*, that rickety old piece of fireworks; in an opposite box sat Lady Blessington, "not very young, somewhat florid, but effectively arranged in a turban, *à la Joséphine*."

Of the evening of 30th March 1835, Crabb Robinson notes: "At half-past seven went to Lady Blessington's, where I dined. The amusing man of the party was a young Irishman — Lover — a miniature painter and an author. He sang and accompanied himself, and told some Irish tales with admirable effect. . . . Among other guests were Chorley and the American Willis. Count d'Orsay, of course, did the honours. Did not leave till near one. . . ."

Lord Lyndhurst was a frequent visitor to Seamore Place. Henry Fothergill Chorley was well-known and respected in his day as a musical critic, as a novelist neither respected nor famous; he was a close friend of D'Orsay. A rude journalist once spoke of "the Chorleys and the *chawbacons* of literature." An intimate friend describes him as "doing all sorts of good and generous deeds in a quiet, unostentatious way." Samuel Lover is best represented by his ballad

of " Rory O'More," and *Handy Andy* still finds
a few readers.

William Archer Shee met Lover under somewhat similar circumstances at another house :—
" He is a man who shines much in a small
circle. There is a brilliancy of thought, a general
versatility of talent about him that makes his
society very charming . . . he is one of the best
raconteurs that ever kept an audience in a roar.
He told two Irish stories with the most racy
humour."

The Blessington of course often showed herself at the Opera, which then as now was a
fashionable lounge for musical and unmusical
folk. Writing to the Countess Guiccioli in
August 1833, she says :—" Our Opera has been
brilliant, and offered a galaxy of talent, such
as we never had before. Pasta, Malibran,
Tamburini, Rubini, Donzelli, and a host of
minor stars, with a *corps de ballet*, with Taglioni
at their head, who more than redeemed their
want of excellency. I did not miss a single
night. . . ."

XIV

D'Orsay was able to be almost anything to any man, or any woman. He was highly accomplished in every art of pleasing, and endowed with the ability not only to enjoy himself but to be the cause of enjoyment in others. He was popular undoubtedly, wonderfully so, and with a wide and varied range of men and women. But there were also many who despised him, looking askance at one who so openly defied the most sacred conventions of society, and who, in many ways, was accounted a mere adventurer. His money transactions with his friends will not bear scrutiny. Yet when all is said, he counted among the multitude of his friends and admirers such men as Bulwer, Landor, Lamartine, Dickens, Byron, Disraeli and Lyndhurst. John Forster warmed to him, and said that his "pleasantry, wit and kindliness gave him a wonderful fascination."

What did life mean to D'Orsay? Being a wise man he looked upon the world as a place of pleasant sojourning, of which it was the whole duty of man to make the very best. That there was, or might be, "another and a better world" was no sort of excuse for being miserable in this one. "*Vive la joie!*" was his motto, and he lived up to it gloriously. Life was meant to be lived; money was made for spending; credit was a device for obtaining good things for which the obtainer had not any means or intention of paying. No one but a fool would lift the cup of pleasure to his lips and then set it down before he had drained it dry. D'Orsay looked upon the externals of a luxurious life, and found them very pleasant. The Spartans pointed out the drunken helot to their children, as a warning against tippling. So we may hold out to our young men the life of D'Orsay as an example of what they should all endeavour to be, and as a warning against the sheer foolishness of taking life seriously. This is a degenerate age.

Exceptional as he was in so many ways, D'Orsay was not unique. He had his doleful dumps and his hours of bitterness; he was, after all, a great *man*, not a petty god. He plucked the roses of life so recklessly that he experienced the sharpness of the thorns, which must often have pierced deep. The conqueror as he tosses uneasily in his sleep is assailed by dreams that terrify. D'Orsay in his hours of greatest triumph must sometimes have asked what would be the end of his career; when would come his Waterloo and St Helena? His thoughts must have sometimes turned toward the young girl he had married so light-heartedly, whose fortune he had squandered, and whose life he had shadowed. Success has its hours of remorse. Life is a riddle; but D'Orsay was not often so foolish as to bother his brains or break his heart over the solution of it; let it solve itself as far as he was concerned. If to-morrow were destined to be

overcast let not that possible mischance darken
the sunshine of to-day. Sufficient for the day are
the pleasures thereof.

There was not a pleasure or extravagance to
which he did not indulge himself to the full;
wine, women and song were all at his command;
he sported with love, and gambled with fortunes.
It was his ambition and his attainment to set the
pace in all pursuits of folly. Did a dancer take
the fancy of the town, D'Orsay must catch her
fancy and be her lover, in gossipings always and
when he so desired it in fact also.

There is not much doubt that D'Orsay followed
irreligiously the following directions for sowing
wild oats and cultivating exotics :—

"Rake discreetly beds of *coryphées*—plant out
chorus-singers in park villas and Montpelier
cottages—refresh *premières danseuses* with champagne and chicken at the Star and Garter, Richmond, varied with cold punch and white-bait at
the Crown and Sceptre, Blackwall—air *prima
donnas* in new broughams up and down Rotten
Row — carefully bind up rising actresses with
diamond rings and pearl tiaras, from Hancock's
—pot ballet-dancers in dog-carts—trail slips of
columbines to box-seat in four-horse drag—
support fairies running to seed by props from
Fortnum & Mason's—leave to dry Apollos that
have done blooming, and cut Don Giovannis that
throw out too many suckers."

Another famous tavern at Blackwall was Love-
grove's "The Brunswick," where the white-bait
was a famous dish. Of this excellent fish as

served there in 1850, Peter Cunningham says :—
"The white-bait is a small fish caught in the
River Thames, and long considered, but errone-
ously, peculiar to this river; in no other place,
however, is it obtained in such perfection. The
fish should be cooked within an hour after being
caught, or they are apt to cling together. They
are cooked in water in a pan, from which they
are removed as required by a skimmer. They
are then thrown on a stratum of flour, contained
in a large napkin, until completely enveloped in
flour. In this state they are placed in a cullender
and all the superfluous flour removed by sifting.
They are next thrown into hot melted lard, contained in a copper cauldron, or stew vessel, placed
over a charcoal fire. A kind of ebullition immediately commences, and in about ten minutes
they are removed by a fine skimmer, thrown into
a cullender to drain, and then served up quite
hot. At table they are flavoured with cayenne
and lemon juice, and eaten with brown bread and
butter; iced punch being the favourite accompanying beverage." A dish fit to place even
before a *première danseuse!*

In the company of the wealthy he gambled as
though he were one of themselves. Whence he
obtained the money to pay his losses must remain a mystery. At the Cocoa Tree he won
£35,000 in two nights off an unfortunate Mr
Welsh.

Of the many "hells" of those days Crockford's was the most famous and the most sumptuous; there D'Orsay played for enormous stakes.

Bernal Osborne speaking through the mouth of Hyde Park Achilles, utters this :—

> " Patting the crest of his well-managed steed,
> Proud of his action, D'Orsay vaunts the breed ;
> A coat of chocolate, a vest of snow,
> Well brush'd his whiskers, as his boots below ;
> A short-napp'd beaver, prodigal in brim,
> With trousers tighten'd to a well-turn'd limb ;
> O'er play, o'er dress, extends his wide domain,
> And Crockford trembles when he calls a main."

Crockford's " Palace of Fortune "—of misfortune to many—was in St James' Street, upon a site and in a building now partly occupied by the Devonshire Club. The house was designed by and built in 1827 under the direction of Sir Jeffrey Wayatville, or Wyatt, the transformer of Windsor Castle, and its proprietor was John Crockford, who it is reputed died worth some £700,000 ; one authority indeed states that he made over £1,000,000 in a few years out of his famous club. The place was " palatial " ; a splendid vestibule and staircase ; a state drawing-room ; a state dining-room ; and—the play-room. The number of members was between 1000 and 1200, the annual subscription being £25 ; the number of candidates were out of all proportion to the vacancies. Supper was the great institution, but as a matter of honour it was " no play, no supper " ; no payment was asked for, so members who did not desire to play in earnest would, after supper, throw a £10-note upon the play-table and leave it there. The cooking was of the finest, Ude being the *chef ;* the cellar admirable.

Of Ude, the following pleasing little tale is told :—

Colonel Damer going into the club one evening met his highness the *chef* tearing up and down in a terrible passion.

"What's the matter?" asked Damer.

"The matter, Monsieur le Colonel! Did you see that man who has just gone out? Well, he ordered a red mullet for his dinner. I made him a delicious little sauce with my own hands. The price of the mullet marked on the *carte* was two shillings; I added sixpence for the sauce. He refuses to pay the sixpence. The *imbécile* apparently believes that the red mullets come out of the sea, with my sauce in their pockets!"

Major Chambre in his amusing *Recollections of West-End Life*, tells us that these free suppers "were on so grand a scale, and so excellent, that the Club became the refuge of all the undinnered members and *gourmets*, who flocked in after midnight from White's, Brookes', and the Opera, to partake of the good cheer, and try their fortunes at the hazard-table afterwards. The wines were of first-rate quality, and champagne and hock of the best growths peeped out of ice-pails, to cool the agitated nerves of those who had lost their money. Some who had begun cautiously, and risked but little, by degrees acquired a taste for the excitement of play, and ended by staking large sums."

During the Parliamentary Session, supper was served from twelve to five, and the fare was such as to satisfy the most refined *gourmet*, and the

Exterior of Fishmongers Hall, or Regular Break Down.

CROCKFORD'S

[TO FACE PAGE 150

most experienced "kernoozer." Crockford started
the business of life by keeping a fish-stall hard
by Temple Bar.

"In the play-room might be heard the clear
ringing voice of that agreeable reprobate, Tom
Duncombe, as he cheerfully called 'Seven,' and
the powerful hand of the vigorous Sefton in
throwing for a ten. There might be noted the
scientific dribbling of a four by 'King' Allen,
the tremendous backing of nines and fives by Ball
Hughes and Auriol, the enormous stakes played
for by Lords Lichfield and Chesterfield, George
Payne, Sir St Vincent Cotton, D'Orsay, and
George Anson, and, above all, the gentlemanly
bearing and calm and unmoved demeanour,
under losses or gains, of all the men of that
generation."

The English Spy speaks quite disrespect-
fully of Crocky's: "We can sup in Crockford's
pandemonium among parliamentary pigeons, un-
fledged ensigns of the Guards, broken-down titled
legs, and *ci-devant* bankers, fishmongers and
lightermen. . . ." Apparently unkindly wags
spoke of the Club as "Fishmongers' Hall."

"Seven's the main! Eleven's a nick!"

It was the hazard of the die! Dice at
£1, 1s. od. a pair cost the Club exchequer some
£2000 per annum.

The play-room was richly decorated and
furnished, and the centre of attraction was an
oval table covered with green baize. This board
of green cloth was marked out in white lines, and
at the corners, if there can be such to an oval,

were inscribed the mystic words " In ' and " Out."
In the centre was a space divided into squares in
each of which was inscribed a number. At the
middle of one side of the board stood two
croupiers with a box before them containing the
" bank " and with rakes in hand ready to gather
in or to pay out as luck would have it. Crockford
himself would be hovering around ; here is a
sketch of him :—

"A little in arrear of the players a tall and
rather spare man stood, with a pale and strongly-
marked face, light grey eyes, and frosted hair.
His dress was common in the extreme, and his
appearance generally might be denominated of
that order. The only peculiarity, if, peculiarity it
can be called, was a white cravat folded so thickly
round his neck that there seemed to be quite a
superfluity of cambric in that quarter. A smile—
it might be of triumph, it might be of good-
nature, of satisfaction, of benevolence, of good-
will—no, it could not be either of these, save the
former, and yet a smile was there . . . there he
stood, turning a pleasant—it almost amounted to
a benevolent look — upon the progress of the
hazard, and at each countenance of the players."

From the same vivacious work, a curious
account of life about town by John Mills, we now
extract an account of an imaginary gamble by
D'Orsay, called herein the Marquis d'Horsay, and
his friend Lord Chesterlane, otherwise the Earl of
Chesterfield :—

"Among the group, sitting and standing
about the table, were the Marquis d'Horsay and

Lord Chesterlane. The former bore a discon-
solate mood; while the latter evinced thorough
satisfaction and confidence in his thoughts, or
want of them, for good-humour shone in his face,
and he now and then snapped his fingers in very
good imitation of castanets, accompanied by a
whistle both merry and loud. Large piles of red
and white counters were before him, showing that
Fortune had favoured his designs upon her
benefits.

"'You're in luck to-night, Tom,' observed
the Marquis.

"'Yes,' replied his lordship, 'I have the pull.
But what are you doing?'

"'Doing!' repeated the Marquis, 'I'm done;
sown up; drawn as fine as spun glass; eased of
all anxiety from having my pockets picked on my
way home; and entertain, as you may see, a
lively satisfaction in the pleasant carelessness of
my situation.'

"'By the nectar, honied look of the sweetest
girl that ever pointed her glass to the omnibus
box!' swore his lordship, 'your looks and tone
carry poor conviction to the sincerity of the
axiom. Help yourself,' continued he, pushing a
heap of counters towards his friend, 'and stick it
on thick. . . .'

"In a heap—yes, in one uncounted, promis-
cuous heap — the Marquis gathered the ivory
checks on to the division in which the monosyllable
'In' was legible, and in a standing posture called
'Five.'

"'Five's the main,' cried one of the croupiers,

looking with as much indifference at the dice as they were sent spinning across the table from the hand of the caster as if they had been a couple of marbles shot from the bent knuckle of a schoolboy.

"'A nick, by Love's sugar-candy kiss!' said the Earl.

"In a trice the counters were examined by one of the attendants, and an addition made to their numbers in the sum gained.

"With a flushed cheek and flashing eye the Marquis scraped the whole again upon the 'In?'"

Again the Marquis—that is to say D'Orsay —wins; he wins again, and again! Again— again — again; never withdrawing his original stake or his winnings, but letting them lie there, growing and growing. Then—the bank was broken!

"'By my coach and 'osses!' exclaimed Sir Vincent Twist, a tall, well-made, strongly-marked, premature wrinkled, toothless—or, in the phraseology of the ring, all the front rails gone—badly-dressed individual. . . . 'By my coach and 'osses! Fishey's bank must be replenished!'"

This frankly unveracious history from which we have quoted is doubtless as near to truthfulness as many a ponderous volume based upon documentary evidence of undoubted authenticity —but that is not saying much.

At Crockford's Lord Lamington, who wrote so understandingly of the dandies, will have met D'Orsay, with whom he was upon excellent terms: "Men did not slouch through life"; he writes, "and it was remarkable how highly they were appreciated by the crowd, not only of the upper but of the lower classes. I have frequently ridden down to Richmond with 'Count d'Orsay. A striking figure he was in his blue coat with gilt buttons, thrown well back to show the wide expanse of snowy shirt-front and buff waistcoat ; his tight leathers and polished boots ; his well-curled whiskers and handsome countenance ; a wide-brimmed, glossy hat, spotless white gloves."

Doubtless it was to the famous old Star and Garter that they rode down, the scene of many a high jink and of much merriment by night. A famous house with a history dating back to the dim age of the year 1738. A very unpretentious place at first, it was rebuilt upon a fairly fine scale in 1780, but did not prosper. It was a certain Christopher Crean, ex-*chef* to his Royal Highness the Duke of York, and after him his widow, who brought good luck to the house. In D'Orsay's days it was owned by a Mr Joseph Ellis. The old building vanished in flames in 1870.

It must have been a delightful place at which to dine and spend the evening in those far-away D'Orsay days, and very pleasant the ride or drive down there through the country now covered with suburbia. Dukes and dandies, pretty women of some repute and of no repute, bright young bucks and hoary-headed old stagers, hawks and pigeons, the *crème de la Bohême*, all the world and other' people's wives, would be there ; immense the popping of corks from bottles of champagne and claret and burgundy — the monarch of wines.   Uproarious the joviality! They were gay dogs in those gay days!

Though, speaking of a somewhat later date, Serjeant Ballantine's account of the place may be quoted :—

"Many also were the pleasant parties at the Star and Garter at Richmond, not then the great ugly staring barrack of a place that occupies the site where Mr Ellis, the picture of a host, used to receive the guests.   The old house was burnt down.   In itself it had not much pretension, but the garden behind was a perfect picture of loveliness; the small garden-rooms, with honey-suckles, jasmine and roses twining themselves up the sides, with a lovely sweep of lawn, on which were scattered trees that had flourished there for many a long day, affording shade as well as beauty; one magnificent spreading beech, itself a sight, and an avenue of limes forming the prettiest of walks at the bottom of the garden."

The view was of better quality than the viands.

There was not a fashionable haunt of virtue or of vice in which D'Orsay was not quite at home.   There was not any fashionable folly or accomplishment in which he was unskilled; a complete man-about-town, gambler, rake and dandy.   We need not pursue him in all his pastimes; dead and gone revelries cannot be resurrected with any satisfaction; they smell musty.   Let them lie.

XV

EARLY in 1836 Lady Blessington moved from
Mayfair out to Kensington, or—as it then prac-
tically was—from the centre of the town to a
suburb, from Seamore Place to Gore House,
which in Grantley Berkeley's blunt phrase became
"the headquarters of the *demi-monde*, with the
Countess of Blessington as their queen." She
wrote to Landor, describing her change of home,
that she had "taken up her residence in the
country, being a mile from London."

The house stood close down to the roadway,
occupying part of the site upon which now stands
the Albert Hall—why *not* named after Alfred,
Count d'Orsay? It was secluded from the traffic
by a high wall and a sparse row of trees, two
large double gates surmounted by old-fashioned
lanterns giving access to the short drive. The
building was low and quite common-place,
painted white, its only external claim to charm
being the beautiful gardens at the back. William
Wilberforce, a previous tenant, writes:—

"We are just one mile from the turnpike at
Hyde Park Corner, having about three acres of
pleasure-ground around our house, or rather
behind it, and several old trees, walnut and
mulberry, of thick foliage. I can sit and read
under their shade with as much admiration of the

beauties of Nature as if I were down in Yorkshire, or anywhere else 200 miles from the great city."

Under those shady trees far other folk now sat, and we doubt not their meditations were of the town rather than of the beauties of Nature. Of such an assemblage D'Orsay painted a picture, which to a certain extent gives the keynote to the history of Gore House for the next fourteen years. It is a view of the garden side of the house and among those portrayed in the groups that occupy the foreground are in addition to D'Orsay and Lady Blessington, the Duke of Wellington and his son, Lord Douro, of which latter Greville says : " Une lune bien pâle auprès de son père, but far from a dull man, and not deficient in information"; Sir Edwin Landseer, sketching a cow, Lord Chesterfield, Lord Brougham, and Lady Blessington's fair nieces, the two Misses Power.

Of course D'Orsay also moved out to Kensington, at first living next door to Gore House at No. 4 Kensington Gore.

Bulwer writing to Lord Durham on many matters, notes the move from Seamore Place :—

" Lady Blessington has moved into Wilberforce's old house at Knightsbridge. . . . She has got Gore House for ten years. It cost her a thousand pounds in repairs, about another thousand in new furniture, entails two gardeners, two cows, and another housemaid; but she declares with the gravest of all possible faces she only does it for—economy! D'Orsay is installed in a cottage *orné* next door, and has set up an aviary of the best-dressed birds in all

Ornithology. He could not turn naturalist in anything else but Dandies. The very pigeons have trousers down to their claws and have the habit of looking over their left shoulder," of course to see that no evil-minded man-of-law was approaching with a writ.

Afterward, doubtless realising that any further pretence at propriety was mere waste of energy and money, he lived in Gore House itself, in the grounds of which he erected his studio. Charles Greville, who so often dipped his pen in gall, speaking of D'Orsay's art work, declares that he "constantly got helped, and his works retouched by eminent artists, whose society he cultivated, and many of whom were his intimate friends." Yet we find Benjamin Robert Haydon recording on 10th July 1839, while he was painting his portrait of Wellington :—

"D'Orsay called, and pointed out several things to correct in the horse. . . . I did them, and he took my brush in his dandy gloves, which made my heart ache, and lowered his hind-quarters by bringing over a bit of the sky. Such a dress! white great-coat, blue satin cravat, hair oiled and curling, hat of the primest curve and purest water, gloves scented with *eau de Cologne*, or *eau de jasmin*, primrose in tint, skin in tight-ness. In this prime of dandyism he took up a nasty, oily, dirty hog-tool, and immortalised Copenhagen by touching the sky. I thought, after he was gone, this won't do—a Frenchman touch Copenhagen! So out I rubbed all he had touched, and modified his hints myself."

So strange that Haydon should not have recognised that the touch of the dandy's handiwork would immortalise the picture! There are many historical painters, but only a few great dandies. So little do great men appreciate greater men! D'Orsay was from now onward to the day of his fall at the top of his fame.

At Gore House the *salon* presided over by D'Orsay and Lady Blessington was even more brilliant than that at Seamore Place, though time was beginning to play his unkindly tricks at the lady's expense, and debt was dogging the footsteps of the gentleman.

Of the former William Archer Shee gives a description too glowing to be true :—

"Gore House last night was unusually brilliant. Lady Blessington has the art of collecting around her all that is best worth knowing in the *male* society of London. There were Cabinet Ministers, diplomats, poets, painters, and politicians, all assembled together. . . . She has the peculiar and most unusual talent of keeping the conversation in a numerous circle *general*, and of preventing her guests from dividing into little selfish *pelotons*. With a tact unsurpassed, she contrives to draw out even the most modest tyro from his shell of reserve, and, by appearing to take an interest in his opinion, gives him the courage to express it. All her visitors seem, by some hidden influence, to find their level, yet they leave her house satisfied with themselves."

But Madden, who was more intimate with her

GORE HOUSE

(*From a Water-colour Drawing by T. H. Shepherd*)

[TO FACE PAGE 160

than perhaps anyone else save D'Orsay, gives us a peep behind the mask of gaiety. He declares that there was no real happiness in those Gore House days; the skeletons in their cupboards were rattling their bones. Lady Blessington's merriment had no longer the sparkle of genuine vivacity, was no longer unforced. Cares and troubles grew upon her; her "conversation generally was no longer of that gay, enlivening, cheerful character, abounding in drollery and humour, which made the great charm of her *réunions* in the Villa Belvedere, and in a minor degree in Seamore Place."

This is supported by Bulwer in a letter to Albany Fonblanque in September 1837 : "I had a melancholyish letter from Lady Blessington the other day. It always seems to me as if D'Orsay's *blague* was too much for her. People who live with those too high-spirited for them always appear to me to get the life sucked out of them. The sun drinks up the dews." So does the passage of years. Lady Blessington was now fading. The background of her life had grown grey; the passage of years was impairing her beauty; money matters troubled her sorely, and it cannot have added to the joy of life to know that her love and her charms no longer satisfied all the requirements of her lover. Banishment from the society of almost every respectable woman must also have grated upon her who was born to reign over society.

As for D'Orsay, his existence was one per-

L

petual gallop after pleasure and to escape the
clutches of duns and their myrmidons. As far
back as his arrival in England he had been
arrested on account of a debt of a mere £300 to
his Paris bootmaker, M'Henry, who, however,
did not enforce imprisonment, but allowed the bill
to run on for several years. The mere fact of
D'Orsay being his patron brought him the custom
of all the exquisites of Paris.

It was a magnificent misery for " the gorgeous "
Lady Blessington ; but D'Orsay possessed a heart
and spirit above trifles ; the conqueror of to-day
does not discount his present pleasure by any foreboding of defeat to-morrow. D'Orsay had conquered London society, almost all the male members
of it and not a few of its female ; with his wit
and his good looks he could gain for love what
only money could obtain for less favoured rivals.

Of the fair, frail ones who were to be met
with at Gore House one of the most distinguished,
if not for good looks, at any rate for the good
fortune of having had a famous lover, was the
Countess Guiccioli. Shee met her there in the
spring of 1837, and was sorely disappointed.
He considered her a "fubsy woman," without
youth, beauty or grace ; short, thick-set, lacking
in style : " She sang several Italian airs to her
own accompaniment, in a very pretentious manner,
and her voice is loud and somewhat harsh." It
is told of her that once at a great house, when
all were alert to hear the song to which she was
playing the introduction, she suddenly clasped
her—waist, exclaiming—

"Good Lord! I've over-eaten myself!"

Lady Blessington gives a kindlier portrait: "Her face is decidedly handsome, the features regular and well proportioned, her complexion delicately fair, her teeth very fine, and her hair of that rich golden tint, which is peculiar to the female pictures by Titian and Giorgione. Her countenance is very pleasing; its general character is pensive, but it can be lit up with animation and gaiety, when its expression is very agreeable. Her bust and arms are exquisitely beautiful. . . ."

Leigh Hunt tells us that she possessed the handsomest nose he had ever seen.

Opinions differ about beauties as about other matters, so it will not hurt to hear what Henry Reeve has to say :—

"October 15th (1839).—I have been a good deal at Gore House lately, attracted and amused by Mme. de Guiccioli, who is staying with my lady. Having recently made the acquaintance of Lady Byron, it is very curious to me to compare the manners and character of her celebrated rival. The Guiccioli is still exceedingly beautiful. She has sunbeams of hair, a fine person, and a milky complexion. Her spirits are wonderful, and her conversation brilliant even in the most witty house in London. Besides which, she alone of all Italian women knows some things. Besides a fine taste, which belongs to them by nature, she has a good share of literary attainments, which, as her beauty fails, will smooth a track from coquetry to pedantry, from the courted beauty to the courted blue."

She and D'Orsay were very good friends; there are constant messages to her from him in Lady Blessington's letters:—"Count d'Orsay charges me with the kindest regards for you; we often think and talk of the pleasant hours passed in your society at Anglesey, when your charming voice and agreeable conversation, gave wings to them." And: "Comte d'Orsay charges me with *mille choses aimables* to you; you have, *malgré all discussions*, secured a very warm and sincere friend in him." And, writing from Gore House on 15th August 1839: "Your friend Alfred charges me with his kindest regards to you. He is now an inmate at Gore House, having sold his own residence; and this is not only a great protection but a great addition to my comfort." A quite pleasantly frank confession to the mistress of a great poet from the mistress of a great dandy. But there have been greater poets than Byron, not any greater dandy than D'Orsay, so the Blessington was the prouder woman of the two.

The following, written in January 1845, must be quoted in full, and read with the remembrance to the fore that Lady Blessington posed in conversation and in print as having been on terms of intimate friendship with Byron. ". . . You have, I daresay, heard that your friend Count d'Orsay has within the last two years taken to painting, and such has been the rapidity of his progress, that he has left many competitors, who have been for fifteen years painters, far behind.

"Dissatisfied with all the portraits that have

THE COUNTESS GUICCIOLI

(By D'Orsay)

[TO FACE PAGE 164

been painted of Lord Byron, none of which
render justice to the intellectual beauty of his
noble head, Count d'Orsay, at my request, has
made a portrait of our great poet, and it has been
pronounced by Sir John Cam Hobhouse, and
all who remember Lord Byron, to be the best
likeness of him ever painted! The picture
possesses all the noble intelligence and fine
character of the poet's face, and will, I am sure,
delight you when you see it. We have had it
engraved, and when the plate is finished, a print
will be sent to you. It will be interesting, *chère
et aimable amie*, to have a portrait of our great
poet, from a painting by one who so truly esteems
you : for you have not a truer friend than Count
d'Orsay, unless it be me. How I wish you were
here to see the picture! It is an age since we
met, and I assure you we all feel this long separation as a great privation. I shall be greatly
disappointed if you are not as delighted with the
engraving as I am, for to me it seems the very
image of Byron."

"Our great poet" would have torn the hair
of his noble head if he had read this quaint production. La Guiccioli did approve the engraving
to the contentment of the artist.

Shee tells us that the Countess on her visits
to Gore House was overwhelmed by her more
showy hostess, and by her sister, the Countess
Saint Marceau, the latter forming a fine foil to
the more exuberant Lady Blessington, being
slight, short, small-featured, but extremely pretty
and piquant, and, as Madden tells us, "always

courted and complimented in society, and coquetted with by gentlemen of a certain age, by humourists in single blessedness, especially like Gell, and by old married bachelors like Landor."

Landor visited Lady Blessington in 1837; he writes to Forster: "I shall be at Gore House on Monday, pray come in the evening. I told Lady Blessington I should not let any of her court stand at all in my way. When I am tired of them, I leave them."

It is very strong proof of the fascination exercised by D'Orsay that such men as Landor, Carlyle and Forster, each one of whom we would think impervious to his charms, should have succumbed to them.

Landor's enslavement by Lady Blessington or her sister is understandable, but what attracted him in D'Orsay? Chorley gives us a glimpse of Landor dining at Gore House when its master was absent: "Yesterday evening, I had a very rare treat—a dinner at Kensington *tête-à-tête* with Lady Blessington and Mr Landor; she talked her best, brilliant and kindly, and without that touch of self-consciousness which she sometimes displays when worked up to it by flatterers and gay companions. Landor, as usual, the very finest man's head I have ever seen, and with all his Johnsonian disposition to tyrannise and lay down the law in his talk, restrained and refined by an old-world courtesy and deference to his bright hostess, for which *chivalry* is the only right word."

Landor conceived quite an affection for

D'Orsay ; perhaps at heart they *both* were dandies ?
Here is a pleasant bit of chaff from Landor,
written to Lady Blessington : " By living at
Clifton, I am grown as rich as Rothschild ; and
if Count d'Orsay could see me in my new coat,
he would not write me so pressingly to come up
to London. It would breed ill-blood between us—
half plague, half cholera. He would say—' I wish
the fellow had his red forehead again—the deuce
might powder it for me.' However, as I go out
very little, I shall not divide the world with him."

Once when Landor was dining at Gore House,
his attire had become slightly disordered, to which
fact D'Orsay smilingly drew attention as they rose
to join the ladies. " My dear Count d'Orsay," exclaimed Landor, " I thank you ! My dear Count
d'Orsay I thank you from my soul for pointing out
to me the abominable condition to which I am
reduced ! If I had entered the drawing-room, and
presented myself before Lady Blessington in so
absurd a light, I would have instantly gone home,
put a pistol to my head, and blown my brains out ! "

In January 1840, Henry Reeve was at dinner
at Gore House, and gives a capital account of the
fun there :—

" Our dinner last night was very good fun,
but we made rather too many puns. Landor
rode several fine paradoxes with savage impetu-
osity : particularly his theory that the Chinese
are the only civilised people in the world. I am
sure the Ching dynasty has not a firmer adherent
than Landor within its own imperial capital.
Landor, you know, is quite as vain of not being

read, as Bulwer is of being the most popular writer of the day. Nothing can equal the contempt with which he treats anybody who has more than six readers and three admirers unless it be that saying of Hegel's, when he declared that nobody understood his writings but himself, and that not always. Lady B(lessington) said the finest thing of Carlyle's productions that ever was uttered; she called them 'spangled fustian.'"

Forster and D'Orsay got on very well together, which was perhaps due to the almost if not quite exaggerated respect paid by the former to the latter. He was heard above the roar of talk at one of his dinners, absolutely shouting to his man Henry: "Good heavens, sir, butter for the Count's flounders!" D'Orsay contrived to misunderstand him very nicely on an occasion. Forster when expecting a visit from the Count was urgently summoned to his printers. He gave his servant strict injunction to tell the Count, should he call before his return, that he had just gone round to Messrs Spottiswoode. He missed his visitor entirely, and his explanation when next he met him was cut short by—"Ah! I know, you had just gone round to *Ze Spotted Dog*—I understand."

In 1835 Lady Blessington writes to Forster from Gore House:

"It has given me the greatest pleasure to hear that you are so much better. Count d'Orsay assures me that the improvement is most satisfactory. To-morrow will be the anniversary of his birthday, and a few friends will meet to celebrate it. How I wish you were to be among the number." Ten years later, when Forster again was on the sick-list, she writes : " If you knew the anxiety we all feel about your health, and the fervent prayers we offer up for its speedy restoration, you would be convinced, that though you have friends of longer date, you have none more affectionately and sincerely attached to you than those at Gore House. I claim the privilege of an *old woman* to be allowed to see you as soon as a visitor in a sick-room can be admitted. Sterne says that ' A friend has the same right as a physician,' and I hope you will remember this. Count d'Orsay every day regrets that he cannot go and nurse you, and we both often wish you were here, that we might try our power of alleviating your illness, if not of curing you. God bless you, and restore you speedily to health."

Macready turns up, if we may use words so flippant of a man so serious, at Gore House in 1837. " Reached Lady Blessington's about a quarter before eight," he writes. " Found there Fonblanque, Bulwer, Trelawney, Procter, Auldjo, Forster, Lord Canterbury, Fred Reynolds and Mr and Mrs Fairlie, Kenney, a young Manners Sutton, Count d'Orsay and some unknown. I passed an agreeable day, and had a long and interesting conversation in the drawing-room (what an elegant and splendid room it is!) with D'Orsay on pictures."

Of the members of the party that Macready found himself amongst—Lord Canterbury, when he was the Right Honourable Charles Manners

Sutton and Speaker of the House of Commons, had married in 1828 Lady Blessington's sister Ellen, of whom Moore speaks as "Mrs Speaker": "Amused to see her, in all her state, the same hearty, lively Irishwoman still." She had first been married to a Mr Purves. Mrs Fairlie was Mrs Purves' eldest daughter, Louisa, who while quite young had married Mr John Fairlie. Trelawney was the "Younger Son," whose "Adventures" are so entertaining and exciting, the intimate of Shelley and Byron, and the model for the old sea captain of Millais' "North-West Passage." Procter was "Barry Cornwall"; John Auldjo had been introduced to Lady Blessington by Gell in 1834; Frederick Mansell Reynolds was a minor poet and writer of tales, a letter from whom shows D'Orsay in a pleasant light. It is written from Jersey in 1837—

"MY DEAR LADY BLESSINGTON,—After having so recently seen you, and being so powerfully and so painfully under the influence of a desire never again to place the sea between me and yourself and circle, I feel almost provoked to find how much this place suits me in every physical respect. . . . You and Count d'Orsay speak kindly and cheerfully to me; but I am *un malade imaginaire*, for I do not fear death; on the contrary, I rather look to it as my only hope of secure and lasting tranquillity. In the lull which has hitherto accompanied my return to this delicious climate, I have had time and opportunity for ample retrospection, and I find that we have both * laid in a stock of regard for Count d'Orsay which is immeasurable : anybody so good-natured and so kind-hearted I never before saw ; it seems to me that it should be considered an inestimable privilege to live in his society. When you write to me, pray be good enough to acquaint me whether you have been told verbatim what a lady said on the subject ; for praise so natural, hearty and agreeable was never before uttered in a soliloquy, which her speech really was, though I was present at the time.

" At the risk of repeating, I really must tell it to you. After Count d'Orsay's departure from our house, there was a pause, when it was broken, by her exclaiming, ' What a very nice man ! ' I assented in my own mind, but I was pursuing also a chain of thought of my own, and I made no audible reply. Our ruminations then proceeded, when mine were once more interrupted by her saying : ' In fact, he is the *nicest man I ever saw.*'

" This is a pleasant avowal to me, I thought ; but still I could not refrain from admitting that she was right. Then again, for a third time, the mental machinery of both went to work in silence, until that of the lady reached a *ne plus ultra* of admiration, and she ejaculated in an ecstasy : ' Indeed, he is the nicest man that can possibly be ! ' " *

The Kenney mentioned by Macready must have been James, who as the author of *Raising the Wind,* and of *Sweethearts and Wives,* was a singularly appropriate friend for the impecunious, amorous D'Orsay.

* Referring to his devoted wife.

XVI

STARS

LADY BLESSINGTON reported that in June 1838, London was "insupportable. The streets and the Park crowded to suffocation, and all the people gone mad"; but in the same month Dizzy writes in a different key: "We had a very agreeable party at D'Orsay's yesterday. Zichy, who has cut out even Esterhazy, having two jackets; one of diamonds more brilliant than E's., and another which he wore at the drawing-room yesterday of turquoises. This makes the greatest sensation of the two. . . . Then there was the Duke of Ossuna, a young man, but a grandee of the highest grade. . . . He is a great dandy and looks like Philip II., but though the only living descendant of the Borgias, he has the reputation of being very amiable. When he was last at Paris he attended a representation of Victor Hugo's *Lucrezia Borgia*. She says in one of the scenes: 'Great crimes are in our blood.' All his friends looked at him with an expression of fear; 'But the blood has degener-ated,' he said, 'for I have committed only weaknesses.' Then there was the real Prince Poniatowsky, also young and with a most brilliant star. Then came Kissiloffs and Strogonoffs, 'and other offs and ons,' and de Belancour, a very agreeable person. Lyndhurst, Gardner, Bulwer and myself completed the party."

D'Ossuna died while quite a young man and was succeeded by his brother, also a friend of D'Orsay.

This must have been a curiously polyglot gathering, and the noble company of dandies was brilliantly represented by D'Orsay, Bulwer and Dizzy, not to mention Zichy of the turquoise jacket.

XVII

THERE is both amusement and interest in the record of the year 1839, during which all pretence at a separate establishment was cast aside, and the D'Orsay-Blessington alliance was publicly acknowledged by the gentleman taking up his residence in the lady's house.

D'Orsay went down this year to Bradenham, on a visit to the Disraelis.

It is not uninteresting to know that Bradenham and Hurstley in *Endymion* are one and the same place, and thus described :—

" At the foot of the Berkshire downs, and itself on a gentle elevation, there is an old hall with gable ends and lattice windows, standing in grounds which once were stately, and where there are yet glade-like terraces of yew-trees, which give an air of dignity to a neglected scene. In the front of the hall huge gates of iron, highly wrought, and bearing an ancient date as well as the shield of a noble house, opened on a village green, round which were clustered the cottages of the parish, with only one exception, and that was the vicarage house, a modern building, not without taste, and surrounded by a small but brilliant garden. The church was contiguous to the hall, and had been raised by the lord on a portion of his domain. Behind the hall and its enclosure the country was common land but picturesque.

It had once been a beech forest, and though the timber had been greatly cleared, the green land was occasionally dotted, sometimes with groups and sometimes with single trees, while the juniper which here abounded, and rose to a great height, gave a rich wildness to the scene, and sustained its forest character." It is easy to fit the author of the *Curiosities of Literature* into this framework, but in this old-world hall two such gorgeous butterflies as D'Orsay and the writer of *Vivian Grey* seem rather astray. It would be almost as startling to find a dog-rose climbing up a lamppost in Pall Mall, or honeysuckle adorning the front of the Thatched House.

Disraeli writes to Lady Blessington :—

"We send you back our dearest D'Orsay, with some of the booty of yesterday's sport as our homage to you. His visit has been very short, but very charming, and everybody here loves him as much as you and I do. I hope that I shall soon see you, and see you well ; and in the meantime, I am, as I shall ever be, your affectionate—"

Concerning an earlier occasion, Disraeli writes from Bradenham on 5th August 1834, to Lady Blessington :—

"I suppose it is vain to hope to see my dear D'Orsay here ; I wish indeed he would come. Here is a wish by no means contemptible. He can bring his horses if he likes, but I can mount him. Adieu, dear Lady Blessington, some day I will try to write you a more amusing letter ; at present I am in truth ill and sad."

Charles Greville was at Gore House on 17th

February, and seems to have enjoyed himself pretty well:—

"February 17th.—I dined at Lady Blessington's yesterday, to meet Durham and Brougham; but, after all, the latter did not come, and the excuse he made was, that it was better not; and as he was taking, or going to take (we shall see) a moderate course about Canada, it would impair his efficacy if the press were to trumpet forth, and comment on, his meeting with Durham. There was that sort of strange omnium gatherum party which is to be met with nowhere else, and which for that reason alone is curious. We had Prince Louis Napoleon and his A.D.C.* He is a short, thickish, vulgar-looking man, without the slightest resemblance to his imperial uncle, or any intelligence in his countenance. Then we had the ex-Governor of Canada, Captain Marriott, the Count Alfred de Vigny (author of *Cinq Mars*, etc.), Sir Edward Lytton Bulwer, and a proper sprinkling of ordinary persons to mix up with these celebrities. In the evening, Forster, sub-editor of the *Examiner*; Chorley, editor of the *Athenæum*; Macready and Charles Buller. Lady Blessington's existence is a curiosity, and her house and society have at least the merit of being singular, though the latter is not so agreeable as from its composition it ought to be. There is no end to the men of consequence and distinction in the world who go there occasionally—Brougham,

* The first mention of His Imperial Majesty Napoleon III., who was an *habitué* of Gore House, and well known to all who frequented it. The A.D.C. was M. de Persigny, who accompanied the Prince everywhere.—[*Note in Greville.*]

EDWARD, FIRST BARON LYTTON
(*From a Painting by A. E. Chalon, R.A.*)

[TO FACE PAGE 176

Lyndhurst, Abinger, Canterbury, Durham, and many others; all the minor poets, *literati*, and journalists, without exception, together with some of the highest pretensions. Moore is a sort of friend of hers; she had been very intimate with Byron, and is with Walter Savage Landor. Her house is furnished with a luxury and splendour not to be surpassed; her dinners are frequent and good; and D'Orsay does the honours with a frankness and cordiality which are very successful; but all this does not make society, in the real meaning of the term. There is a vast deal of coming and going, and eating and drinking, and a corresponding amount of noise, but little or no conversation, discussion, easy quiet interchange of ideas and opinions, no regular social foundation of men of intellectual or literary calibre ensuring a perennial flow of conversation, and which, if it existed, would derive strength and assistance from the light superstructure of occasional visitors, with the much or the little they might individually contribute. The reason of this is that the woman herself, who must give the tone to her own society, and influence its character, is ignorant, vulgar, and commonplace.* Nothing can be more

---

* Lady Blessington had a good deal more talent and reading than Mr Greville gives her credit for. Several years of her agitated life were spent in the country in complete retirement, where she had no resources to fall back upon but a good library. She was well read in the best English authors, and even in translations of the Classics; but the talent to which she owed her success in society was her incomparable tact and skill in drawing out the best qualities of her guests. What Mr Greville terms her vulgarity might be more charitably described as her Irish cordiality and *bonhomie*. I have no doubt that her *Conversations with Lord Byron* were entirely written by herself.—[*Note in Greville.*]

M

dull and uninteresting than her conversation, which is never enriched by a particle of knowledge, or enlivened by a ray of genius or imagination. The fact of her existence as an authoress is an enigma, poor as her pretensions are; for while it is very difficult to write good books, it is not easy to compose even bad ones, and volumes have come forth under her name for which hundreds of pounds have been paid, because (Heaven only can tell how) thousands are found who will read them. Her 'Works' have been published in America, in one huge folio, where it seems they meet with peculiar success; and this trash goes down, because it is written by a Countess, in a country where rank is eschewed, and equality is the universal passion. They have (or some of them) been likewise translated into German; and if all this is not proof of literary merit, or at least of success, what is? It would be not uninteresting to trace this current of success to its source, and to lay bare all the springs of the machinery which sustains her artificial character as an authoress. The details of course form the mystery of her craft, but the general causes are apparent enough. First and foremost, her magnificent house and luxurious dinners; then the alliance offensive and defensive which she has contrived (principally through the means of said house and dinners) to establish with a host of authors, booksellers, and publishers, and above all with journalists. The first lend her their assistance in composition, correction, or addition; with the second she manages to establish an interest and an interchange of services; and the last everlastingly puff her performances. Her name is eternally before the public; she produces those gorgeous inanities, called *Books of Beauty*, and other trashy things of the same description, to get up which all the fashion and beauty, the taste and talent, of London are laid under contribution. The most distinguished artists and the best engravers supply the portraits of the prettiest women in London; and these are illustrated with poetical effusions of the smallest possible merit, but exciting interest and curiosity from the notoriety of their authors; and so, by all this puffing, and stuffing, and untiring industry, and practising on the vanity of some, and the good-nature of others, the end is attained; and though I never met with any individual who had read any of her books, except the *Conversations with Byron*, which are too good to be hers, they are unquestionably a source of considerable profit, and she takes her place confidently and complacently as one of the literary celebrities of her day."

The *Conversations* were in all probability almost entirely the composition of Lady Blessington, more so indeed than they had any right to be, Byron's sayings being the invention to some extent at any rate of the lively imagination of the so-called recorder. But it is not necessary here —or anywhere—to discuss Lady Blessington's performances as a writer of fiction.

The Durham referred to by Greville was John George Lambton, first Earl of Durham, who in 1838 had been appointed Governor-

General of the British provinces of North America,
and whose somewhat arbitrary proceedings there
had not met with universal approbation. But there
cannot be any doubt that in the main he was
right and wise. Charles Buller, his secretary,
is reputed to have been the author of Durham's
famous *Report on the Affairs of British North
America*.

When Lord Durham was making ready for his
departure to Canada, he included among his immense
baggage a large number of musical instruments.
"What on earth are they for?" said a wonderer.
To whom Sydney Smith: "Don't you know he
is going to make overtures to the Canadians?"

George Ticknor describes Durham in 1838 as
"little, dark-complexioned, red-faced-looking."
Charles Greville had many severe things to say
of him—and said them.

Durham seems to have been on fairly intimate
terms with Lady Blessington. In 1835 he writes
from Cowes :—

"I thank you much for your very agreeable letter, which I received this morning, and
for your kind inquiries after my health, which
is wonderfully improved, if not quite restored, by
this fine air, and *dolce far niente* life. I antici-
pate with horror the time when I shall be obliged
to leave it, and mix once more in the *troublous*
realities of *public life*."

Durham died in 1840, and of the event Alfred
de Vigny wrote to Lady Blessington :—

"PARIS.

"Moi qui me souviens, milady, de vous avoir

trouvé un soir si profondément affecté de la mort d'une amie, je puis mesurer toute la peine que vous avez éprouvée à la perte de Lord Durham. J'aimais toujours à me figurer que je le retrouverai à Gore House à coté de vous, et je ne puis croire encore qu'en si peu de temps il ait été enlevé à ses amis. Je ne crains point avec vous de parler d'une chose déjà ancienne, comme on dirait à Paris, car je sais quel religieux souvenir vous gardez à ceux qui ne sont plus, et qui vous furent chers.

"Je regrette dans Lord Durham tout l'avenir que je me promettois de sa vie politique, et le développement des idées saines et larges, que, chez vous il m'avait montrées. Si je ne me suis trompé sur lui, l'alliance de la France lui semblait précieuse à plus d'un titre, et il connaissait pro- pondément les vues de la Russie. S'il tenoit à cette géneration de vos hommes d'état qui prennent part aux plus grandes luttes, il était pourtant jeune d'esprit et de cœur, et un homme de passé et d'avenir à la fois sont bien rares.

"Vous pensez à voyager en Italy, y songez vous encore, milady, je le voudrois puisque Paris est sur le chemin, et je suis assuré par toute la grâce avec laquelle vous m'avez ouvert Gore House, que vous ne seriez point affligée de me voir vous porter en France l'assurance du plus sincère et du plus durable dévouement.

"ALFRED DE VIGNY."

De Vigny was the popular French poet and novelist, author of *Cinq Mars* and *Chatterton*, of

whom Lady Blessington remarked that he was
"of fine feelings as well as genius, but were they
ever distinct?"

Charles Buller will perhaps be chiefly remembered as the pupil of Carlyle and the friend
of Thackeray, who on his death in 1848 wrote to
Mrs Brookfield :—

"MY DEAR LADY—I am very much pained
and shocked at the news brought at dinner
to-day that poor dear Charles Buller is gone.
Good God! think about the poor mother surviving, and what an anguish that must be!
If I were to die I cannot bear to think of my
mother living beyond me, as I daresay she will.
But isn't it an awful, awful sudden summons?
There go wit, fame, friendship, ambition, high
repute! Ah! *aimons nous bien.* It seems to me
that is the only thing we can carry away. When
we go let us have some who love us wherever we
are. . . . Good-night."

Thackeray, himself "no small beer" as a
dandy in his young days, was a visitor to Gore
House, and we fancy liked its mistress better than
its master, with whom, however, he was on
quite friendly terms. Lady Ritchie remembers
a morning call paid by D'Orsay to her father :—

"The most splendid person I ever remember
seeing had a little pencil sketch in his hand, which
he left behind him on the table. It was a very
feeble sketch; it seemed scarcely possible to
admiring little girls that so grand a being should
not be a bolder draughtsman. He appeared to us

one Sunday morning in the sunshine. When I came hurrying down to breakfast I found him sitting beside my father at the table with an untasted cup of tea before him ; he seemed to fill the bow-window with radiance as if he were Apollo ; he leant against his chair with one elbow resting on its back, with shining studs and curls and boots. We could see his horse looking in at us over the blind. . . . I think my father had a certain weakness for dandies, those knights of the broadcloth and shining fronts. Magnificent apparitions used to dawn upon us in the hall sometimes, glorious beings on their way to the study, but this one outshone them all."

By the way, Chorley was never editor of the *Athenæum* as Greville states.

As for Brougham, what shall we say of that curious mixture of a man? Three parts genius and one part humbug?

It was at Gore House on 21st October 1839, that Alfred Montgomery read out the letter he had received which purported to come from Mr Shafto at Penrith, at Brougham Hall. It announced that Brougham had been killed by the overturning of a postchaise in which he was driving. The company present were completely deceived and the news was communicated to the papers, which with the exception of *The Times* gave it currency.

Henry Reeve was dining at the club when he heard a rumour that Brougham was ill, and straightway went up to Gore House, to find if there were any news. The letter had been brought over by Alfred Montgomery to Gore House early in the morning ; Shafto was the only uninjured survivor of the party of three in the chaise; Brougham had been stunned by a kick from one of the horses, thrown down and the carriage had turned over on to him, crushing him to death. D'Orsay spread the news round the town in the afternoon, when he took his walk abroad. Reeve had better be left to tell the rest of the story of that evening :—

"It was the most melancholy evening I ever spent there. In no house was Brougham so entirely tamed; in none, except his own, so much beloved. Only last Sunday week—not ten days ago—just six before his death—he dined there, and stayed very late, which he rarely did, leaving them dazzled with the brilliancy of his unflagging spirit. I was to have dined there too; they very earnestly pressed me; but I had promised to go to Richmond. They tried hard, too, to get Sir A. Paget; but we both stayed away, and they sat down to table *thirteen*. I can only say that the deaths which have struck me most in my life have always been preceded by a dinner of thirteen, in spite of efforts to avoid it."

Brougham, it is said, was very much interested in reading his obituary notices! Shafto promptly denounced the letter as a forgery. Who then wrote it? The Duke of Cambridge among many others suspected the corpse, and greeted Brougham at a Privy Council meeting with: "Damn you, you dog, *you* wrote that letter, you know you did!" and chased him round the room. D'Orsay apparently held the same opinion and was in turn himself accused of the hoax. Fonblanque writes to Lady Blessington :—

"The falsehood that Count d'Orsay had anything to do with the hoax was sufficiently refuted by all who knew him, by the two circumstances that it was stupid and cruel; and the unique characteristic of D'Orsay is, that the most brilliant wit is uniformly exercised in the most good-natured way. He can be wittier with kindness than the rest of the world with malice."

Reeve asserts roundly that Brougham wrote later to Montgomery, admitting that he was the perpetrator of the "thoughtless jest," and continues: "D'Orsay drew a capital sketch of Brougham in his plaid trousers, from memory, which we thought invaluable; and nobody could look at his wild, uncouth handwriting without tears in his eyes. In short, so bad a joke was never played off on so large a scale before; but one can't look forward without a good deal of amusement to Brougham's telling the story."

We meet Lyndhurst and Brougham together at Gore House this year, just as they appeared together in *Punch* later on in that famous cartoon "The Mrs Caudle of the House of Lords," drawn by Leech and invented by Thackeray. The picture represents Lyndhurst as Lord Chancellor reposing in bed, his head upon the woolsack, beside him Mrs Caudle Brougham, very much awake, and saying: "What do you say? *Thank heaven! You are going to enjoy the recess—and you'll be rid of me for some months?* Never mind. Depend upon it, when you come back, you shall have it again. No: I don't raise the House, and set everybody in it by the ears;

but I'm not going to give up every little privilege ;
though it's seldom I open my lips, goodness knows!"

Charles Sumner, the famous American senator
and jurist, visited Gore House in March, and records:

"As I entered her brilliant drawing-room, she
came forward to receive me with that bewitching
manner and skilful flattery which still give her
such influence. 'Ah, Mr Sumner,' she said,
'how sorry I am that you are so late! Two of
your friends have just left us—Lord Lyndhurst
and Lord Brougham ; they have been pronounc-
ing your *éloge.*' She was, of course, the only
lady present ; and she was surrounded by D'Orsay,
Bulwer, Disraeli, Duncombe, the Prince Napoleon,
and two or three lords. The house is a palace of
Armida, about two miles from town. . . . The
rooms are furnished in the most brilliant French
style, and flame with costly silks, mirrored doors,
bright lights, and golden ornaments. But Lady
Blessington is the chief ornament. The world
says she is almost fifty-eight ; by her own confession
she must be over fifty, and yet she seems hardly
forty: at times I might believe her twenty-five."

Of D'Orsay, Sumner writes, he "surpasses all
my expectations. He is the divinity of dandies ;
in another age he would have passed into the
court of the gods, and youths would have sacri-
ficed to the God of Fashion. . . . I have seen
notes and letters from him, both in French and
English, which are some of the cleverest I have
ever read ; and in conversation, whether French
or English, he is excessively brilliant."

But most amazing of all his conquests was

D'Orsay's subduing of Carlyle. Would it not have been thought that the dandy would have been a type peculiarly irritating to the author of *Sartor Resartus* ?

On 16th April 1839, Carlyle writes from Cheyne Row to his brother John :—

". . . I must tell you of the strangest compliment of all, which occurred since I wrote last—the advent of Count d'Orsay. About a fortnight ago, this Phœbus Apollo of dandyism, escorted by poor little Chorley, came whirling hither in a chariot that struck all Chelsea into mute amazement with splendour. Chorley's under jaw went like the hopper or under riddle of a pair of fanners, such was his terror on bringing such a splendour into actual contact with such a grimness. Nevertheless, we did amazingly well, the Count and I. He is a tall fellow of six feet three, built like a tower, with floods of dark auburn hair, with a beauty, with an adornment unsurpassable on this planet ; withal a rather substantial fellow at bottom, by no means without insight, without fun, and a sort of rough sarcasm rather striking out of such a porcelain figure. He said, looking at Shelley's bust, in his French accent : ' Ah, it is one of those faces who weesh to swallow their chin.' He admired the fine epic, etc., etc. ; hoped I would call soon, and see Lady Blessington withal. Finally he went his way, and Chorley with re-assumed jaw. Jane laughed for two days at the contrast of my plaid dressing-gown, bilious, iron countenance, and this Paphian apparition. I did not call till the other day, and left my card merely. I do not see well what good I can get by meeting him much, or Lady B. and demirepdom, though I should not object to see it once, and then oftener if agreeable."

But Carlyle was not always so complacent. In August 1848, the Carlyles received from Forster "An invaluable treat; an opera box, namely, to hear Jenny Lind sing farewell. Illustrious indeed. We dined with Fuz * at five, the hospitablest of men; at eight, found the Temple of the Muses all a-shine for Lind & Co. —the piece, *La Sonnambula*, a chosen bit of nonsense from beginning to end—and, I suppose, an audience of some three thousand *expensive-looking* fools, male and female, come to see this Swedish nightingale 'hop the twig,' as I phrased it. . . . 'Depend upon it,' said I to Fuz, 'the Devil is busy *here* to-night, wherever he may be idle!' Old Wellington had come staggering in to attend the thing. Thackeray was there; D'Orsay, Lady Blessington—to all of whom (Wellington excepted!) I had to be presented and give some kind of foolery—much against the grain."

A curious company this that D'Orsay moved in: Brougham, Lyndhurst, Sumner, Carlyle, Landor, Macready, Haydon, Bulwer, the Disraelis, father and son; men of brains and men without, of morals and of no morals; comedians and heavy tragedians; he himself the prince of comedians, though, as is often the case, beneath the light, lilting melodies there surged a solemn, minatory bass. An absolutely happy man this D'Orsay ought to have been, but—?

* Forster.

CARLYLE IN 1839
(*By D'Orsay*)

[TO FACE PAGE 188

XVIII

NOT only in the sports of the town but also in those of the country, and with equal success, did D'Orsay indulge, paying many a pleasant country visit. Thus in January 1840 he was down in Staffordshire hunting and shooting with Lord Anglesey, Lord Hatherston and other good sportsmen, and at the end of the same year he spent some weeks in the country with Lord Chesterfield. At Chesterfield House in town, too, D'Orsay passed many a pleasant hour with the generous, kindly Earl.

D'Orsay had a fondness for the theatre, both the regions before and behind the curtain, and for those connected with it in any way. J. R. Planché, herald, dramatist and student of costume, was at Gore House on 6th May 1840, there being a brilliant company and much bright talk. Bright companions and gay converse : no wonder that D'Orsay said that " he had never known the meaning of the word *ennui.*" To the production of Lytton's *Money* D'Orsay lent a hand in 1840, helping Macready in various ways to secure an accurate representation of club-life and so forth, introducing the actor to his hatter and so forth, and showing the innocent man how play-accounts and so forth were kept. Actors in those days must have been as innocent of the ways of the world as statesmen and politicians are in these times.

Of another play of Bulwer's, Charles Greville records :—

"March 8th, 1839.—I went last night to the first representation of Bulwer's play *Richelieu ;* a fine play, admirably got up, and very well acted by Macready, except the last scene, the conception of which was altogether bad. He turned Richelieu into an exaggerated Sixtus V., who completely lost sight of his dignity, and swaggered about the stage, taunting his foes, and hugging his friends with an exultation quite unbecoming and out of character. With this exception it was a fine performance ; the success was unbounded, and the audience transported. After Macready had been called on, they found out Bulwer, who was in a small private box next the one I was in with Lady Blessington and D'Orsay, and were vociferous for his appearance to receive their applause. After a long delay, he bowed two or three times, and instantly retreated. Directly after he came into our box, looking very serious and rather agitated ; while Lady Blessington burst into floods of tears at his success, which was certainly very brilliant."

Macready himself notes of this occasion : "Acted Cardinal Richelieu very nervously : lost my self-possession, and was obliged to use too much effort ; it did not satisfy me at all. How can a person get up such a play and do justice at the same time to such a character !"

It was in truth a dazzling circle of dandies with whom Lady Blessington and D'Orsay were surrounded : Disraeli, Bulwer, Ainsworth, Dickens

—in fact Gore House was the haunt of the
novelists, for to the above may be added
Thackeray and Marryat. Ainsworth aped D'Orsay
in matters of costume and attitudinising, but as is
so often the case with imitators the copy did not
nearly equal the great original. The author of
Jack Shepherd and many other capital stories was
"a fine, tall, handsome, well-whiskered fellow,
with a profusion of chestnut curls, and bore himself with no inconsiderable manifestation of self-
consciousness." Ainsworth started business life
as a publisher, but made fame and money as a
writer. In order to correct the above somewhat
acrid description of him, here is a pleasanter one
of later years :—

"The time is early summer, the hour about
eight o'clock in the evening ; dinner has been
removed from the prettily-decorated table, and
the early fruits tempt the guests, to the number
of twelve or so, who are grouped around it. At
the head there sits a gentleman no longer in his
first youth, but still strikingly handsome ; there is
something artistic about his dress, and there may
be a little affectation in his manners, but even
this may in some people be a not unpleasing
element. He was our host, William Harrison
Ainsworth, and, whatever may have been the
claims of others, and, in whatever circles they
might move, no one was more genial, no one
more popular."

Charles Dickens first visited Gore House in
1840, and soon gained and always retained the
friendship of D'Orsay. Dickens was a very vivid

dresser, his gay spirit loved riotous colours. He has been described as "rather florid in his dress, and gave me an impression of gold chain and pin and an enormous tie." Dickens thoroughly enjoyed the conviviality of Gore House, as is shown by the following letter :—

"COVENT GARDEN,
"*Sunday, Noon, December* 1844.

"MY DEAR LADY BLESSINGTON,—Business for other people (and by no means of a pleasant kind) has held me prisoner during two whole days, and will so detain me to-day, in the very agony of my departure for Italy again, that I shall not even be able to reach Gore House once more, on which I had set my heart. I cannot bear the thought of going away without some sort of reference to the happy day you gave me on Monday, and the pleasure and delight I had in your earnest greeting. I shall never forget it, believe me. It would be worth going to China—it would be worth going to America, to come home again for the pleasure of such a meeting with you and Count d'Orsay—to whom my love, and something as near it to Miss Power and her sister as it is lawful to send. . . ."

And this message in another letter to Lady Blessington, written in the following year :—

"Do not let your nieces forget me, if you can help it, and give my love to Count d'Orsay, with many thanks to him for his charming letter. I was greatly amused by his account of ——. There was a cold shade of aristocracy about it, and a dampness of cold water, which entertained me beyond measure."

There were three dandies in this Gore House circle of strangely different temperaments and abilities. Dickens, a thorough Englishman in almost every habit and instinct, who dressed violently rather than well, sported somewhat fantastic costumes simply because it was the fashion so to do among the young men with whom his growing fame had brought him into contact. In the inner meaning of the word Dickens was no dandy, but simply a dressy man ; his was not the dandiacal temper. Of this, indeed, there was far more in the Oriental Disraeli, though he, like his *Vivian Grey*, used high dressing as a pose. Whatever he undertook he loved to do well, and in his youth even to do to extremes. The effeminate dandy pose was excellently acted in the following which he tells of himself, writing from Malta to his father in 1830 :—

" Affectation tells here even better than wit. Yesterday, at the racket court, sitting in the gallery among strangers, the ball entered, and lightly struck me and fell at my feet. I picked it up, and observing a young rifleman excessively stiff, I humbly requested him to forward its passage into the court, as I really had never thrown a ball in my life. This incident has been the general subject of conversation at all the messes to-day ! "

And this from Gibraltar :—

" Tell my mother that as it is the fashion among the dandies of this place—that is, the

N

officers, for there are no others—not to wear
waistcoats in the morning, her new studs come
into fine play and maintain my reputation of
being a great judge of costume, to the admiration and envy of many subalterns. I have also
the fame of being the first who ever passed the
Straits with two canes, a morning and an evening
cane. I change my cane as the gun fires, and
hope to carry them both on to Cairo. It is
wonderful the effect these magical wands produce.
I owe to them even more attention than to being
the supposed author of—what is it?—I forget!"

Disraeli in his dress had a touch of the
fantastic, as thus, when he appeared at a dinner
party attired in a coat of black velvet lined
with satin, purple trousers with a gold stripe down
the seam, a scarlet waistcoat, lace ruffles down to
the fingers' tips, white gloves with rings worn outside them and his hair in long, black ringlets.

Dickens was only a clothes-deep dandy;
Disraeli was a true dandy as far as he went, but
he did not go all the way. He trifled with politics,
he did not realise that to be a perfect, complete
dandy, calls for the devotion of a lifetime.
D'Orsay made no such mistake; he was a dandy
through and through and all the way; a dandy
in love affairs, in his toilet, in his clothes, in his
sport, and in all the arts of life from cookery
down to sculpture. Thus it must be with every
great man; he aims at one target, pulls his bow
with all his strength, and shoots only at that
one mark. D'Orsay had but one aim, to lead
a life of dandified pleasure.

XIX

NAP

CHARLES SUMNER writes in March 1840 : " Lady Blessington is as pleasant and time-defying as ever, surrounded till one or two of the morning with her brilliant circle. . . . Prince Napoleon is always there, and of course D'Orsay."

Says Edmund Yates, writing of the great folk in Hyde Park at a later date :—

" There, in a hooded cabriolet, the fashionable vehicle for men-about-town, with an enormous champing horse, and the trimmest of tiny grooms —' tigers,' as they were called—half standing on the footboard behind, half swinging in the air, clinging on to the straps, would be Count d'Orsay, with clear-cut features and raven hair, the king of the dandies, the cynosure of all eyes, the greatest ' swell' of the day. He was an admirable whip— he is reported on one occasion, by infinite spirit and dash, to have cut the wheel off a brewer's dray which was bearing down upon his light carriage, and to have spoken of it afterwards as ' the triumph of mind over matter '—and always drove in faultless white kid gloves, with his shirt wristbands turned back over his coat-cuffs, and his whole ' turn-out' was perfection. By his side was occasionally seen Prince Louis Napoleon, an exile too, after his escape from Ham, residing in lodgings in King Street, St James'—he pointed out the house to the Empress Eugénie when, as Emperor of the French, on his visit to Queen Victoria, he drove by it. He was a constant visitor of Lady Blessington's at Gore House. Albert Smith, in later years, used to say he wondered whether, if he called at the Tuileries, the Emperor would pay him 'that eighteenpence,' the sum which one night at Gore House he borrowed from A. S. to pay a cabman."

A strange, almost uncanny personage in some ways, this Louis Napoleon, with his dogged, not to be daunted belief in his high destiny.

George Augustus Sala thus describes him :—

" A short, slight form he had, and not a very graceful way of standing. His complexion was swarthily pale, if I may be allowed to make use of that somewhat paradoxical expression. His hair struck me as being of a dark brown ; it was much lighter in after years ; and while his cheeks were clean-shaven, the lower part of his face was concealed by a thick moustache and an 'imperial' or chin-tuft. He was gorgeously arrayed in the dandy evening costume of the period . . . he wore a satin 'stock,' green, if I am not mistaken ; and in the centre of that stock was a breastpin in the image of a gold eagle encircled with diamonds."

Shee notes in May 1839, of an evening at Gore House : " Among the company last night was Prince Louis Napoleon. He was quiet, silent, and inoffensive, as, to do him justice, he generally is, but he does not impress one with the idea that he has inherited his uncle's talents any more than his fortunes. He went away before the circle quite broke up, leaving, like Sir Peter Teazle, 'his character behind him,' and the few remaining did not spare him, but discussed him in a tone that was far from flattering. D'Orsay, however, who came in later with Lord Pembroke, stood up manfully for his friend, which was pleasant to see."

Said D'Orsay : " C'est un brave garçon, mais pas d'esprit " ; yet stood manfully by him.

There is not the slightest doubt that very intimate relations existed between D'Orsay and Louis Napoleon during his days of exile in England. Napoleon III. was the son of Louis Napoleon, King of Holland and his wife Hortense, whom Lady Blessington met in Italy. Of this meeting the following entry from Lady Blessington's Journal, dated Rome, March 1828, is a quite interesting account :—

" Though prepared to meet in Hortense Bonaparte, ex - Queen of Holland, a woman possessed of no ordinary powers of captivation, she has, I confess, far exceeded my expectations. I have seen her frequently ; and spent two hours yesterday in her society. Never did time fly with greater rapidity than while listening to her conversation, and hearing her sing those charming little French *romances*, written and composed by herself, which, though I had always admired them, never previously struck me as being so expressive and graceful as they now prove to be. Hortense, or the Duchesse de St Leu, as she is at present styled, is of the middle stature, slight and well formed ; her feet and ankles remarkably

fine ; and her whole *tournure* graceful, and distinguished. Her complexion and hair are fair,
and her countenance is peculiarly expressive ; its
habitual character being mild and pensive, until
animated by conversation, when it becomes arch
and *spirituelle*. I know not that I ever en-
countered a person with so fine a tact, or so quick
an apprehension, as the Duchesse de St Leu :
these give her the power of rapidly forming an
appreciation of those with whom she comes in
contact ; and of suiting the subjects of conversation to their tastes and comprehensions. Thus,
with the grave she is serious, with the lively gay ;
and with the scientific, she only permits just a
sufficient extent of her own *savoir* to be revealed
to encourage the development of theirs. She is,
in fact, 'all things to all men,' without at the
same time losing a single portion of her own
natural character ; a peculiarity of which seems to
be, the desire, as well as the power, of sending
away all who approach her satisfied with themselves, and delighted with her. Yet there is no
unworthy concession of opinions made, or tacit
acquiescence yielded to conciliate popularity ; she
assents to, or dissents from, the sentiments of
others, with a mildness and good sense that
gratifies those with whom she coincides, or dis-
arms those from whom she differs. The only
flattery she condescends to practise is that most
refined and delicate of all, the listening with
marked attention to the observations of those
with whom she converses ; and this tacit symptom
of respect to others is not more the result of an

extreme politeness, than of a fine nature, attentive
to the feelings of those around her. . . .

"It is not often that a woman so accomplished
unites the more solid attraction of a highly-culti-
vated mind : yet in Hortense this is the case ;
for, though a perfect musician, a most successful
amateur in drawing, and mistress of three
languages, she is well read in history and *belles-
lettres ;* has an elementary knowledge of the
sciences, and a general acquaintance with the
works of the most esteemed authors of ancient
and modern times. Her remarks denote an
acute perception, and a superior understanding ;
and are delivered with such a perfect freedom
from all assumption of the self-conceit of a *bas-
bleu,* or the dictatorial style of one accustomed
to command attention, that they acquire an
additional charm from the modest grace with
which they are uttered. . . .

"She showed me her diamonds yesterday,
and some of them are magnificent, particularly
the necklace presented to the Empress Josephine
by the city of Paris. It is a *rivière* of large
diamonds, of such immense value that none but a
sovereign, or some of our own princely nobility,
could become the purchaser. Her other diamonds
are very fine, and consist of many *parures*, some
presented to her as Queen of Holland; and others
bequeathed to her, with the necklace, by her
mother. Her bed, furniture, and toilette service
of gilt plate, are very magnificent, and are the
same that served her in her days of regal state.
The arrangement of her apartments indicates a

faultless taste, uniting elegance and comfort with grandeur. She has some fine portraits of Napoleon and Josephine in her possession: on our contemplating them, she referred to her mother with as much sensibility as if her death had been recent.

"Prince Louis Bonaparte lives with his mother, and never did I witness a more devoted attachment than subsists between them. He is a fine, high-spirited youth, admirably well educated, and highly accomplished, uniting to the gallant bearing of a soldier all the politeness of a *preux chevalier;* but how could he be otherwise, brought up with such a mother? Prince Louis Bonaparte is much beloved and esteemed by all who know him, and is said to resemble his uncle, the Prince Eugène Beauharnois (*sic*), no less in person than in mind ; possessing his generous nature, personal courage, and high sense of honour."

It is not necessary to follow in any detail the career of Louis Napoleon, so we will skip on to the year 1840, when on 6th August he made his absurd descent upon France, landing at Boulogne with about sixty followers.

Lord Malmesbury, who was often a visitor at Gore House, mentions a curious little happening.

"*7th August.*—News arrived this morning of Louis Napoleon having landed yesterday morning at Boulogne with fifty followers. None of the soldiers, however, having joined him, the attempt totally failed, and he and most of those who accompanied him were taken. This explains an expression he used to me two evenings ago. He was standing on the steps of Lady

Blessington's house after a party, wrapped up
in a cloak, with Persigny by him, and I observed
to them : ' You look like two conspirators,' upon
which he answered : ' You may be nearer right
than you think.' "

Disraeli writes on the same day :—

" The morning papers publish two editions,
and Louis Napoleon, who last year at Bulwer's
nearly drowned us by his bad rowing, has now upset himself at Boulogne. Never was anything so
rash and crude to all appearances as this ' invasion,'
for he was joined by no one. A fine house in Carl-
ton Gardens, his Arabian horses, and excellent cook
was hardly worse than his present situation."

He was captured, tried, condemned to perpetual imprisonment, and consigned to the fortress
of Ham, where he remained for five years, and
then escaped to England.

On August 2nd, 1840, Planché relates that he
went between ten and eleven to Gore House,
where there had been a small dinner party, of
which four men had stayed on, Lord Nugent,
" Poodle " Byng, and two strangers. " The
youngest immediately engaged my attention.
It was the fashion in that day to wear black
satin kerchiefs for evening dress ; and that of the
gentleman in question was fastened by a large
spread eagle in diamonds, clutching a thunder-
bolt of rubies. There was but one man in
England at that period who, without the im-
peachment of coxcombry, could have sported so
magnificent a jewel ; and, though I had never
to my knowledge seen him before, I felt con-

vinced that he could be no other than Prince
Louis Napoleon. Such was the fact; and his
companion was Count Montholon." Planché
walked home with Nugent and Byng, one of
whom remarked: "What could Louis Napoleon
mean by asking us to dine with him this day
twelvemonths at the Tuileries?" The ill-
starred landing at Boulogne a few days later
explained the mystery.

But earlier in this same year (1840), D'Orsay
had supported the Prince in another adventure.

For many years a peculiar Count Léon had
been looked on as one of the curiosities of Paris;
in appearance he was an enlarged replica of
Napoleon the Great, which was not surprising
seeing that he was reputed—probably wrongly
—to be his son by the Polish Countess Walewska.
Napoleon provided for the education of his
offspring, who in 1830 attained the dignity of a
colonelcy in the Legion of the Garde Nationale.

In February 1840, Count Léon came over to
London, it being absurdly stated afterward that
he had been entrusted by the Tuileries with the
pleasing duty of removing Louis Napoleon.

The Prince refused to receive the Count,
from whom after some heated correspondence he
received a challenge, borne by Lieutenant-
Colonel Ratcliffe. Léon refused to engage with
swords, so pistols were decided upon; the hour
chosen being seven o'clock on the morning of
3rd March, and the place Wimbledon Common.
Napoleon was accompanied by D'Orsay and
Colonel Parquin. It was not until the parties

were on the ground that Count Léon raised the difficulty about the weapons to be used, and the delay caused by the discussion on the point gave time to the authorities to arrive and put an end to the contemplated breach of the peace. The upshot of this fiasco was an appearance at Bow Street. Before the Court proceeded to deal with the ordinary night charges, Prince Louis and Count Léon were charged before Mr Jardine with having attempted a breach of the peace by fighting a duel ; Ratcliffe, Parquin, D'Orsay, and Martial Kien, a servant, were brought in as being aiders and abettors. They were all "bound over," Mr Joshua Bates, of Baring Brothers, becoming surety for Prince Louis and Colonel Parquin, and the Honourable Francis Baring for D'Orsay. So ended the encounter.

On January 13th, 1841, Napoleon wrote from Ham to Lady Blessington, in reply to a letter from her :—

"I am very grateful for your remembrance, and I think with grief that none of your previous letters have reached me. I have received from Gore House only one letter, from Count d'Orsay, which I hastened to answer when I was at the Conciergerie. I bitterly regret that my letter was intercepted, for in it I expressed all the gratitude at the interest he took in my misfortunes. ... My thoughts often wander to the place where you live, and I recall with pleasure the time I have passed in your amiable society, which the Count d'Orsay still brightens with his frank and *spirituel* gaiety."

On the 26th of May 1846, there was gathered

together a gay dinner-party at Gore House, among those assembled, beside the host and hostess, being Landor and John Forster. A message was brought in to D'Orsay that a person, who preferred not to give his name, desired to see him. To the amazement of D'Orsay the unknown turned out to be Louis Napoleon, just landed after his escape from Ham. He came in and entertained the party with a vivacious account of his adventures.

Serjeant Ballantine describes a curious visit paid to him at his chambers in June 1847 by Louis Napoleon and D'Orsay, which certainly strengthens the statements made by others that the dandy was upon very intimate terms with the prince. The visit was concerned with some of Napoleon's money-raising endeavours, which had resulted in his being swindled by a rascally bill-discounter, but in which the Serjeant could not assist to right the wrong. Ballantine dubs D'Orsay, "the prince of dandies," adding that he "never saw a man who in personal qualities surpassed him"; continuing, he "was courteous to everyone, and kindly. He put the companions of his own sex perfectly at their ease, and delighted them with his varied conversation, and I never saw anyone whose manner to ladies was more pleasing and deferential."

Louis Philippe toppled over; a Republic was set up in February 1848, and Napoleon promptly and effectively took advantage of the situation thus created to push himself to the front. In December of the same year he was

elected President. The oath that he swore on
the occasion was : " In the presence of God and
before the French people represented by the
National Assembly, I swear to remain faithful to
the Democratic Republic, one and indivisible, and
to fulfil all the duties imposed on me by the
Constitution." And on the 2nd of December
1851, he dissolved the said Assembly, upset the
Republic, and shortly became Napoleon III,
Emperor of the French.

Among Napoleon's English advisers was
Albany Fonblanque, who through D'Orsay sent him
some suggestions as to the policy it would be wise for
the President of the French Republic to pursue.
How far that advice promised to produce fruit, the
following letter shows :—

"GORE HOUSE, 26th January 1849.

" MON CHER FONBLANQUE,—J'espère que vous
avez vu que notre conseil à été écouté ; les
réductions dans l'armée et la marine sont très
fortes, et Napoleon à éprouvé, je vous assure, une
grande opposition pour en arriver là. L'armée,
qui était en 1845 de 502,196 hommes et de 100,
432 horses, sera réduite en 1849 à 380,824
hommes et 92,410 chevaux. Le Budget de la
Marine est diminué de vingt deux millions et
plus ; la flotte en activité est réduite à dix
vaisseaux de ligne, huit frégates, etc.—et il y a
aussi une grande réduction dans les travaux des
arsenaux. Tout cela devrait plaire à John Bull
et à Cobden. Je vous promets que ces réductions n'en resteront pas là ; mais il faut considérer
la difficulté qu'il y a de toucher aux joujoux des

enfants français, car chez nous l'armée est l'objet principal; chez vous ce n'est qu'un accessoire. Votre affectionné, D'Orsay."

Madden, in his description of this "man-mystery," for once in a way is graphic. " I watched his pale, corpse-like, imperturbable features, not many months since, for a period of three hours. I saw eighty thousand men in arms pass before him, and I never observed a change in his countenance or an expression in his look which would enable the bystander to say whether he was pleased or otherwise at the stirring scene. . . . He did not speak to those around him, except at very long intervals, and then with an air of *nonchalance*, of *ennui* and eternal occupation with self; he rarely spoke a syllable to his uncle, Jérôme Bonaparte, who was on horseback somewhat behind him. . . . He gave me the idea of a man who had a perfect reliance on himself, and a feeling of complete control over those around him. But there was a weary look about him, an aspect of excessive watchfulness, an appearance of want of sleep, of over-work, of over-indulgence, too, that gives an air of exhaustion to face and form, and leaves an impression on the mind of a close observer that the machine of the body will break down soon, and suddenly—or the mind will give way—under the pressure of pent-up thoughts and energies eternally in action, and never suffered to be observed or noticed by friends or followers."

Louis Napoleon is, as everybody knows, the

NAPOLEON III

(*By D'Orsay*)

[TO FACE PAGE 206

Colonel Albert who plays so large a part in Lord Beaconsfield's unjustly neglected *Endymion*, quite one of the most delightful of his novels, although it contains that strange caricature of Thackeray in the grotesque personage of St Barbe. Says "Colonel Albert" :—". . . I am the child of destiny. That destiny will again place me on the throne of my fathers. That is as certain as I am now speaking to you. But destiny for its fulfilment ordains action. Its decrees are inexorable, but they are obscure, and the being whose career it directs is as a man travelling in a dark night ; he reaches his goal even without the aid of stars and moon."

Louis Napoleon emerged from the dark night of his exile and sat in the limelight that beats upon a throne, and he achieved his destiny without accepting the aid or advice of his friend, D'Orsay. He did not trust the latter with his counsels and could scarcely have been expected to ask him to accompany him to France. D'Orsay would have been the central figure ; the Prince of the Dandies would have basked in the popularity which the future Emperor of the French knew he must focus upon himself.

After his escape to London from Ham, Louis Napoleon, however, does seem to have consulted with D'Orsay, and acting upon his advice to have written to the French Ambassador to the Court of St James, stating that it was his intention to settle down quietly as a private individual ; which statement was doubtless taken for what it was worth. D'Orsay may have helped, also, toward Napoleon's election as President by interesting friends in his cause, but of the schemes upon the empty imperial throne D'Orsay appears to have been ignorant. Indeed, he went so far as to express his opinion of the *coup d'état*, that "it is the greatest political swindle that ever has been practised in the world!"

The following letter to Landor from Lady Blessington is interesting:—

"GORE HOUSE, *28th February* 1848.

"I will not admit that the eruption of the Parisian volcano has brought out only cinders from your brain, *au contraire*, the lava is glowing and full of fire—your honest indignation has been ignited and has sent forth a bright flame.

"It gave me great pleasure to see your handwriting again, for I had thought it long since I had heard from you. I saw it stated to-day in the *Daily News* that Count d'Orsay had set out for Paris with Prince Louis. This report is wholly untrue. Prince Louis has gone to Paris alone. Here no one pities Louis Philippe, nor has the report of his death mitigated the indignation excited against him. His family are to be pitied, for I believe they were not implicated in his crooked policy. Seldom has vengeance so rapidly overtaken guilt."

Still more interesting this from Landor to Lady Blessington, written about a year later, on 9th January 1849—

"Possibly you may never have seen the two articles I enclose. I inserted in the *Examiner* another, deprecating the anxieties which a truly patriotic and, in my opinion, a singularly wise man, was about to encounter, in accepting the

Presidency of France. Necessity will compel him to assume the Imperial Power, to which the voice of the army and people will call him.

"You know (who know not only my writings, but my heart) how little I care for station. I may therefore tell you safely, that I feel a great interest, a great anxiety, for the welfare of Louis Napoleon. I told him if ever he were again in prison, I would visit him there ; but never, if he were upon a throne, would I come near him. He is the only man living who would adorn one, but thrones are my aversion and abhorrence. France, I fear, can exist in no other condition. Her public men are greatly more able than ours, but they have less integrity. Every Frenchman is by nature an intriguer. It was not always so, to the same extent ; but nature is modified, and even changed, by circumstances. Even garden statues take their form from clay.

"God protect the virtuous Louis Napoleon, and prolong in happiness the days of my dear, kind friend, Lady Blessington. W. S. L."

"I wrote a short letter to the President, and not of congratulation. May he find many friends as disinterested and sincere."

Wellington also judged Napoleon's rise to power in France as propitious, and wrote to D'Orsay on 9th April 1849 :—"*Je me réjouis de la prospérité de la France et du succès de M. le Président de la République. Tout tend vers la permanence de la paix de l'Europe qui est nécessaire pour le bonheur de chacun. Votre ami très devoué.* WELLINGTON."

o

Though D'Orsay was not Napoleon's active ally, he watched his progress with interest, and, despite the opinion he held of the means employed, apparently with approbation also up to a point. To Madden on the first day of the Presidential election, a Sunday—but really we must here have Madden's own words :—" He came to my house before church-time, and diverted me from graver duties, to listen to his confident anticipations of the result of that memorable day. ' Think,' said he, ' what is the ordinary November weather in Paris : and here is a beautiful day. I have watched the mercury in my garden. I have seen where is the wind, and I tell you, that on Paris is what they will call the sun of Austerlitz. To-morrow you shall hear that, while we are now talking, they vote for him with almost one mind, and that he has the absolute majority.' "

And later, he wrote to Richard Lane, the artist : " *Rely upon it, he will do more for France than any sovereign has done for the last two centuries, if only they give him time.*"

Even previous to this exciting period, at the time of the Boulogne descent, Lady Blessington was shedding ink in the defence of D'Orsay; writing to Henry Bulwer :—

"GORE HOUSE, 17*th September* 1840.

" I am never surprised at evil reports, however unfounded, still less so at any acts of friendship and manliness on your part. . . . Alfred is at Doncaster, but he charges me to authorise you to contradict, in the most positive terms, the reports about his having participated in, or even known, of the intentions of the Prince Louis. Indeed, had he suspected them, he would have used every effort in his power to dissuade him from putting them into execution. Alfred, as well as I, entertain the sincerest regard for the Prince, with whom, for fourteen years, we have been on terms of intimacy ; but of his plans we knew no more than you did. Alfred by no means wishes to conceal his attachment to the Prince, and still less that any exculpation of himself should in any way reflect on him ; but who so well as you, whose tact and delicacy are equal to your good-nature, can fulfil the service to Alfred that we require ?

" Lady C——* writes to me that *I*, too, am mixed up in the reports. But I defy the malice of my greatest enemy to prove that I ever dreamt of the Prince's intentions or plans."

Both D'Orsay and Lady Blessington had to do with Napoleon as Emperor.

D'Orsay, to a certain extent, tried to run both with the fox and with the hounds, for, in 1841, an attempt was made to procure for him the appointment of Secretary to the French Embassy in London. The Count St Aulaire was then Ambassador, and much influence was brought to bear upon him in this matter.

Among Lady Blessington's papers was found the following memorandum by her, which throws considerable light upon this affair :—

" With regard to the intentions relative to our Count, there is not even a shadow of truth in

* Possibly Lady Canterbury.

them. Alfred never was presented here at Court, and never would, though I, as well as his other friends, urged it : his motive (for declining) being, never having left his name at any of the French Ambassadors of Louis Philippe (not even at Count Sebastiani's, a connection of his own) or at Marshal Soult's, also nearly connected with his family, he could not ask to be presented at Court by the French Ambassador, and did not think it right to be presented by anyone else . . . and the etiquette of not having been engaged to meet the Queen, unless previously presented at Court, is too well known to admit of any mistake. . . . I enter into these details merely to show the utter falsehoods which have been listened to against Alfred. Now with regard to his creditors, his embarrassments have been greatly exaggerated ; and when the sale of the northern estates in Ireland shall have been effected, which must be within a year, he will be released from all his difficulties.* In the meantime he has arranged matters, by getting time from his creditors. So that all the fuss made by the nomination, being only sought as a protection from them, falls to the ground. . . . I mention all these facts to show how ill Alfred has been treated. If the appointment in London is still deemed impracticable, why should not they offer him the secretaryship at Madrid, which is vacant ?

"Alfred entrusted the affair (of the appointment) to M—— and W——. He received posi-

---

* If Lady Blessington wrote this in good faith, "our Count" must have deceived her grossly as to the amount of his debts.

tive assurances from both that he would receive
an appointment in the French Embassy here,
and that it was only necessary, as a mere matter
of etiquette, that St Aulaire was to ask for his
nomination to have it granted. The assurances
were so positive that he could not doubt them,
and he accordingly acted on them. The highest
eulogies on Alfred's abilities and power of rendering service to the French Government were
voluntarily pronounced to St Aulaire by Lord
B——, the Duke of B——, and other persons of
distinction. M. St Aulaire, not satisfied with these
honourable testimonies, consulted a *coterie* of foolish
women, and listening to their malicious gossiping,
he concluded that the nomination would not be
popular in London, and so was afraid to ask for it.

"It now appears that the Foreign Office at
Paris is an inquisition into the private affairs of
those who have the misfortune to have any reference to it; a bad plan when clever men are so
scarce in France, and particularly those well-
born and well-connected : a Government like the
present should be glad to catch any such that
could be had.　　　　MARGT. BLESSINGTON."

To which may be added a letter from Henry
Bulwer to Lady Blessington, written in December
1841 :—

"MY DEAR LADY BLESSINGTON, — I think
D'Orsay wrong in these things you refer to : to
have asked for London especially, and not to
have informed me * how near the affair was to its

* Bulwer was at this time *chargé d'affaires* at Paris.

maturity when St Aulaire went to the D. of B——'s, because I might then have prepared opinion for it here; whereas, I first heard the affair mentioned in a room, where I had to contend against every person present, when I stated what I think—that the appointment would have been a very good one. But it does not now signify talking about the matter, and saying that I should have wished our friend to have given the matter rather an air of doing a favour than of asking one. It is right to say that he has acted most honourably, delicately, and in a way which ought to have served him, though, perhaps, it is not likely to do so. The French Ambassador did not, I think, wish for the nomination. M. Guizot, I imagine, is, at this moment, afraid of anything that might excite discussion and opposition, and it is idle to disguise from you that D'Orsay, both in England and here, has many enemies. The best service I can do him is by continuing to speak of him as I have done amongst influential persons, viz., as a man whom the Government would do well to employ; and my opinion is, that if he continues to wish for and to seek employment, he will obtain it in the end. But I don't think he will obtain the situation he wished for in London, and I think it may be some little time before he gets such a one as he ought to have, and that would suit him. The Secretaryship in Spain would be an excellent thing, and I would aid the Marshal in anything he might do or say respecting it. I shall be rather surprised, however, if the present man is recalled. Well do not let D'Orsay lose courage. Nobody succeeds in these things just at the moment he desires : ——, with his position here" (speaking of a French nobleman), "has been ten years getting made an ambassador, and at last is so by a fortunate chance. Remember also how long it was, though I was in Parliament, and had some little interest, before I was myself fairly launched in the *diplomatic career*. Alfred has all the qualities for success in anything, but he must give the same trouble and pains to the pursuit he now engages in that he has given to other pursuits previously. At all events, though I speak frankly and merely what I think to him, I am here and always a sincere and affectionate friend, and most desirous to prove myself so."

To Madden, Henry Bulwer expressed the opinion :—" It was altogether a great pity D'Orsay was not employed, for he was not only fit to be so, but to make a most useful and efficient agent, had he been appointed."

But Governments, as well as individuals, are fallible, and often blind to their best interests. Yet it really is difficult to understand why D'Orsay was refused his modest request ; what more distinguished ornament to an Embassy could be desired than a splendid libertine and a man distinguished for the vastness of his debts ? Unfortunately, mediocrity succeeds often enough when transcendent genius fails.

XX

WALTER SAVAGE LANDOR, who was born in 1775,
lived on hale and hearty till 1864. As he himself
wrote :—

> " I warm'd both hands before the fire of life ;
> It sinks, and I am ready to depart."

He was, as we have seen, the very good friend
of both D'Orsay and Lady Blessington, whom he
first met when he was living in Italy.

In a letter to Lady Blessington, in 1837,
Landor presented her with his autobiography in
brief :—

"Walter Landor, of Ipsley Court, in the
county of Warwick, married first, Maria, only
daughter and heiress of J. Wright, Esq., by
whom he had an only daughter, married to her
cousin, Humphrey Arden, Esq., of Longcroft,
in Staffordshire; secondly, Elizabeth, eldest
daughter and co-heiress of Charles Savage, of
Tachebrooke, who brought about eighty thousand
pounds into the family. The eldest son of this
marriage, Walter Savage Landor, was born 30th
January 1775. He was educated at Rugby—
his private tutor was Dr Heath, of St Paul's.
When he had reached the head of the school, he
was too young for college, and was placed under
the private tuition of Mr Langley of Ashbourne.
After a year, he was entered at Trinity College,

Oxford, where the learned Beonwell was his private tutor. At the peace of Amiens, he went to France, but returned at the end of the year.

"In 1808, on the first insurrection of Spain, in June he joined the Viceroy of Gallicia, Blake. The *Madrid Gazette* of August mentions a gift from him of twenty thousand reals. On the extinction of the Constitution, he returned to Don P. Cavallos the tokens of royal approbation, in no very measured terms. In 1811, he married Julia, daughter of J. Thuillier de Malaperte, descendant and representative of J. Thuillier de Malaperte, Baron de Nieuveville, first gentleman of the bed-chamber to Charles the Eighth. He was residing at Tours, when, after the battle of Waterloo, many other Englishmen, to the number of four thousand, went away. He wrote to Carnot that he had no confidence in the moderation or honour of the Emperor, but resolved to stay, because he considered the danger to be greater in the midst of a broken army. A week afterwards, when this wretch occupied Tours, his house was the only one without a billet. In the autumn of that year, he retired to Italy. For seven or eight years, he occupied the Palazzo Medici, in Florence, and then bought the celebrated villa of Count Gherardesea, at Fiesole, with its gardens, and two farms, immediately under the ancient villa of Lorenzo de Medici. His visits to England have been few and short."

This is but the bare bones of a very interesting life; but its very bluntness seems to illustrate the character of its writer, a member of the *genus irritabile*, whom many hated, many loved and most men admired. For several years he made his home at Bath, living there from 1838 to 1858, when again he retired to Italy, where he died at Florence.

He is, perhaps, best known to the world at large under the slight disguise of Lawrence Boythorn in *Bleak House*.

Charles Sumner describes him thus in 1838 :—
" Dressed in a heavy frock-coat of snuff colour, trousers of the same colour, and boots . . . with an open countenance, firm and decided, and a head grey and inclining to baldness . . . conversation . . . not varied, but it was animated and energetic in the extreme. We crossed each other several times; he called Napoleon the weakest, littlest man in history."

Forster's account is more vivid :—
" He was not above the middle stature, but had a short stalwart presence, walked without a stoop, and in his general aspect, particularly the set and carriage of his head, was decidedly of what is called a distinguished bearing. His hair was already silvered grey, and had retired far upward from his forehead, which wide and full but retreating, could never in the earlier time have been seen to such advantage. What at first was noticeable, however, in the broad white massive head, were the full yet strangely-lifted eyebrows. In the large, grey eyes there was a depth of compound expression that ever startled by its contrast to the eager restlessness looking out from the surface of them ; and in the same variety and quickness of transition the mouth was extremely striking. The lips, that seemed com-

pressed with unalterable will would in a moment
relax to a softness more than feminine ; and a
sweeter smile it was impossible to conceive."

Carlyle says that "he was really stirring company ; a proud, irascible, trenchant, yet generous,
veracious and very dignified old man ; quite a
ducal or royal man in the temper of him."

He was very frequently at Gore House, and
they must have made a curious trio, the fascinating Lady Blessington, the ducal Landor and
dandy D'Orsay.

He addressed these lines to her :—

> "What language, let me think, is meet
> For you, well called the Marguerite.
> The Tuscan has too weak a tone,
> Too rough and rigid is our own ;
> The Latin—no—it will not do,
> The Attic is alone for you."

Of some of his many visits here are a few
notes :—

Writing Friday, 7th May 1841 :—

" I did not leave my cab at Gore House gate
until a quarter past six. My kind hostess and
D'Orsay were walking in the garden and never
was more cordial reception. After dinner we
went to the English opera, *The Siege of Rochelle*
and *A Day at Turin*. Nothing could be worse
than the first except the second. The Hanoverian
minister, very attentive to Miss Power, a Carlist
viscount, and Lord Pembroke were the only
persons who stayed any time in the box," and on
8th May he writes again from Gore House : " We
went this evening to the German Opera. Never
was music so excellent. The pieces were *A
Night in Grenada* and *Fidelio*. Madame Schodel

sings divinely, and her acting is only inferior to
Pasta's. . . . Both D'Orsay and Lord Pembroke
were enchanted with Madame Schodel, and Lady
B. and Miss Power, both good judges, and the
latter a fine composer, were breathless. To-night
we go to the Italian Opera."

Landor writing from Gore House in June 1842 :

" We have not been to the Opera this evening,
as Lord Pembroke and the Duc de Guiche came
to dinner. He is on a visit to Lord Tankerville,
but has the good taste to prefer the society he
finds here, particularly D'Orsay's. D'Orsay was
never in higher spirits or finer plumage."

On July 20th he writes :—

" A few days after my arrival in town, the
Duc de Grammont dined at Gore House. He is
on a visit to Lord Tankerville. . . . D'Orsay has
just finished an exquisite painting of the Duchesse."

Then on September 7th :—

" I arrived at Gore House early on Monday.
In the morning, beside Lord Allen and some
other people, there called Lord Auckland. . . .
At dinner the Duc de Guiche, Sir Francis Burdett
and Sir Willoughby Cotton. . . . Those were
bright hours ; even my presence could not
interrupt their brilliancy. . . . The Duc de
Guiche left us this morning to shoot with his
cousin, Lord Ossulton.* We miss the liveliness
of his conversation—he talked Memoirs."

When he was not at Gore House he kept up
a very lively correspondence with his two friends,
some of which it will be useful to quote, for in
familiar letters we become almost on speaking

* Son of Lord Tankerville.

terms with their writers, and who of us would not be glad to chat with Lady Blessington, Landor and D'Orsay?

This from her to him, when sending him her portrait :—

"I send you the engraving, and have only to wish that it may sometimes remind you of the original. You are associated in my memory with some of my happiest days; you were the friend, and the highly-valued friend, of my dear and lamented husband, and as such, even without any of the numberless claims you have to my regard, you could not be otherwise than highly esteemed. It appears to me that I have not quite lost him, who made life dear to me, when I am near those he loved * and that knew how to value him. Five fleeting years have gone by since our delicious evenings on the lovely Arno, evenings never to be forgotten, and the recollections of which ought to cement the friendships then formed. This effect I can, in truth, say has been produced on me, and I look forward, with confidence, to keeping alive, by a frequent correspondence, the friendship you owe me, no less for that I feel for you, but as the widow of one you loved, and that truly loved you. We, or more properly speaking I, live in a world where friendship is little known, and were it not for one or two individuals like yourself, I might be tempted to exclaim with Socrates : 'My friends, there are no friends.' Let us prove that the philosopher was wrong, and if Fate has denied us the comfort of meeting, let us by letters keep

* Did he love D'Orsay?

up our friendly intercourse. You will tell me what you think and feel in your Tuscan retirement, and I will tell you what I do, in this modern Babylon, where thinking and feeling are almost unknown. Have I not reason to complain that in your sojourn in London you do not give me a single day? And yet methinks you promised to stay a week, and that of that week I should have my share. I rely on your promise of coming to see me again before you leave London, and I console myself for the disappointment of seeing so little of you, by recollecting the welcome and the happiness that await you at home. Long may you enjoy it, is the sincere wish of your attached friend, M. BLESSINGTON."

He to her, in the shape of "bits" out of a long letter written from Florence in March 1835 :—

"Poor Charles Lamb, what a tender, good, joyous heart had he! What playfulness! what purity of style and thought! His sister is yet living, much older than himself. One of her tales is, with the sole exception of the *Bride of Lammermoor*, the most beautiful tale in prose composition in any language, ancient or modern. A young girl has lost her mother, the father marries again, and marries a friend of his former wife. The child is ill reconciled to it, but being dressed in new clothes for the marriage, she runs up to her mother's chamber, filled with the idea how happy that dear mother would be at seeing her in all her glory—not reflecting, poor soul, that it was only by her mother's death that she appeared in it. How natural, how novel is all this! Did you ever imagine that a fresh source of the pathetic would burst forth before us in this trodden and hardened world? I never did, and when I found myself upon it, I pressed my temples with both hands, and tears ran down to my elbows.

" The Opium-eater calls Coleridge ' the largest and most spacious intellect, the subtlest and most comprehensive that has yet existed among men.' Impiety to Shakespeare! treason to Milton! I give up the rest, even Bacon. Certainly, since their day, we have seen nothing at all comparable to him. Byron and Scott were but as gun-flints to a granite mountain; Wordsworth has one angle of resemblance; Southey has written more, and all well, much admirably. . . .

" Let me add a few verses as usual :—

> ' Pleasures—away, they please no more :
> Friends—are they what they were before?
> Loves—they are very idle things,
> The best about them are their wings.
> The dance—'tis what the bear can do;
> Music—I hate your music too.
> Whene'er these witnesses that time
> Hath snatch'd the chaplet from our prime
> And called by nature (as we go
> With eyes more wary, step more slow),
> And will be heard, and noted down,
> However we may fret or frown;
> Shall we desire to leave the scene
> Where all our former joys have been?
> No! 'twere ungrateful and unwise :
> But when die down our charities
> For human weal and human woes,
> 'Tis then the hour our days should close.' "

And this :—

" D'Orsay's mind is always active. I wish it would put his pen in motion. At this season of the year (January) I fancied he was at Melton. Does not he lament that this bitter frost allows him no chance of breaking his neck over gates and double hedges? Pray offer him my kind remembrances."

And here a chatty little note from D'Orsay :—

"It is a fact, that my brave nephew has been acting the part of Adonis, with a *sacré cochon*, who nearly opened his leg;* his presence of mind was great, he was on his lame leg in time to receive the second attack of the infuriated beast, and killed him on the spot, plunging a *couteau de chasse* through his heart—luckily the wild boar had one. The romantic scene would have been complete, if there had been another Gabrielle de Vergy looking at this modern Raoul de Courcy. We think and speak of you often, and are in hopes that you will pay us a visit soon. Poor Forster is ill and miserable at the loss of his brother. I am sure that Forster is one of the best, honestest and kindest men that ever lived. I had yesterday a letter from Eugene Sue, who is in raptures with Macready as an actor and as a man. We saw lately that good, warm-hearted Dickens—he spoke of you very affectionately. . . . —Most affectionately,   D'ORSAY."

* The Duke de Guiche, son of D'Orsay's sister, had been attacked by a wild boar while out hunting.

XXI

THE ARTIST

It behoves us now to pay some attention to D'Orsay's claims as an artist; if he had posed simply as an amateur, silence would be possible, but he worked for money, entered the lists with other artists, and therefore laid himself open to judgment. In his own day he was highly thought of by many—here we have what was written of him in *La Presse* on November 10th, 1850, when D'Orsay's bust of Lamartine was exhibited :—

"M. le comte d'Orsay est un amateur de l'art plutôt qu'un artiste. Mais qu'est-ce qu'un amateur ? C'est un volontaire parmi les artistes ; ce sont souvent les volontaires qui font les coup d'éclat dans l'atelier comme sur les champs de bataille. Qu'est ce qu'un amateur ? C'est un artiste dont le génie seul fait la vocation. Il est vrai qu'il ne reçoit pas dans son enfance et pendant les premières années de sa vie cette éducation du métier d'où sort Michel Ange, d'où sort Raphaël . . . mais s'il doit moins au maître, il doit plus à la nature. Il est son œuvre. . . . M. d'Orsay exerça dans les salons de Paris et de Londres la dictature Athénienne du goût et de l'élégance. C'est un de ces hommes qu'on aurait cru préoccupé de succès futiles,—parce que la nature semble les avoir créés uniquement pour son plaisir—mais qui trompent la nature, et qui, après avoir recueilli les légères admirations des jeunes gens et des femmes de leur âge, échappent à cette atmosphère de

légèreté avant le temps où ils laissent ses idoles
dans le vide, et se transforment par l'étude et par
le travail en hommes nouveaux, en hommes de
mérite acquis et sérieux. M. d'Orsay a habité
longtemps l'Angleterre ou il donnait l'exemple et
le ton à cette société aristocratique, un peu raide
et déforme, qui admire surtout ce qui lui manque,
la grâce et l'abandon des manières. . . .

"Dès cet époque, il commenca à jouer avec
l'argile, le marbre, le ciseau, lié par un attache-
ment devenu une parenté d'esprit, avec une des
plus belles et des plus splendides femmes de son
époque, il fit son buste pendant qu'elle vivait ; il
le fit idéal et plus touchant après sa mort. Il
moula en formes après, rudes, sauvages, de grandeur fruste, les traits paysanesque d'O'Connell.
Ces bustes furent à l'instant vulgarisés en
millièrs d'exemplaires en Angleterre et à Paris.
C'étaint des créations neuves. . . .

"Ces premiers succès furent des plus com-
plets. Il cherchait un visage. Il en trouva
un. Lord Byron, dont il fut l'ami et avec lequel
il voyagea pendant deux ans * en Italie, n'était
plus qu'un souvenir aimé dans son cœur. . . . Il fit
le buste de Lamartine, . . ." and then there is
something approaching very closely to a rhapsody
on this work of art, and then a set of verses by
Lamartine himself !

Debt drove D'Orsay to seek in art a means of
adding to his income ; in the case of Mr. Mitchell
of Bond Street, who published a series of portrait
drawings, it is even possible that he used his art
to cancel his debt for Opera boxes, etc. ! These

---

* The inaccuracies here are obvious.

portraits were 14 inches high and 10½ inches wide
and were sold at 5s. each. The set must have
been almost a pictorial " Who's Who," and among
those honoured with inclusion may be named
Byron, Disraeli, Theodore Hook, Carlyle, Liszt,
D'Orsay himself, the Duke of Wellington, Greville,
Louis Napoleon, Bulwer Lytton, Trelawney,
Landor, Dickens, Lady Blessington, Henry
Bulwer, Captain Marryat and Sir Edwin Landseer.

Richard James Lane, the engraver and litho-
grapher, saw much of D'Orsay, and judging by
the following letter held him in esteem :—

" As a patron, his kind consideration for my
interest, and prompt fulfilment of every engagement, never failed me for the more than twenty
years of my association with him ; and the friendship that arose out of our intercourse (and which
I attest with gratitude) proceeded at a steady
pace, without the smallest check, during the
same period ; and remained unbroken, when on
his final departure from England, he continued to
give me such evidence of the constancy of his
regard, as will be found conveyed in his letters.

" In the sketches of the celebrities of Lady
Blessington's *salons*, which he brought to me
(amounting to some hundred and fifty, or more),
there was generally an appropriate expression and
character, that I found difficult to retain in the
process of elaboration ; and although I may have
improved upon them in the qualities for which I
was trained, I often found that the final touches of
his own hand alone made the work satisfactory.

" Of the amount and character of the assistance of which the Count availed himself, in the

production of his pictures and models, I have a clear notion. . . .

"When a gentleman would rush into the practice of that which, in its mechanism, demands experience and instruction, he avails himself of the help of a craftsman, whose services are sought for painting-in the subordinate parts, and working out his rude beginnings. In the first rank of art, at this day, are others who, like the Count d'Orsay, have been unprepared, excepting by the possession of taste and genius, for the practice of art, and whose merits are in no way obscured by the assistance which they *also* freely seek in the manipulation of their works; and it is no less easy to detect, in the pictures of the Count, the precise amount of mechanical aid which he has received from another hand, than the graces of character and feeling that are superadded by his own. I have seen a rough model, executed entirely by himself, of such extraordinary power and simplicity of design, that I begged him to have it *moulded*, and not to proceed to the details of the work, until he could first place this model side by side with the cast in clay, to be worked up. He took my advice, and his equestrian statue of the first Napoleon may fairly justify my opinion.

"In art, he had a heartfelt sympathy, a searching eye, and a critical taste, fostered by habitual intercourse with some of our first artists."

This letter from D'Orsay to Lane shows the Count in an amiable light :—

"PARIS, 21st *February* 1850.

"MY DEAR LANE,—I cannot really express to you the extent of my sorrow about your dear and good family. You know that my heart is quite open to sympathy with the sorrows of others. But judge therefore, how it must be, when so great a calamity strikes a family like yours, which family I always considered one of the best I ever had the good fortune to know. What a trial for dear Mrs Lane, after so many cares, losing a son like yours, just at the moment that he was to derive the benefit of the good education you gave him. . . . There is no consolation to offer. The only one that I can imagine, is to think continually of the person lost, and to make oneself more miserable by thinking. It is, morally speaking, an homœopathic treatment, and the only one which can give some relief. . . . Give my most affectionate regards to your dear family, and believe me always —far or near. Your sincere friend, D'ORSAY."

In 1843 D'Orsay writes jestingly of himself : " I am poetising, modelling, etc., etc. In fact, I begin to believe that I am a Michael Angelo *manqué.*"

Concerning the Wellington statuette, D'Orsay writes to Madden : " You must have seen by the newspapers that I have completed a great work, which creates a revolution in the Duke of Wellington's own mind, and that of his family. It is a statuette on horseback of himself, in the costume and at the age of the Peninsular war. They say that it will be a fortune for me, as every regiment in the service will have one, as the Duke says publicly, that it is the only work by which he desires to be known, physically, by portraits. They say that he is very popular in Portugal and Spain. I thought possibly that you could sell for me the copyright at Lisbon, to some speculator to whom I could send the mould."

Shortly before his death he completed a smaller equestrian statuette of the Duke, an account of which was given in the *Morning Chronicle* of 23rd December 1852 :—

"One of the last of the late lamented Count d'Orsay's studies was a statuette of the Duke on horseback, the first copy of which, in bronze, was carefully retouched and polished by the artist. The work is remarkable for its mingled grace and sprightliness. The Duke, sitting firmly back in his saddle, is reining in a pawing charger, charmingly modelled, and a peculiar effect is obtained by the rider dividing the reins, and stretching that on the left side completely back over the thigh. The portrait is good, particularly that of the full face, and very carefully finished, and the costume is a characteristic closely-fitting military undress, with hanging cavalry sabre. Altogether, indeed, the statuette forms a most agreeable memorial, not only of the Duke, but, in some degree, of the gifted artist."

Henry Vizetelly roundly states that there was no secrecy about the help rendered to D'Orsay in his equestrian statuettes, etc., by T. H. Nicholson, a draughtsman of horses, and that the faces of these works of art were modelled by Behnes. He goes on to say: "The statuette of the Duke of Wellington on horseback was undoubtedly Nicholson's, and that famous bust of the Iron Duke which was to make the fortune of the lucky manufacturer who reproduced it in porcelain, is said to have been his and Behnes' joint work."

Then follows this amusing story :—

"Sir Henry Cole—Old King Cole of the Brompton toilers,* and Felix Flummery of the art-manufacture craze—used to tell an amusing story of the high estimate, artistic and pecuniary, which D'Orsay set upon this production. The Count had written to ask him to call at Gore House, and on his proceeding there, after handing his card through the wicket, he was cautiously admitted to the grounds and safely piloted between two enormous mastiffs to the door of the house. He was then conducted to the Count, whom he found pacing up and down Lady Blessington's drawing-room in a gorgeous dressing-gown.

"D'Orsay, Cole used to say, at once broke out with—'You are a friend of Mr Minton's! I can make his fortune for him!' Then turning to his servant, 'François,' said he, 'go to my studio and in the corner you will find a bust. Cover it over with your handkerchief and bring it carefully here.' François soon returned carrying his burthen as tenderly as though it were a baby, and when he had deposited it on the table, the Count removed the handkerchief and posing before the bust with looks of rapt admiration, he promptly asked Cole—

"'What do you think of that?'

"'It's a close likeness,' Cole cautiously replied.

"'Likeness! indeed it is a likeness!' shouted the Count, 'why, Douro when he saw it exclaimed : "D'Orsay, you quite appal me with the likeness to my father!"'

"The Count then confided to Cole that the Duke had given him four sittings, after refusing, said he, a single sitting to 'that fellow Landseer.'

* Now (1910) no more.

" The Duke it seems came to inspect the bust after it was completed. In D'Orsay's biassed eyes he was as great in art as he was in war, and he always went, the Count maintained, straight up to the finest thing in the room to look at it. Naturally, therefore, he at once marched up to the bust, paused, and shouted :—

" ' " By God, D'Orsay, you have done what those damned busters never could do." '

" The puff preliminary over, the Count next proceeded to business.

" ' The old Duke will not live for ever,' he sagely remarked ; ' he must die one of these days. Now, what I want you to do is to advise your friend Minton to make ten thousand copies of that bust, to pack them up in his warehouse and on the day of the Duke's death to flood the country with them, and heigh presto ! his fortune is made.'

" The Count hinted that he expected a trifle of £10,000 for his copyright, but Cole's friend, Minton, did not quite see this, and proposed a royalty upon every copy sold. D'Orsay, who was painfully hard up for ready cash, indignantly spurned the offer. . . ."

D'Orsay is most generally known as an artist by reason of his large portrait of the Duke of Wellington now in the National Portrait Gallery, upon the completion of which the Duke is said to have shaken hands with the painter, saying : " At last I have been painted like a gentleman ! I'll never sit to anyone else." And he certainly did write to Lady Blessington :— " You are quite right. Count d'Orsay's work is of a higher description of art than is described by the word portrait! But I described it by that word, because the likeness is so remarkably good, and so well executed as a painting, and that this is the truest of all artistic ability, truest of all in this country." Which last sentence is rather enigmatical.

Anent the statuette of O'Connell, referred to already, may be quoted a letter written by D'Orsay on 16th March 1847 to John Forster:—

"Prince Napoleon told me to-night at the French play, that he read in an evening paper, the *Globe*, I think, an article copied from an Irish paper, stating that I had made a statuette of O'Connell, and praising it, etc. I suppose that it is from Osborne Bernal,* who is in Ireland. But I would be glad it were known that I have associated him in the composition with the Catholic Emancipation, and also that I intend to make a present of the copyright to Ireland, for the benefit of the subscription for the poor."

Of other works from his hand we may name the bust of Emile de Girardin, a portrait of Sir Robert Peel, and the picture of which some details have already been given, showing a group in the garden of Gore House.

We have already quoted an account of one visit paid by D'Orsay to Haydon, here is that of a second, from an entry in the painter's Diary, dated 31st June 1838 :—

"About seven, D'Orsay called, whom I had not seen for long. He was much improved, and looking the glass of fashion and the mould of form ; really a complete Adonis, not made up at all. He made some capital remarks, all of which

* Better known to us now as Bernal Osborne.

must be attended to. They were sound impressions, and grand. He bounded into his cab, and drove off like a young Apollo, with a fiery Pegasus. I looked after him. I like to see such specimens."

In conclusion on this subject, from the *New Monthly Magazine* of August 1845, this :—

" Whatever Count d'Orsay undertakes, seems invariably to be well done. As the arbiter elegantiatum he has reigned supreme in matters of taste and fashion, confirming the attempts of others by his approbation, or gratifying them by his example. To dress, or drive, to shine in the gay world like Count d'Orsay was once the ambition of the youth of England, who then discovered in this model no higher attributes. But if time, who ' steals our years away,' steals also our pleasures, he replaces them with others, or substitutes a better thing ; and thus it has befallen with Count d'Orsay.

" If the gay equipage, or the well-apparelled man be less frequently seen than formerly, that which causes more lasting satisfaction, and leaves an impression of a far more exalted nature, comes day by day into higher relief, awakening only the regret that it should have been concealed so long. When we see what Count d'Orsay's productions are, we are tempted to ask, with Malvolio's feigned correspondent, ' Why were these things hid ? ' "

All things considered we may write down Count d'Orsay as a quite first-rate amateur, as skilful in the arts as any dandy has ever been. What more fitting than that his skill and accomplishment were best shown in his bust of Lady Blessington ?

LADY BLESSINGTON

(*From the Bust by D'Orsay*)

[TO FACE PAGE 234

XXII

D'ORSAY, had he devoted his time and his mind to the matter, could doubtless have attained high eminence as a painter and sculptor, but he was wise and refused to be bitten by the temptation; he well knew that there are many artists, but few dandies. The gifts that other men would have cultivated exclusively, he used to heighten and perfect his genius as a master of dandyship. It is perhaps the highest attribute of genius to be able to recognise genius—in oneself; only mediocre men are modest. Modesty is a sign of incompetency or stupidity.

Could D'Orsay have achieved greatness as a writer? Byron thought very highly of the journal which, it will be remembered, D'Orsay wrote during his first visit to London, but we cannot accept this criticism as final, for the poet's literary judgment was often faulty.

He is reputed to have been a contributor to some of the journals of the day and he was put forward as the "editor" of the translation published in London in 1847 of a French novel, *Marie, Histoire d'une Jeune Fille*. But other men have gained fame with as little regular literary baggage as the Count, literature in the form of familiar letters, written always, or almost always, without a thought that they would meet the public eye. Of casual letters we have a fair number of D'Orsay's, and some of them make quite pleasant reading. At any rate they are as good as those which are not written by dandies, which is saying much, for dandies have many important affairs to fill their time. They are chatty epistles, serve to shed a light upon their writer's character; by his letters to his friends you may know the man.

Here is a note from him to Landor, written in September 1828 :—

' I have received, dear Mr Landor, your letter. It has given us great pleasure. You ought to feel sure that we should particularly appreciate a letter from you, and it will appear that our intimacy in Florence counted for nothing with you if you doubt the pleasure that your news arouses in us. As soon as I have received the pictures I will carry out your commission carefully. I do wish you would come to Paris, for we have some fine things to show you, particularly pictures. Apropos, I am sending you herewith the portrait of Prince Borghese, which I hope you will find to be a good likeness. . . . We talk and think often of you. It is really strange that you are in the odour of sanctity in this family, for it seems to me it is not exactly this sort of reputation you pique yourself on possessing.

"Lady B. and all our ladies send you a thousand good wishes and I renew the assurance of the sincerity of mine.—Yours very affectionately,   D'Orsay."

" All our ladies," included Lady d'Orsay.

Then of a much later date, probably 1842 or 1843 :—

"I think that Henry the Eighth was at Richmond-on-the-Hill when Anne Boleyn was beheaded. They say that he saw the flag which was erected in London as soon as her head fell. Therefore, as you make him staying at Epping Forest at that time, and as I am sure you have some good reasons for it, I will thank you to give them to me.

"We regretted much not to have seen you at Bath, and I was on the moment to write to you, like Henry the Fourth did to the brave Crillon after the battle!

"'Pends toi, brave Landor, nous avons été à Bath, et tu n'y étois pas—'

"You will be glad to hear that the second son of my sister has been received at the Ecole of St Cyr, after a ticklish examination. Hoping to see you soon, believe me, yours most affectionately,

"D'ORSAY."

There is not very much of distinction, perhaps, in these two letters, but they serve to show the familiar friendship of the two men and also that the dandy studied his English History, at any rate as far as concerns the disposal of wives.

With John Forster he kept up a fairly lively correspondence, some of the letters containing points of interest :—

"GORE HOUSE, 25th October 1844.

"It is really an age since you've been here. It's a poor joke! Where *have* you been? . . . Macready has sent me a Boston paper, in which I

have read with great interest of his success. . . .
I have not seen 'De la Roche' Maclise. Give
him a thousand good wishes.

"Eugene Sue gets better and better ; he leads
you to his moral by somewhat perilous roads, but
once you get there you find it pure and beautiful.
The fecundity of his imagination surpasses all
previous works ; the Jesuits are smashed up, the
convents broken down and the workman raised
upon their debris. Amen.—Yours ever,

D'Orsay."

Was it not to this practical Forster that D'Orsay
wrote upon his project for establishing a means of
communication between the guard and the engine-
driver of a train ?   But the "sacrés directeurs de
rail road" would not adopt his idea because of
their own ideas of economy.

"P.M., *4th August* 1845.

"I am determined to follow up the directors
until they take up my scheme, and if you will
assist me" (*i.e.* by writing in the papers), "these
continual accidents will establish a 'raw,' which we
will tickle continually with cayenne pepper, and in
the end they will take real steps to heal the
wound.   My idea is this, that they shall have a
seat behind the last carriage of every train, just
like the coachman's of a hansom cab.   It would
be in communication with the engine by a long
cord passing along the whole length of the roof of
the carriages ; on pulling the cord a hammer would
strike a gong by the engine and would indicate
that a halt must be made. . . ."

There was also to be an arrangement of lamps

and a cord—very similar to that now in use—for the benefit of travellers in trouble. Quite sufficient in all this to prove that a dandy need not be a fool.

"GORE HOUSE, 25*th September* 1845.

" I am sorry to tell you that Lady Blessington a reçu des nouvelles " (from here the letter is in French) ; " very alarming concerning the health of Lady Canterbury. There is no doubt she is gradually sinking, surrounded by those who choose to blind themselves to her condition. . . . It will be best, I think, for you to tell our dear Dickens why for the moment we must abandon our plans. I should most willingly have gone with you to Knebworth, we will arrange to go there together when I can manage a day. . . ." Knebworth was Lord Lytton's country seat.

The letter continues, throwing a light upon the dark side of our comedy :—

" Think of poor Lady Blessington losing in so short a time her niece, her little niece, her nephew, her brother-in-law, and her sister dying. . . ."

Then again he returns to his railway scheme :—

" I was just going to write to you from the country, where I have been some time, to tell you that Lady C—— and Lady Sophie de V—— went to Derby by rail ; they were in the last carriage of the train. One of the connections is broken, the carriage is tossed from right to left and left to right so violently, that the two unhappy people think they are lost, and wave their handkerchiefs out of the window. They call out ; no one sees them ; no one hears them, and happily they reach the station, not a moment too soon—

the carriage could not have held out. You will
see that a guard in such a case would have saved
this? Do you think we had better drop the
subject or take it up again? *Au revoir*, brave
Forster."

"BOURNEMOUTH, HANTS, 9*th September* 1848.

" We are in the most charming neighbourhood
in the world, a kind of Wheemby Hill with the
sea : it is three hours from Southampton. Come
and see us! You will be delighted, it is perfection
for bathing, and the weather is superb ; it is the
climax of summer. . . ."

Of Mathews' friendship with D'Orsay in Italy,
an account has already been given ; the following
letters show that it was continued on paper :—

"17*th November* 1831.

" MY DEAR CHARLES . . . I have lost my poor
friend Blessington and my mother within two
months ; they died in my arms, and when I think
of them it is always their last moments that come
to my mind. I would it were in other times, but
that is difficult. . . ."

The following from London :—

"1*st September*.

" MY DEAR CHARLES . . . I was the other
day at Goodwood. . . . Since I learnt that you
had taken the Adelphi I agreed with Lord
Worcester that we would do all we could to
interest society in your favour by thinking and
talking about it. I understand that the first idea
of Y (ates)* is to put you at a disadvantage, he
himself will leave you, in order to make you feel

* Frederick Henry Yates, actor and theatrical manager. Father
of Edmund Yates.

that he is indispensable ; this season is a trial that he gives you, hoping that in case of a failure you will give everything up into his hands. No matter what happens you must remedy this. Reeves, also, goes to America. Mrs Honey is engaged elsewhere ; in short, most of the old names connected with the theatre are going. I therefore recommend you to make an arrangement with the proprietor of the Queen's Theatre, who would join his company with yours ; union gives strength, and thanks to your talents you will triumph completely over the trap which Y (ates) has set for you. The Queen's Theatre has been very successful this season ; to-day they have taken £90 ; it is wonderful for the time of year. Chesterfield, Worcester and myself have a box there and we wish to have one at the Adelphi, and speaking this evening on the matter to Bond, he told me that he would be delighted to join his company with yours and then to close the Queen's Theatre. Think it over, see if you would not find it to your advantage, and let me know.—Your sincere friend, etc. D'ORSAY."

The Adelphi was opened by Yates and Mathews on 28th September 1835 ; the house was full, but the season was not satisfactory.

The details of acting and stage production were not beneath D'Orsay's notice :—

" MY DEAR CHARLES,—I like your new piece very much, and you acted very well. You must ask the orchestra to accompany you a little less noisily, for the noise they made made it impossible to follow a quarter of your Aria. You

Q

would do well, also, in my opinion, to cut out two verses of the Welsh song. Your French-woman is perfect ; it is the best that I have yet seen presented in an English theatre. Use your influence to make Oxberry wear a·black wig, he will be the image of George Wombwell,* he has the dress and the manner to perfection, and it will be a hit. Wombwell won't be annoyed, on the *contrary.* . . . *Au revoir,* dear Charles.—Your affectionate,   D'ORSAY."

The bright vivacity of the following letter to Dr Quin had best be left in its native French :—

"*8th Août* 1831,

"SEAMORE PLACE, MAYFAIR.

CHER ET ESTIMABLE QUIN,—Régénérateur de l'humanité souffrante ! Nouveau Prophète dont les disciples s'essoufflent à chanter les louanges, et qui finira par triompher comme la civilisation régnante ; comment se fait il que vous oubliez entièrement votre disciple Alfred, n'attendez pas en vain l'arrivée d'un ange du ciel pour m'éclairer mais déroulez vos Papyrus pour y graver les progrès de la marche gigantesque de cette *methodus medendi,* qui jointe à votre intelligence vous assure pour votre vieillesse un outrage de Lauriers dont l'épaisseur permettroit à peine que vous soyez encore plus eclairé par le rayon de gloire que le Ciel dirigera sur vous—Maintenant que je vous ai dit ma façon de penser à votre égard, parlons de moi dans un style *moins laconique.*

"Depuis mon arrivée dans ce pays il étoit difficile de pouvoir donner un *Fair Trial,* à la

* Probably the founder of the famous menagerie.

méthode, étant toujours obligé à diner et boire un verre de vin, avec tous ceux qui ont soif. Ainsi je l'ai abandonné trop tôt pour me guérir, mais toujours à temps pour me pénétrer que jusqu'à ce jour le genre de humain a vegeté au lieu de vivre—Il faut donc que je recommence malgré que je souffre moins ; repénêtrez vous de ma santé, consultez vos oracles, et voyez à me reprendre en main comme vous l'aviez fait. Je suivrai ponctuellement vos airs, et vous aurez au moins la gloire d'avoir guéri une des trompettes de la renommée de la méthode, et un ami sincère. Détaillez bien la manière de prendre, les remèdes, et prescrivez non pas en *paraboles*, mais dans votre style persuasif. . . . Adieu, brave Quin. Je vous serre la main non pas de toutes mes forces, mais de tout mon cœur.—Votre devoué et sincère ami, ALFRED D'ORSAY."

Dr Quin was the first homœopathic practitioner in England, and in his early days was denounced as a quack. He was endowed with an inexhaustible fund of good humour, was a wit and a master of repartee. In a postscript to another letter D'Orsay writes :—

"You have, my friend, an unbearable mania, that of always defending the absent. Don't you know that there is a French proverb which says, 'Les absens ont toujours tort ?' This fashion never goes out, and, the devil, you who are the 'pink of fashion,' you must be in the mode."

Jekyll declared to Lady Blessington that he "was asked gravely if quinine was invented by Doctor Quin!"

Here is a quaint little note to the Doctor :—

"GORE HOUSE, *Saturday.*

"MY DEAR DR QUIN,—M. Pipelet (D'Orsay) requests that you will send him the letter about Mr —— you promised he should have. I suppose it is in vain to tell you we are going to the Opera to-night. Of course you have 999 impatient patients who *must* see you every five minutes throughout the course of the day and night, and as many more friends who expect you to dinner. However, *en passant*, I venture to hint that we go with Mdme. Calabrella, so if you manage to kill off the maladies, and put the friends under the table in turn, we shall be delighted to see you ready and waiting, as Homer says in the fifth book of the *Iliad*, line forty-nine. Farewell, may you be happy whilst I— Sobs choke my utterance. Adieu."

XXIII

D'ORSAY might have been a great artist and a great man of letters ; of his genius as a financier there is no doubt. He solved the question of how to obtain unlimited credit ; he paid such debts as he did cancel with money which legally was his, but which almost any other man would not have cared to touch.

Lord Blessington is said, when he persuaded D'Orsay to abandon his career in the French army, to have undertaken to provide for the Count's future, and he fulfilled his promise at the expense of his daughter's happiness and of the family estates.

In the return made of " The Annuities, Mortgages, Judgments and other Debts, Legacies, Sums of Money, and Incumbrances, charged upon or affecting the Estates of the said Charles John, Earl of Blessington, at the Time of his Decease," we find that the mortgages and sums of money charged on D'Orsay's account from 1837 to 1845, amounted to the quite respectable sum of £20,184. In Blessington's will all his estates in Dublin, bringing in a rental of £13,322, 18s. 8d. were left to whichever of his daughters married D'Orsay.

By the marriage settlement £20,000 was to be paid to trustees, the Duc de Guiche, and Robert Power, within twelve months of the solemnisation, and a further £20,000 on Blessington's decease; the money to be invested in the funds, and the interest thereupon to be paid to D'Orsay during his life.

As we have seen, the happy couple separated actually in 1831, legally in 1838.

In 1834 an order was made by the Court of Chancery in Ireland, upon which was thrown the task of clearing up the mess made of his property by Blessington, granting D'Orsay an income of £500, and to his wife £450.

How great that mess was, for which D'Orsay and his wife were partly to blame, will be seen from the following facts. The Countess had run up debts to the tune of £10,000, which sum, however, is scarcely worth mentioning beside that incurred by her husband. By the deed of separation between them, D'Orsay relinquished all his claims on the Blessington estates, in consideration—

i. Of £2467 of annuities granted by him being redeemed, which cost £23,500.

ii. In consideration of the sum of £55,000 being paid to him, £13,000 of which was to be raised as soon as possible, and £42,000 within ten years.

A grand total of money which all went in one way or another to pay off D'Orsay's debts.

As to the estate: the trustees were empowered by Act of Parliament to make sales to the amount of £350,000 to pay off all encumbrances and claims. Thus ended the glory of the Blessington fortune; thus often has it been in Ireland.

D'Orsay found fortune and lost it; he could

not even retain the wife with which it was encumbered.

Over £100,000 of debts we know he paid, and still he owed very much. For at least two years previous to his final departure from England he went in constant dread of arrest at the instigation of sordid persons, who had not sufficient understanding of the fact that it was an honour to them to help in the support of a great man. There are too many petty-minded people in the world! Just heavens! That a man of D'Orsay's calibre should be confined to his house and grounds all the days of the week save Sunday, excepting that he could creep forth under cover of darkness! That the Prince of the Dandies should go in danger of the vile clutch of a sinister myrmidon of the law and of the degradation of a sponging-house.

In 1845 D'Orsay apparently realised that his pecuniary condition was irreparable, and sought in vain for means of escape. He prepared a schedule of his liabilities, the total sum of his indebtedness amounting to £107,000, not including a number of debts to private friends, which made an additional sum of £13,000. It was even contemplated that he should go through the Court of Bankruptcy, but a difficulty was found in the fact that it could not be proved that he was a commercial man or an agriculturalist. He only sowed wild oats.

The situation so pressed upon him, that he allowed himself for a time to become the prey of impostors, who declared that they had achieved what the alchemists of old had so long looked for in vain, the conversion of the baser metals into gold!

From an unveracious chronicle we quote a passage which is veracious :—

"Now, among the shyest birds that ever ducked from a missile of the law was, without an exception the Marquis d'Horsay (D'Orsay). His maxim had long been 'catch me who can;' at the same time, acting up to the patent-safety rule of 'prevention being so much better than cure,' he afforded no facilities whatever of being hobbled in the chase. At bay he kept the yelping pack, and within the good, stout, rich walls of his covert he maintained both a pleasant and a secure retreat from the dangers besetting him. He now no longer ventured to frame himself, as it were, in his cab, and exhibit his colours and attractions to the curious crowds, except on that privileged day—when even the debtor is at liberty to rest—the seventh of the week.* Then, indeed, he issued forth, decked as of old, and, like a bird free from the confines of his cage, made the most of the brief hours of his freedom.

"Every art, every manœuvre within the subtle and almost inexhaustible resources of those apt functionaries of the law who are ever on the alert to deprive the subject of his liberty, let him be never so chary of the preservation of it, had been put in force to trap our hero ; but hitherto in vain. Mr Sloughman,† truly, arrived within a short journey of accomplishing this much-desired end ; still he was frustrated, and now among the

---

* The first is meant.
† *Alias* Sloman, a well-known catchpole

ranks of bums there was a cloud which damped
their hopes and mildewed their energies. The
Marquis was not to be grabbed, and they knew
it. With flagging spirits the attempts were
renewed over and over again. Bribes and offers
of rewards were extended liberally to his menials
for their traitorous assistance in obtaining the
design, but they had been too well selected, and
knew their own interests depended on no such
frail or fleeting benefits. False messengers in all
garbs and disguises, upon all kinds of errands and
excuses, applied for admission and interviews.
Even—yes, even the fair sex were at last made
not bearers of Love's despatches, but conveyancers
of stern writs, notices of declarations, trials, and
suchlike means to the end and breaking up
of a man of fashion. Still the Marquis was proof
against all these attacks, let them come in what
shape they would."

That may be fancy, but it is close akin to fact.

In *The English Spy* we read of the crowd
in Hyde Park of a Sunday afternoon at the
fashionable hour :—

> "The low-bred, vulgar, Sunday throng,
> Who dine at two, are ranged along
>   On both sides of the way ;
> With various views, these honest folk
> Descant on fashions, quiz and joke,
>   Or march a *shy cock** down ;
> For many a star in fashion's sphere
> Can only once a week appear
>   In public haunts of town,
>   Lest those two ever *watchful* friends,
> The *step*-brothers, whom sheriff sends,
>   John Doe and Richard Roe,

* A shy cock being a "Sunday" man, such as D'Orsay.

A *taking* pair should deign to borrow,
To wit, until *All Souls* the morrow,
   The body of a beau ;
But Sunday sets the prisoner free,
He *shows* the Park, and laughs with glee,
   At creditors and Bum."

Henry Vizetelly used on occasion to make an early call upon Thackeray, and walk into town with him from Kensington. "On one of these journeys," he says, "soon after Lady Blessington gave up Gore House to reside in Paris, I remember his taking me with him to look over the little crib, adjacent to the big mansion, where Count d'Orsay, Lady Blessington's recognised lover, was understood to have resided, with the view of saving appearances. For years past the ringleted and white-kidded Count, although his tailor and other obliging tradespeople dressed him for nothing, or rather, in consideration of the advertisement that his equivocal patronage procured for them, had been a self-constituted prisoner through dread of arrest for debt. It was only on Sundays that he ventured outside the Gore House grounds, and for his protection on other days the greatest possible precaution was exercised when it was necessary for any of Lady Blessington's many visitors to be admitted. D'Orsay's friend, Thomas Slingsby Duncombe, who was mixed up with him in numerous bill transactions, used to say that the Count's debts amounted to £120,000, and that before he retired to the safe asylum of Gore House, he was literally mobbed by duns."

Tom Duncombe describes Lady Blessington's parties as gay, "where all the men about town

HYDE PARK CORNER IN 1824

[TO FACE PAGE 250

assembled, and sunned themselves in her charms ;
and where, for certain reasons, she was secure from
the intrusion of rivals. There Count d'Orsay,
tied by the leg with 120,000*l.* of debt, was sure
to welcome his '*cher Tomie.*'"

"*Cher Tomie*" saw and knew much of D'Orsay,
and did his best to help him in his money troubles.
The following letters tell a tale of woe :—

Saturday, 12th February 1842.

"MY DEAR TOMMY,—I know that you have
been to C. Lewis, and that he told you it was
settled. It is not so ; he expected that I would
have signed the renewals at sixty per cent. which
he sent me, and which I delivered. Therefore,
if you have a moment to lose, have the kindness
to see him this morning and persuade him of the
impossibility of my renewing at that rate ; say
anything you like on the subject, but that is the
moral of the tale. You must come and dine with
us soon again.—Yours faithfully,

"D'ORSAY."

Thursday, 6th April 1842.

"MY DEAR TOMMY,—I see by the papers that
Lord Campbell and Mr T. S. Duncombe received
a petition against the *Imprisonment for Debt !*
It is the moment to immortalise yourself, and
also the *sweetest* revenge against all our gang of
Jews, if you succeed in carrying this petition
through. I have taken proper means to keep
this proposal alive in the Press. Will you come
and dine with us ?—Yours affectionately,

"D'ORSAY."

This last *may* refer to the schedule above-mentioned :—

" My Dear Tommy,—I send you this precious document ; the only one I could obtain. It is a flaring-up page of the *History of the Nineteenth Century!* God is great, and will be greater the day He will annihilate our persecutors. *En attendant*, I am always,—Your affectionate friend,

" D'Orsay."

The following refers again to the Imprisonment Abolition Bill :—

" Mon Cher Tommy,—I think that we ought to try to ascertain how far the humbugging system can go. As soon as I received your note this morning I wrote to Brougham, and explained all the unfructuous attempts of Mr Hawes.* I enclose the first answer. *Now*, he has just been here, after having had a long conversation with Lyndhurst, who is decided to spur the Solicitor-General, stating, as the Parliament will last until Thursday week, there will be time enough to pass the bill. See what you can do with Mr Hawes. I am sure that if he will strike the iron now, when it is hot, that we have still a chance. Lyndhurst, I assure you, is very anxious about it, and expressed it strongly to Brougham. Do not be discouraged.—Yours affectionately,

" D'Orsay."

The enclosed note from Brougham ran :—

" Mon Cher A.,—Je suis *coloré* plutôt que *désespéré*. Il faut que je mette ordre à tout cela. Je vais chez Lyndhurst dans l'instant, H. B."

* M.P. for Southwark.

Tom Duncombe was himself a capital hand at getting into debt; we read :—"Duncombe is playing good boy, having completely drawn in; he has given up his house and carriages, and taken his name out of the Clubs. He had become so involved that he could not carry on the war any longer. They say that he has committed himself to the amount of 120,000*l.*"

Readers of *Vanity Fair* will recall " Mr Moss's mansion in Cursitor Street," "that dismal place of hospitality," to which Colonel Crawdon was an unwilling visitor. It was such an ordeal, that D'Orsay was determined not to undergo. Shame upon those who threatened him with it.

Madden tells us that D'Orsay's sister " makes no concealment of her conviction that Count d'Orsay's ignorance of the value of money—the profuse expenditure into which he was led by that ignorance, the temptation to play arising from it, the reckless extravagance into which he entered, not so much to minister to his own pleasure, as to gratify the feelings of an inordinate generosity of disposition, that prompted him to give whenever he was called on, and to forget the obligations he contracted for the sake of others, and the heavy penalties imposed on his friends by the frequent appeals for pecuniary assistance—were very grievous faults, and great defects in his character."

Mice nibbling at the reputation of a lion! Faults and defects; it is so easy to see spots on the sun! The world is often cruel to its greatest men; and who can deny that D'Orsay was much ill-used? Who can realise the suffering inflicted on his generous heart by the lack of generosity in others? How absurd to insult his memory by calling "reckless extravagance" that which in ordinary men would be so, but which in him was the striving to fulfil his great destiny. If his spirit haunts the earth it must be torture, worse than any in the place to which he may have gone, to find that he should have been so greatly misunderstood. It is a lovable trait in a man that he should give to others of his superfluity; it is adorable in D'Orsay that he should have distributed with open hand and tender heart the spare cash of others. Petty questionings as to right and wrong, *meum et tuum*, to which commonplace men rightly pay attention, have no claim upon such a man as D'Orsay. To the good all things are good.

He had the tongue of the charmer. Mr Mitchell, to whom he owed much money, would in moments of despair, write and demand immediate payment In all his glory D'Orsay would answer in person; would calm the tempest with fair words and would usually succeed in *increasing* his indebtedness.

CHAPTER XXIV

THERE cannot, indeed, be any question but that D'Orsay possessed the gift of fascination; his personality was one that compelled both admiration and attention. It is impossible to define or describe wherein exactly lies this power of personality. Of two women equally beautiful and apparently equally attractive, one will fascinate and the other will not, but it surpasses the ability of even those who are fascinated to say wherein is the difference between the two charmers.

D'Orsay had charm, and for our part we believe that with him, at any rate, part of this charm lay in the fact that he did not grow old; those whom the gods love die young despite the passage of years. He was young and he was gay; and joyousness is singularly and strongly attractive in a world where the majority of men and women are apt to be unjoyous. Gaiety of spirits, and unconquerable, unquenchable *joie de vivre*, are treasures above all price because they cannot be purchased.

Especially with those who make pleasure a pursuit, and it was with such that D'Orsay chiefly forgathered, the amusements of life too frequently become "stale, flat and unprofitable"; such folk make pleasure the business of life, pleasure does not come to them naturally, spontaneously; they suffer from that most wearing of mental troubles, boredom. Far otherwise was it with D'Orsay. We have been with him now in many places and with many companies, and never once has there been a hint that he was either satiated with enjoyment or depressed when things went astray. He often said himself: "I have never known the meaning of the word *ennui*."

Beneath all the tinsel and unreality of some of Disraeli's novels, there is always a stratum of keen observation and shrewd knowledge of men and women. It will help us, therefore, in our understanding of D'Orsay to see how he appeared to his friend and fellow-dandy.

Disraeli sketched D'Orsay's portrait as Count Alcibiades de Mirabel in *Henrietta Temple*: "The satin-lined coat thrown open . . . and revealing a breastplate of starched cambric . . . ," the wristbands were turned up with "compact precision," and were fastened by "jewelled studs." "The Count Mirabel could talk at all times well. . . . Practised in the world, the Count Mirabel was nevertheless the child of impulse, though a native grace, and an intuitive knowledge of mankind, made every word pleasing and every act appropriate. . . . The Count Mirabel was gay, careless, generous. . . . It seemed that the Count Mirabel's feelings grew daily more fresh, and his faculty of enjoyment more keen and relishing. . . ." Into Count Mirabel's mouth is put this, which sounds very D'Orsayish: "Between ourselves, I do not understand what this being bored is," said the Count. "He who is bored appears to me a bore. To be bored supposes the

inability of being amused. . . . Wherever I may
be, I thank heaven that I am always diverted."
Then this: "I live to amuse myself, and I do
nothing that does not amuse me." And this:
"Fancy a man ever being in low spirits. Life is
too short for such *bêtises*. The most unfortunate
wretch alive calculates unconsciously that it is
better to live than to die. Well then, he has
something in his favour. Existence is a pleasure,
and the greatest. The world cannot rob us of
that, and if it be better to live than to die, it is
better to live in a good humour than a bad one.
If a man be convinced that existence is the
greatest pleasure, his happiness may be increased
by good fortune, but it will be essentially independent of it. He who feels that the greatest
source of pleasure always remains to him, ought
never to be miserable. The sun shines on
all; every man can go to sleep; if you cannot
ride a fine horse, it is something to look upon
one; if you have not a fine dinner, there is
some amusement in a crust of bread and
Gruyère. Feel slightly, think little, never
plan, never brood. Everything depends upon
the circulation; take care of it. Take the
world as you find it, enjoy everything. *Vive la
bagatelle!*"

Then further on :—

"The Count Mirabel was announced. . . .

"The Count stood before him, the best-dressed
man in London, fresh and gay as a bird, with
not a care on his sparkling visage, and his eye
bright with *bonhomie*. And yet Count Mirabel
had been the very last to desert the recent

R

mysteries of Mr Bond Sharpe;* and, as usual,
the dappled light of dawn had guided him to his
luxurious bed—that bed that always afforded him
serene slumbers, whatever might be the adventures of the day, or the result of the night's
campaign. How the Count Mirabel did laugh
at those poor devils, who wake only to moralise
over their own folly with broken spirits and
aching heads. Care, he knew nothing about;
Time, he defied; indisposition he could not com-
prehend. He had never been ill in his life, even
for five minutes.

"Melancholy was a farce in the presence of
his smile; and there was no possible combination
of scrapes that could withstand his kind and
brilliant raillery."

Then to his friend, Armine, who is *distrait* :—

"A melancholy man! *Quelle bêtise!* I will
cure you; I will be your friend, and put you all
right. Now we will just drive down to Richmond; we will have a light dinner—a flounder,
a cutlet, and a bottle of champagne, and then we
will go to the French play. I will introduce you
to Jenny Vertpré. She is full of wit; perhaps
she will ask us to supper. Allons, mon ami, mon
cher Armine; allons, mon brave!"

Could Armine resist a tempting invitation so
irresistible? No, "so, in a few moments, he was
safely ensconced in the most perfect cabriolet in
London, whirled along by a horse that stepped
out with a proud consciousness of its master."

We hold that portrait to be excellent not only
as regards the outer but also the inner man

* At Crockford's.

D'Orsay. He was the "child of impulse," not a
cold, cynical, calculating voluptuary; he did not
deliberately "feel slightly, think little"; it was
not in him to suffer deep emotion or to think
deeply. "*Vive la bagatelle!*" that was his
motto, because for him there was not in life anything else than "*bagatelle*"; existence for him
was compounded of "trifles light as air." His
good spirits, as Disraeli hints, were based upon
his splendid physical vitality as infectious good
spirits must ever be. The joy of life may be
apparent to and partially enjoyed by those whose
physical health is weak, but complete realisation
of the joy of living, of merely being alive, is only
for those whose vitality is abundant and superb.
Further, he had the faculty of enjoying himself;
it was not that he would not but that he could
not be bored.

Even children felt his fascination. Madden
writes :—

"One of the proofs of the effect on others of
his insinuating manners and prepossessing appearance, was the extreme affection and confidence he
inspired in children, of whom he was very fond,
but who usually seemed as if they were irresistibly
drawn towards him, even before he attempted to
win them. The shyest and most reserved were
no more proof against this influence than the most
confiding. Children who in general would hardly
venture to look at a stranger, would steal to his
side, take his hand, and seem to be quite happy
and at ease when they were near him."

Nor, as we have learned, was it merely the
butterflies who found pleasure in his sunny nature;

he had a striking faculty of suiting himself to his company, an adaptability which is essential for success in general society. Landor loved him, so almost it may be said did the somewhat stern Macready. Indeed the actor was one of the most ardent of D'Orsay's admirers; he wrote after his death :—

"No one who knew and had affections could help loving him. When he liked he was most fascinating and captivating. It was impossible to be insensible to his graceful, frank and most affectionate manner. I have reason to believe that he liked me, perhaps much, and I certainly entertained the most affectionate regard for him. He was the most brilliant, graceful, endearing man I ever saw—humorous, witty and clear-headed. But the name of D'Orsay alone had a charm; even in the most distant cities of the United States all inquired with interest about him."

A few notes from Macready's Diary, and from records kept by others, will serve to confirm the testimony already adduced of the great variety and interest of the friends with whom D'Orsay was surrounded in the Gore House days.

On February 16th, 1839, there was a pleasant company there, of which Macready makes this record :—

"Went to Lady Blessington's with Forster, who had called in the course of the day. Met there the Count de Vigny, with whom I had a most interesting conversation on *Richelieu*. . . . Met also with D'Orsay, Bulwer, Charles Buller, Lord Durham, who was very cordial and courteous to me, Captain Marryat, who wished to be reintroduced to me, Hall, Standish, Chorley, Greville, who wished to be introduced to me also, Dr Quin, etc. Passed a very agreeable two hours."

With most of these we have already met on other occasions. On May 31st, 1840, Macready met at Gore House the Fonblanques, Lord Normanby, Lord Canterbury, Monckton Milnes, Chorley, Rubini and "Liszt, the most marvellous pianist I ever heard. I do not know when I have been so excited." And in April 1846, we hear of him dining at Gore House in the company of, amongst others, Liston, Quin, Chesterfield, Edwin Landseer, Forster, Jerdan and Dickens.

And on the other hand many a time did D'Orsay dine with Macready to meet good company, but Lady Blessington was not and could not be included in the invitations. It is a feather in their caps for men to conquer beautiful ladies, but *væ victis*. On the evening of May 6th, 1840, Planché "was present at a very large and brilliant gathering at Gore House. Amongst the company were the Marquis of Normanby and several other noblemen, and, memorably, Edwin Landseer. During the previous week there had been a serious disturbance at the Opera, known as 'The Tamburini Row,' and it naturally formed the chief subject of conversation in a party, nearly every one of whom had been present. Lord Normanby, Count d'Orsay, and Landseer were specially excited; there was some difference of opinion, but no quarrelling, and the great animal painter was in high spirits and exceedingly amusing till the small hours of the morning, when we

all gaily separated, little dreaming of the horrible
deed perhaps at that very moment perpetrating,
the murder of Lord William Russell by his valet
Courvoisier."

Of James Robinson Planché, herald and writer
of extravaganzas and student of the history of
costume, Edmund Yates gives a thumbnail
sketch in later years :—

" Such a pleasant little man, even in his extreme
old age—he was over eighty at his death *— and
always neatly dressed, showing his French origin
in his vivacity and his constant gesticulation."

The murder of Lord William Russell created
an unpleasant sensation, though there was not
anything mysterious in it, or particularly interesting to the amateur in crime. François Benjamin
Courvoisier, a Swiss and Lord William's valet,
two maid - servants aud Lord William, aged
seventy-two, formed the household at the establishment in Norfolk Street, Park Lane. On the
morning of 7th May, the housemaid found her
master's writing-room in a state of disarray, and
in the hall a cloak, an opera-glass and other
articles of wearing apparel done up together as if
prepared to be taken away. The maid roused
Courvoisier, who exclaimed, when he came upon
the scene : " Some one has been robbing us ; for
God's sake go and see where his lordship is ! "

They went together to Lord William's room,
where a shocking sight presented itself, their
master lying dead upon the bed, his head nearly
severed from his body. The police were
summoned, and money, banknotes, and some

* In 1880. He was born in 1796.

jewellery, believed to have been stolen from Lord William, being found concealed behind the skirting in the pantry, Courvoisier was arrested, tried, condemned, and then acknowledged his crime. He was executed on 6th July, before an immense mob of men, women and children.

Of another evening at Gore House Planché has this to relate of Lablache :—

" It was after dinner at Gore House that I witnessed his extraordinary representation of a thunderstorm simply by facial expression. The gloom that gradually overspread his countenance appeared to deepen into actual darkness, and the terrific frown indicated the angry lowering of the tempest. The lightning commenced by winks of the eyes, and twitchings of the muscles of the face, succeeded by rapid sidelong movements of the mouth which wonderfully recalled to you the forked flashes that seem to rend the sky, the motion of thunder being conveyed by the shaking of his head. By degrees the lightning became less vivid, the frown relaxed, the gloom departed, and a broad smile illuminating his expansive face assured you that the sun had broken through the clouds and the storm was over."

Another house to which D'Orsay frequently went was that of Charles Dickens, and we read of in 1845 an entertainment which no doubt was a festive jollification. In September of that year an amateur performance, with Dickens at the head of the troupe, was given of *Every Man in His Humour*, at Miss Kelly's Theatre, in Dean Street, Soho, now known as the Royalty. After the " show " it was decided to wind up with a supper, concerning which Dickens writes to Macready :—

"At No. 9 Powis Place, Great Ormond Street, in an empty house belonging to one of the company. There I am requested by my fellows to beg the favour of thy company and that of Mrs Macready. The guests are limited to the actors and their ladies—with the exception of yourselves and D'Orsay and George Cattermole, 'or so'— that sounds like Bobadil a little."

In the company were included Douglas Jerrold, John Leech and Forster.

Referring to yet another dinner, Lady Blessington writes to Forster from Gore House, on 12th April 1848 :—

"Count d'Orsay repeated to me this morning the kind things you said of him when proposing his health. He, I assure you, was touched when he repeated them, and his feelings were infectious, for mine responded. To be highly appreciated by those we most highly value, is, indeed, a source of heartfelt gratification. From the first year of our acquaintance with you, we had learned to admire your genius, to respect your principles, and to love your goodness of heart, and the honest warmth of your nature. These sentiments have never varied. Every year, by unfolding your noble qualities to us, has served to prove how true were our first impressions of you, and our sole regret has been that your occupations deprive us of enjoying half as much of your society as all who have once enjoyed it must desire. Count d'Orsay declares that yesterday was one of the happiest days of his life. He feels proud of having assisted at the triumph of a friend whose heart is as genial as his genius is great. Who can resist being delighted at the success of one who wins for himself thousands of friends (for all his readers become so), without ever creating an enemy, even among those most envious of another's fame, and simply by the revelations of a mind and heart that excite only the best feelings of our—nature ? I cannot resist telling you what is passing in my heart. You will understand this little outbreak of genuine feeling in the midst of the toil of a literary life."

There were almost as many writers of genius then as now!

Forster and Dickens were together at Gore House early in 1848, when Madden tells us "there was a remarkable display of D'Orsay's peculiar ingenuity and successful tact in drawing out the oddities or absurdities of eccentric or ridiculous personages—mystifying them with a grave aspect, and imposing on their vanity by apparently accidental references of a gratulatory description to some favourite hobby or exploit, exaggerated merit or importance of the individual to be made sport of for the Philistines of the fashionable circle." Bear-baiting was succeeded in those polite days by bore-baiting. Anent this particular evening, one of those present wrote to Lady Blessington :—

" Count d'Orsay may well speak of our evening being a happy one, to whose happiness he contributed so largely. It would be absurd, if one did not know it to be true, to hear D——— (Dickens ?) talk as he has done ever since of

Count d'Orsay's power of drawing out always the best elements around him, and of miraculously putting out the worst. Certainly I never saw it so marvellously exhibited as on the night in question. I shall think of him hereafter unceasingly, with the two guests that sat on either side of him that night,"

It was but fitting that the Prince of Dandies and the future Poet Laureate should come together. Tennyson writes:—"Count d'Orsay is a friend of mine, co-godfather to Dickens' child with me." This was Dickens' sixth child and fourth son, christened Alfred Tennyson after his godfathers.

D'Orsay was not so unkind as to neglect his native country entirely, and we find him now and again running over to Paris.

As pendants to the Disraeli portrait of D'Orsay, here are two others, one from a man's hand, the other from a woman's.

Chesterfield House was the headquarters of a racing set, and was gossiped about as also the centre of some heavy gambling, probably untruly so.

The Honourable F. Leveson Gore in *Bygone Years* expresses himself bluntly: "I used to wonder that Lady Chesterfield admitted into her house that good-for-nothing fellow, Count d'Orsay. He was handsome, clever and amusing, and I am aware that in the eyes of some people such qualities cover a multitude of sins. But his record was a bad one. No Frenchman would speak to him because he had left the French army at the breaking out of the war between his own

country and Spain, in order to go to Italy with
Lord and Lady Blessington, and his conduct
with regard to his marriage was infamous." How
uncharitable is the judgment of a virtuous world.
Reading on we find that the writer holds that
Lady Blessington induced D'Orsay "entirely to
neglect his young wife. She, moreover, en-
deavoured to undermine her faith and her morals
by getting her to read books calculated to do so,
and what was still worse, she promoted the
advances of other men, who made up to this
inexperienced and beautiful young woman. Her
life at Gore House * became at last so intolerable
that she fled from it never to return."

Mr Leveson Gore also calls Lady Harriet the
only daughter of Lord Blessington, which is really
not doing his lordship justice.

It is much more helpful, however, to have the
opinion of a keen, shrewd woman ; one who cannot have been disposed to like D'Orsay, yet who
seems, as did her husband, to have a soft place
in her heart for him.

Jane Welsh Carlyle was a capital hand at a
pen portrait; here is what she has to say of
D'Orsay :—

"*April* 13, 1845.—To-day, oddly enough,
while I was engaged in re-reading Carlyle's
Philosophy of Clothes, Count d'Orsay walked in.
I had not seen him for four or five years. Last
time he was as gay in his colours as a humming-
bird—blue satin cravat, blue velvet waistcoat,
cream-coloured coat, lined with velvet of the same
hue, trousers also of a bright colour, I forget what ;

* She never was there. Seamore Place is meant.

white French gloves, two glorious breastpins attached by a chain, and length enough of gold watch-guard to have hanged himself in. To-day, in compliment to his five more years, he was all in black and brown—a black satin cravat, a brown velvet waistcoat, a brown coat some shades darker than the waistcoat, lined with velvet of its own shade, and almost black trousers, one breast-pin, a large pear-shaped pearl set into a little cup of diamonds, and only one fold of gold chain round his neck, tucked together right on the centre of his spacious breast with one magnificent turquoise. Well! that man understood his trade; if it be but that of dandy, nobody can deny that he is a perfect master of it, that he dresses himself with consummate skill! A bungler would have made no allowance for five more years at his time of life, but he had the fine sense to perceive how much better his dress of to-day sets off his slightly enlarged figure and slightly worn complexion, than the humming-bird colours of five years back would have done. Poor D'Orsay! he was born to have been something better than even the king of dandies. He did not say nearly so many clever things this time as on the last occasion. His wit, I suppose, is of the sort that belongs more to animal spirits than to real genius, and his animal spirits seem to have fallen many degrees. The only thing that fell from him to-day worth re-membering was his account of a mask he had seen of Charles Fox, 'all punched and flattened as if he had slept in a book.'

"Lord Jeffrey came, unexpected, while the Count was here. What a difference! the prince of critics and the prince of dandies. How washed out the beautiful dandiacal face looked beside that little clever old man's! The large blue dandiacal eyes, you would have said, had never contemplated anything more interesting than the reflection of the handsome personage they pertained to in a looking-glass; while the dark penetrating ones of the other had been taking note of most things in God's universe, even seeing a good way into millstones."

XXV

SUNSET

SUNSET of the glories of Gore House came in the
year 1849, a cold, bitter sunset, presaging a stormy
morrow. Lady Blessington was nearly sixty years
old, well-preserved indeed, but Time's footsteps
are crow's-feet. D'Orsay was nearing fifty.
Darby and Joan; only the former at fifty is more
than ten years younger than the latter at sixty.

Behind all the gaiety of Gore House there had
long been a dark background, ever growing more
sinister. Without the harassment of any cares it
would have been difficult for a woman of Lady
Blessington's age to maintain a sovereignty which
depended almost entirely upon her beauty.
Troubles met her at every turn, and the last few
years at Gore House must have been to her years
of torment and despair. She heard her doom
approaching with sure foot, and knew that she
was unable to stay the advance.

Her jointure of £2000 was entirely inadequate
to maintain the expenses of either Seamore Place
or Gore House, to the exchequers of which
D'Orsay cannot have contributed ; any capital that
came into his hands was rapidly dispersed by them
among hungry debtors, and his income of £500
was probably hypothecated in the same way. It
was essential for her, therefore, to add to her
revenue, for the reduction of expenditure does not

seem to have occurred to this luxury-loving soul. She does indeed seem to have been careful to see that she obtained her money's worth, and kept a tight hand on the household expenses and accounts. One habit of hers was to keep a " book of dinners," noting down the names of the guests at each entertainment.

When no other way of securing an income suggests itself to the needy or hard-up, they invariably take up their pens and write. Lady Blessington, if it had not been for her beauty and notoriety, could scarcely have earned a livelihood as a hack writer for the lesser journals, but her name gave to her writings a market value which their intrinsic merit did not. Her *Conversations with Byron* have already been mentioned, and sufficiently dealt with ; she also wrote books of travel, novels, verses, edited such periodicals as *The Keepsake* and *The Book of Beauty*, to which the eminent authors who fluttered round her at Gore House contributed, and in the end when these enterprises were failing became a contributor to the *Daily News* of "exclusive intelligence," that is to say of "any sort of intelligence she might like to communicate, of the sayings, doings, memoirs or movements in the fashionable world," for which she received payment at the rate of £400 a year ; Dickens and Forster were her editors.

The death in 1848 of Heath, the publisher, in insolvency brought a loss to Lady Blessington of about £700. Her earnings have been placed at a thousand a year, but William Jerdan in his *Autobiography* declares them to have been much higher. " I have known her to enjoy from her pen an amount somewhere midway between £2000 and £3000 per annum, and her title, as well as talents, had considerable influence in 'ruling high prices' as they say in Mark Lane and other markets. To this, also, her well-arranged parties with a publisher now and then, to meet folks of a style unusual to men in business, contributed their attractions ; and the same society was in reality of solid value towards the production of such publications as the Annuals, the contents of which were provided by the editor almost entirely from the pens of private friends."

In 1833 by a robbery of jewellery and plate at Seamore Place, Lady Blessington lost something like £1000.

These losses, the continual strain of working to obtain the funds necessary for her luxurious mode of life and the difficulties in which D'Orsay was involved told heavily upon her health and spirits. As she herself writes in her commonplace book :—

" Great trials demand great courage, and all our energy is called up to enable us to bear them. But it is the minor cares of life that wear out the body, because, singly, and in detail, they do not appear sufficiently important to engage us to rally our force and spirits to support them. . . . Many minds that have withstood the most severe trials, have been broken down by a succession of ignoble cares ;" and there is a touch of sorrowful bitterness in this : " Friends are the thermometers by which we may judge the temperature of our fortunes."

Not that she was ill-served by her friends,

rather the contrary ; few women have had so many or so faithful.

The following letter paints the situation better than can any words of ours ; it was written to Lady Blessington in or about 1848 :—

"My Dearest Friend,—You do not do me more than justice in the belief that I most fully sympathise with all your troubles, and I shall be only too happy if my advice can in any way assist you.

"First. As to your jointure, nothing in law is so indisputable—as that a widow's jointure takes precedence of every other claim on an estate. The very first money the agent or steward receives from the property should go to the discharge of this claim. No subsequent mortgages, annuities, encumbrances, law-suits, expenses of management, etc., can be permitted to interfere with the payment of jointure ; and as, whatever the distress of the tenants, or the embarrassments of the estate, it is clear that some rents must have come in half-yearly ; so, on those rents you have an indisputable right ; and, I think, on consulting your lawyer, he will put you in a way, either by a memorial to Chancery, or otherwise, to secure in future the regular payment of this life-charge. Indeed, as property charged with a jointure, although the rents are not paid for months after the proper dates, the jointure must be paid on the regular days, and if not, the proprietor would become liable to immediate litigation. I am here presuming that you but ask for the jointure, due quarterly, or half-yearly, and not in advance, which, if the affairs are in Chancery, it would be illegal to grant.

s

" Secondly. With respect to the diamonds, would it be possible or expedient, to select a certain portion (say half), which you least value on their own account; and if a jeweller himself falls too short in his offer, to get him to sell them on commission? You must remember, that every year, by paying interest on them,* you are losing money on them, so that in a few years you may thus lose more than by taking at once less than their true value. There are diamond merchants, who, I believe, give more for those articles than jewellers, and if you know Anthony Rothschild, and would not object to speak to him, he might help you. . . .

" I know well how, to those accustomed to punctual payments, and with a horror of debt, pecuniary embarrassments prey upon the mind, but I think they may be borne, not only with ease, but some degree of complacency, when connected with such generous devotions and affectionate services as those which must console you amidst all your cares. In emptying your purse you have at least filled your heart with consolations, which will long outlast what I trust will be but the troubles of a season."

The last sentences refer to the generous charity which was one of Lady Blessington's saving graces: parents, brothers, sisters, friends, lover, all benefited by her aid. Two very pleasing letters from Mrs S. C. Hall may be quoted on this and other points :—

" I have never had occasion to appeal to Lady Blessington for aid for any kind or charitable

* Apparently they had been pawned.

purpose, that she did not *at once*, with a grace peculiarly her own, come forward cheerfully and 'help' to the extent of her power."

And :—

"When Lady Blessington left London, she did not forget the necessities of several of her poor dependants, who received regular aid from her after her arrival, and while she resided in Paris.* She found time, despite her literary labours, her anxieties and the claims which she permitted society to make upon her time, not only to do acts of kindness now and then for those in whom she felt an interest, but to give what seemed perpetual thought to their well-doing : and she never missed an opportunity of doing a gracious act or saying a gracious word. . . .

" I have no means of knowing whether what the world said of this beautiful woman was true or false, but I am sure God intended her to be good, and there was a deep-seated good intent in whatever she did that came under my observation.

" Her sympathies were quick and cordial, and independent of worldiness ; her taste in art and literature womanly and refined ; I say ' womanly,' because she had a perfectly feminine appreciation of whatever was delicate and beautiful. . . . Her manners were singularly simple and graceful ; it was to me an intense delight to look at beauty, which though I never saw in its full bloom, was charming in its autumn time ; and the Irish accent, and soft, sweet, Irish laugh, used to make my heart beat with the pleasures of memory. . . . Her conversation was not witty nor wise, but it

* See *Infra*.

was in good tune and good taste, mingled with a great deal of humour, which escaped everything bordering on vulgarity. It was surprising how a tale of distress or a touching anecdote would at once suffuse her clear intelligent eyes with tears, and her beautiful mouth would break into smiles and dimples at even the echo of wit or jest."

This is singularly interesting as the evidence of a woman, one of the few who were intimate with Lady Blessington. Of an Irish woman too, who could perceive and appreciate the womanly side of Lady Blessington's simple nature. Simple, yes; she was just a simple, emotional, luxury-loving, laughter-loving sympathetic Irish woman, who under favourable circumstances might have been a true and adorable wife and helpmate; who under the circumstances that did rule her life, became—Lady Blessington.

Such first-hand testimony as that of Mrs S. C. Hall is worth a wilderness of commentary; to it we will add this from Lady Blessington's maid, Anne Cooper :—

"My lady's spirits were naturally good; before she was overpowered with difficulties, and troubles on account of them, she was very cheerful, droll, and particularly amusing. This was natural to her. Her general health was usually good; she often told me she had never been confined to her bed one whole day in her life. And her spirits would have continued good, but that she got so overwhelmed with care and expenses of all kinds. The calls for her assistance were from all quarters. Some depended wholly on her (and had a regular pension,

quarterly paid) — her father and mother, for
many years before they died; the education of
children of friends fell upon her. . . . Constant
assistance had to be given to others—(to the
family, in particular, of one poor lady, now dead
some years, whom she loved very dearly). She
did a great many charities; for instance, she gave
very largely to poor literary people, poor artists;
something yearly to old servants . . . and from
some, whom she served, to add to all her other
miseries, she met with shameful ingratitude.

"Labouring night and day at literary work,
all her anxiety was to be clear of debt. She was
latterly constantly trying to curtail all her
expenses in her own establishment, and constantly
toiling to get money. Worried and harassed at
not being able to pay bills when they were sent
in; at seeing large expenses still going on, and
knowing the want of means to meet them, she
got no sleep at night. She long wished to give
up Gore House, to have a sale of her furniture,
and to pay off her debts. She wished this for
two years before she left England; but when the
famine in Ireland rendered the payment of her
jointure irregular, and every succeeding year
more and more so, her difficulties increased, and,
at last, Howell & James put an execution in
the house. . . . Poor soul! her heart was too
large for her means."

Still Lady Blessington fought on, and faced
the footlights without outward faltering; she
played her part in the comedy and received the
applause of her friends, few of whom realised that
the comedy was a tragedy. "Passion! Posses-

sion! Indifference!" she writes, "what a history
is comprised in these three words! What hopes
and fears succeeded by a felicity as brief as in-
toxicating—followed in its turn by the old consequence of possession — indifference! What
burning tears, what bitter pangs, rending the very
heartstrings—what sleepless nights and watchful
days form part of this everyday story of life,
whose termination leaves the actors to search
again for new illusions to finish like the last."
But what new illusions can be looked for by a
tried, sad woman of sixty?

D'Orsay was locked up in Gore House during
these last two years of sunset for six days out of
each seven; debt hung like a millstone round
his neck also. These two, who had sailed over
happy seas with favourable winds, were now together drifting on the rocks.

One day in April a sheriff's officer, effectually
disguised, managed to enter the house, and then
the end of this second act of our play came rapidly.
Lady Blessington informed of the mishap, realising
that once it was known that an execution was
laid upon her property there would no more be
any safety for the Count's person, sent to D'Orsay's
room to warn him of his danger.

"Bah!" exclaimed D'Orsay, unable or unwilling to believe that the hour for flight had
at last come upon him; and again and again
"Bah!" Not until Lady Blessington herself added
her personal persuasion did he grasp the situation.

De Contades gives a somewhat different
account. Just before the dinner hour, a pastry-
cook's boy presented himself at Gore House with

a dish, sent in, so he said, by the confectioner. Having left this in the kitchen, he deliberately walked upstairs to the Count's dressing-room.

" Well, who's that?" asked D'Orsay.

It was a sheriff's officer!

" Really!" exclaimed D'Orsay, and demanded that he should be permitted to complete the tying of his tie—*salon* or prison—his tie must be perfect.

" But, Count—"

" Bah, bah! All in good time."

The officer was quite interested in the tying of that tie ; few men had been so honoured as to be allowed to see how D'Orsay tied his tie—and, lo! by the time the tie *was* tied, the sun had sunk to rest and D'Orsay was free till sunrise!

" John," said D'Orsay, calmly walking off to the drawing-room, "kick this chap out of the door."

The which was executed and the writ was not.

.   .   .   .

In the grey of the morning, however, D'Orsay, taking every precaution against capture on the way, set out for Paris with a valet, a valise, and an umbrella. The words of a great man at any moment of crisis in his affairs are worth recording ; one of D'Orsay's last remarks in London was : " Well, at least, if I have nothing else, I will have the best umbrella!"

That was the bravado of a brave man. What really was in his mind? What were Napoleon's thoughts as he turned his back upon Moscow? What were D'Orsay's as he fled that morning, conquered, from the town he had captured and enslaved so long?

XXVI

THE END OF GORE HOUSE

BEFORE following D'Orsay to Paris, we will witness the end of the Blessington *régime* at Gore House. The harassed lady's creditors swarmed round her; she had given bills and bonds in anticipation of her jointure for something like £1500; Howell & James' account seems to have amounted to £4000!! Money-lenders, bill-discounters, tax-collectors, tradesmen of every kind, all rushed in to see what could be saved. In the event it was found impossible to avoid a sale of her goods and effects.

On April 9th, 1849, Lady Blessington writes to Forster from Gore House:

"As I purpose leaving England in a few days, it will pain me very much to depart without personally wishing you farewell; and though I am in all the fever of packing up, I will make time to receive a visit from you, if you can call any day this week between eleven o'clock in the forenoon, or after nine in the evening. Count d'Orsay was called to Paris so suddenly, that he had not time to take leave of any of his friends, but he charged me to say a thousand kind things to you."

The following from Disraeli reached her in Paris:—

25th April 1849.

"We returned to town on the 16th, and a few days after, I called at Gore House, but you were gone. It was a pang; for though absorbing

GARDEN VIEW OF GORE HOUSE

[TO FACE PAGE 280

duties of my life have prevented me of late from passing as much time under that roof as it was once my happiness and good fortune through your kindness to do ; you are well assured, that my heart never changed for an instant to its inmates, and that I invariably entertained for them the same interest and affection.

" Had I been aware of your intentions, I would have come up to town earlier, and specially to have said ' Adieu ! ' mournful as that is.

" I thought I should never pay another visit to Paris, but I have now an object in doing so. All the world here will miss you very much, and the charm with which you invested existence ; but for your own happiness, I am persuaded you have acted wisely. Every now and then, in this life, we require a great change ; it wonderfully revives the sense of existence. I envy you ; pray, if possible, let me sometimes hear from you."

Thackeray writes to Mrs Brookfield :—

" I have just come away from a dismal sight ; Gore House full of snobs looking at the furniture. Foul Jews ; odious bombazine women, who drove up in mysterious flys which they had hired, the wretches, to be fined (? fine), so as to come in state to a fashionable lounge ; brutes keeping their hats on in the kind old drawing-room—I longed to knock some of them off, and say, ' Sir, be civil in a lady's room. . . .' There was one of the servants there, not a powdered one, but a butler, a *whatd'youcallit.* My heart melted towards him and I gave him a pound. Ah ! it was a strange, sad picture of *Vanity Fair.*"

The catalogue of the sale gives an idea of the "household gods":—

"Costly and elegant effects: comprising all the magnificent furniture, rare porcelain, sculpture in marble, bronzes, and an assemblage of objects of art and decoration; a casket of valuable jewellery and *bijouterie*, services of chased silver and silver-gilt plate, a superbly-fitted silver dressing-case; collection of ancient and modern pictures, including many portraits of distinguished persons, valuable original drawings, and fine engravings, framed and in portfolios; the extensive and interesting library of books, comprising upwards of 5000 volumes, expensive table services of china and rich cut glass, and an infinity of useful and valuable articles. All the property of the Right Hon. the Countess of Blessington, retiring to the Continent."

So wrote Mr Phillips, "that eminent author of auctioneering advertisements."

The sale took place in May, and was attended by a crowd of fashionables, and the net sum realised was £11,985, 4s. 0d. Lawrence's portrait of Lady Blessington, now in the Wallace Collection, fetched £336 and was purchased by Lord Hertford, who also acquired D'Orsay's portrait of the Duke of Wellington for £189. Chalon's portrait of Lady Blessington was saved from the wreck; it is now in the National Portrait Gallery.

Lady Blessington's French valet, Avillon, writes to her:—

"GORE HOUSE, KENSINGTON,
May 8th, 1849.

"MY LADY,—J'ai bien reçu votre lettre, et je me serais empressé d'y répondre le même jour, mais j'ai été si occupé étant le premier de la vente qu'il m'a été impossible de le faire. J'ai vu M. P.—— dans l'après midi. Il avais un commis ici pour prendre le prix des différents objets vendu le 7 May, et que vous avez sans doute reçu maintenant, au dire des gens qui ont assisté à la vente. Les choses se sont vendus avant agencement et je dois ajouter que M. Phillips n'a rien negligé pour rendre la vente intéressante a toute la noblesse d'ici.

" Lord Hertford a acheté plusieurs choses, et ce n'est que dimanche dernier fort tard dans l'après midi, qu'il est venu voir la maison. En un mot je pense sans exagération, que le nombre de personnes qui sont venus a la maison pendant les 5 jours quelle a été en vue, que plus de 20,000 personnes y sont entrées ; une très grande quantité de Catalogue ont été vendus, et nous en vendons encore tous les jours, car vous le savez, personne n'est admis sans cela. Plusieurs des personnes qui fréquantent la maison sont venus les deux premiers jours. . . .

" Le Dr. Quin est venu plusieurs fois, et á paru prendre le plus grand intêret a ce qui se passait ici. M. Thackeray est venu aussi, et avait les larmes aux yeux en partant. *C'est peut-être la seule personne que j'ai vu réellement affècté a votre depart.*"

Lady Blessington and her two nieces had left for Paris on 14th April.

XXVII

LADY BLESSINGTON returned to the city where her husband had died ; D'Orsay to serve under another Napoleon than he to whom he had once aspired to render duty. Lady Blessington took a suite of rooms in the Hôtel de la Ville l'Evêque, but shortly moved into an *appartement* in the Rue du Cerq, hard by the Champs Elysées, which she furnished, partly with some of the salvage from the sale, and where she lived very cosily upon her jointure.

The following letter is from Henry Bulwer :—

"*May* 6, 1849.

" I was very glad to get your letter. I never had a doubt (I judged by myself) that your friends would remain always your friends, and I was sure that many who were not Alfred's when he was away, would become so when he was present.* It would be great ingratitude if Prince Louis forgot former kindnesses and services, and I must say, that I do not think him capable of this.

" I think you will take a house in Paris or near it, and I hope some day there to find you, and to renew some of the many happy hours I have spent in your society. I shall attend the sale, and advise all my friends to do so. From what I hear, things will probably sell well. I am sure that Samson will execute any commission for you

* *I.e.* in Paris.

when he goes to Paris, and I gave Douro your message, who returns it. . . ."

Napoleon as President, however, was a different man from a mere Prince in Exile, and could scarcely show himself as intimate in Paris with Lady Blessington and D'Orsay as he had done in London. Accompanied by the Misses Power they dined at the Elysée Palace, and then social intercourse apparently ceased. That D'Orsay had in other days been of great assistance to Napoleon, and that Lady Blessington had been to him a most kind hostess, there is no denying ; they expected much now in return, but Napoleon could scarcely in decency give much.

It is narrated that Napoleon said to Lady Blessington : "Are you going to stay long in France ? "

And that she with more wit than wisdom replied : " I don't know. *Are you ?* "

Lady Blessington was warmly welcomed by many of her old friends, notably by various members of the family of de Grammont. She tried to resume in a minor key at Paris the life she had led at Gore House ; but the endeavour failed.

A letter from Lady Blessington's niece, Margaret Power, brings us to the closing scene of this portion of our story :—

" On arriving in Paris, my aunt followed a mode of life differing considerably from the sedentary one she had for such a length of time pursued ; she rose earlier, took much exercise, and, in consequence, lived somewhat higher than was her wont, for she was habitually a remarkably small eater ; this appeared to agree with her *general* health, for she looked well, and was cheerful ; but she began to suffer occasionally (especially in the morning) from oppression and difficulty of breathing. These symptoms, slight at first, she carefully concealed from our knowledge, having always a great objection to medical treatment ; but as they increased in force and frequency, she was obliged to reveal them, and medical aid was immediately called in. Dr Léon Simon pronounced there was *énergie du cœur*, but that the symptoms in question proceeded probably from bronchitis—a disease then very prevalent in Paris—that they were nervous, and entailed no danger, and as, after the remedies he prescribed, the attacks diminished perceptibly in violence, and her general health seemed little affected by them, he entertained no serious alarm.

"On the 3rd of June, she was removed from the hotel we had occupied during the seven weeks we had passed in Paris, and entered the residence which my poor aunt had devoted so much pains and attention to the selecting and furnishing of, and that same day dined *en famille* with the Duc and Duchesse de Guiche (Count d'Orsay's nephew). On that occasion, my aunt seemed particularly well in health and spirits, and it being a lovely night, we walked home by moonlight. As usual, I aided my aunt to undress—she never allowed her maid to sit up for her—and left her a little after midnight. She passed, it seems, some most restless hours (she was habitually a bad sleeper), and early in the morning, feeling the commencement of one of the attacks, she called for assistance, and Dr Simon was immediately sent for, the symptoms manifesting themselves with considerable violence, and in the meantime, the remedies he had ordered—sitting upright, rubbing the chest and upper stomach with ether, administering ether, internally, etc.—were all resorted to without effect; the difficulty of breathing became so excessive, that the whole of the chest heaved upwards at each inspiration, which was inhaled with a loud whooping noise, the face was swollen and purple, the eyeballs distended, and utterance almost wholly denied, while the extremities gradually became cold and livid, in spite of every attempt to restore the vital heat. By degrees, the violence of the symptoms abated ; she uttered a few words ; the first, ' The violence is over, I can breathe freer ' ; and soon after, ' *Quelle heure est-il ?* ' Thus encouraged, we deemed the danger past ; but, alas ! how bitterly were we deceived ; she gradually sank from that moment, and when Dr Simon, who had been delayed by another patient, arrived, he saw that hope was gone ; and, indeed, she expired so easily, so tranquilly, that it was impossible to perceive the moment when her spirit passed away."

D'Orsay was alone.

The autopsy showed that death was caused by enlargement of the heart. The body was embalmed and lay in the vaults of the Madeleine until the monument at Chambourcy, where was the seat of the de Grammonts, a few miles from St Germain-en-Laye, was ready to receive it. The mausoleum, designed by D'Orsay, stands upon a slight eminence ; a railing of bronze encloses a pyramid of granite rising from a square platform

of black stone. Entering the burial chamber,
against the opposite wall is a copy in bronze of
Michael Angelo's crucified Christ. On either side
the chamber stands a sarcophagus—in that to the
left lies Lady Blessington. " It stands," writes
Miss Power, " on a hillside, just above the village
cemetery, and overlooks a view of exquisite beauty
and immense extent, taking in the Seine winding
through the fertile valley and the forest of St
Germain ; plains, villages and far distant hills, and
at the back and side it is sheltered by chestnut
trees of large size and great age; a more
picturesque spot it is difficult to imagine." The
ivy growing over the green turf·was sent from
Ireland by Bernal Osborne.

On the wall above the tomb of Lady Blessington are two epitaphs, one in Latin by Landor ; the
other by Barry Cornwall, which runs as follows :—

IN HER LIFETIME
SHE WAS LOVED AND ADMIRED,
FOR HER MANY GRACEFUL WRITINGS,
HER GENTLE MANNERS, HER KIND AND GENEROUS HEART.
MEN, FAMOUS FOR ART AND SCIENCE,
IN DISTANT LANDS,
SOUGHT HER FRIENDSHIP :
AND THE HISTORIANS, AND SCHOLARS, THE POETS, AND WITS, AND
PAINTERS, OF HER OWN COUNTRY,
FOUND AN UNFAILING WELCOME
IN HER EVER HOSPITABLE HOME.
SHE GAVE, CHEERFULLY, TO ALL WHO WERE IN NEED,
HELP, AND SYMPATHY, AND USEFUL COUNSEL ;
AND SHE DIED
LAMENTED BY HER FRIENDS.
THEY WHO LOVED HER BEST IN LIFE, AND NOW LAMENT HER MOST,
HAVE RAISED THIS TRIBUTARY MARBLE
OVER HER PLACE OF REST.

So far truth, and it is not to be expected of an
epitaph that it should tell the whole truth.
Requiescat.

MAUSOLEUM OF LADY BLESSINGTON
(*From a Photograph* (?) *by D'Orsay*)

[TO FACE PAGE 288

XXVIII

In April 1849, D'Orsay writes to Dr Quin from Paris :—

"38 RUE DE LA VILLE L'EVEQUE.

"MON BON QUIN,—J'ai eu un départ imprévu heureusement, que je suis *safe* de ce côté. Il a fallu que je me décide de partir à 3 hrs de la nuit pour ne pas manquer le Dimanche. Ces dames vous racontent qu'une de mes prèmieres pensées ici ont été pour vous. Vous le voyez par ce peu de mots —aimez moi toujours de loin, car je vous aimais bien de près.—Votre meilleur ami, ALFRED."

The death of Lady Blessington was a blow to him from which he never really recovered. Writing to Madden from Chambourcy on 12th July, Miss Power says :—

"Count d'Orsay would himself have answered your letter, but had not the nerve or the heart to do so ; although the subject occupies his mind night and day, he cannot speak of it but to those who have been his fellow-sufferers. It is like an image ever floating before his eyes, which he has got, as it were, used to look upon, but which he cannot yet bear to grasp and feel that it is real. Much as she was to us, we cannot but feel that to him she was all ; the centre of his existence, round which his recollections, thoughts, hopes and plans turned, and just at the moment she was about to commence a new mode of life, one that promised a rest from the occupation and anxieties that had for some years fallen to her share, death deprived us of her."

The first visit that he paid to her tomb had a heart-breaking effect upon him; at one moment he would be stunned, at another driven to frenzy by his grief. What thoughts of past times must have assailed him : of his first meeting with her in London so many years ago; of the long days and nights of delight in Italy; of his marriage, perchance; of Seamore Place, of Gore House; of hours of merriment and of sorrow; of her tried faithfulness to him ; of his occasional faithlessness. That his love for her survived even the advance of years we cannot doubt; but the love of man is different far from the love of woman.

In a letter, already partly quoted, to Lane, D'Orsay says, writing early in 1850 :—

"Poor Miss Power is very much affected. There is no consolation to offer. The only one that I can imagine, is to think continually of the person lost, and to make oneself more miserable by thinking. It is, morally speaking, an homœopathic treatment, and the only one which can give some relief. You cannot form an idea of the *soulagement* that I found, in occupying myself in the country (at Chambourcy) in building the monument which I have erected to dear Lady Blessington's memory. I made it so solid and so fine, that I felt all the time that death was the reality and life only the dream of all around me. When I hear anyone making projects for the future, I laugh, feeling as I do now, that we may to-morrow, without five minutes' notice, have to follow those

we regret. I am prepared for that, with a satisfactory resignation."

D'Orsay wrote to Forster on April 23rd,
1850 :—

" Miss Power has told you how much I love
you, and how often we talk about you. The fact
is, I am full of reminiscences, and they are such a
medley of displeasure and pleasure that I hesi-
tate to write even to those who are most likely to
understand me. Just think that I have not even
yet written to Edward Bulwer. You'll understand, I'm sure. To-day I dined with Lamartine
and Victor Hugo at Girardin's. . . .

" Do not let Fonblanque think I have forgotten him? Give a thousand friendly wishes
from me to Dickens and his wife, and embrace
my godson for me. I count also on your speaking kindly of me to Macready and his wife, and
to the good Maclise. It seems to me almost as
if I had only gone away to-day, my recollections
are so vivid ; it is truly a daguerreotype of the
heart that nothing can efface. I adore old
England, and long to return there. Never did
man so suffer as I have done for my loss.*

" I wonder at those religious people who hold
religion so high that they quickly find consolation.
They do not understand, the idiots, that there is
a great, a greater faith in a true sorrow which
does not heal.

" Adieu, *mon brave ami,* count always on my
affection, D'ORSAY."

He found comfort in the companionship of

* Of Lady Blessington.

Lady Blessington's two nieces, Margaret and Ellen. To a certain extent he avoided mixing in society, but we hear of him now and again.

In 1850 he rented a large studio and some smaller rooms in the house of Theodore Gudin, the marine painter, to which he conveyed all his belongings, and where he settled down to work and sedate entertaining. Here Thackeray visited him :—

"To-day I went to see D'Orsay, who has made a bust of Lamartine,* who . . . is mad with vanity. He has written some verses on his bust, and asks : 'Who is this ? Is it a warrior ? Is it a hero ? Is it a priest ? Is it a sage ? Is it a tribune of the people ? Is it an Adonis ?' meaning that he is all these things,—verses so fatuous and crazy I never saw. Well, D'Orsay says they are the finest verses that ever were written, and imparts to me a translation which Miss Power has made of them ; and D'Orsay believes in his mad rubbish of a statue, which he didn't make ; believes in it in the mad way that madmen do,— that it is divine, and that he made it ; only as you look in his eyes, you see that he doesn't quite believe, and when pressed hesitates, and turns away with a howl of rage. D'Orsay has fitted himself up a charming *atelier*, with arms and trophies, pictures and looking-glasses, the tomb of Blessington, the sword and star of Napoleon, and a crucifix over his bed ; and here he dwells without any doubts or remorses, admiring himself in the most horrible pictures which he has painted, and the statues which he gets done for him."

* *Vide supra*, p. 225.

Lord Lamington gives a curious account of a visit :—

I "found his room all hung with black curtains, the bed and window-curtains were the same ; all the souvenirs of one so dear were collected around him."

Of the friends that rallied around him, Madden names as among the most faithful the ex-King Jérôme and his son, Prince Napoleon, and Emile de Girardin. Of the man of the bust, D'Orsay writes, in April 1850 : " Lamartine me disait hier : ' Plus je vois de représentants du peuple, plus j'aime mes chiens.' "

Early in February 1851 we find Dickens in Paris, stopping at the Hôtel Wagram ; D'Orsay dined with him on the 11th and Dickens went in return to the *atelier* the next day. " He was very happy with us," he writes, " and is much improved both in spirits and looks."

In May 1850 Abraham Hayward was in Paris, and dined at Philippe's with a highly-distinguished company, including Brougham, Alexandre Dumas, Lord Dufferin, the Hon. W. Stuart, a Mr Dundas of Carron, Hayward himself and D'Orsay. Lord Dufferin, who, however, gives 1849 as the date, describes this dinner as "noisy but amusing." The object of the dinner was the bringing together of Brougham and Dumas :—" Brougham was punctual to the hour, and they were formally introduced by Count d'Orsay, who, observing some slight symptoms of stiffness, exclaimed : ' *Comment, diable, vous, les deux grands hommes, embrassez-vous donc, embrassez-vous.*' They fraternised accordingly *à la française*, Brougham looking very much during the operation as if he were in the grip of a bear, though nobody could look more cordial and satisfied than Dumas. The dinner was excellent. Some first rate *Clos de Vougeot,* of which Dumas had an accurate foreknowledge, sustained the hilarity of the company ; the conversation was varied and animated ; each of the distinguished guests took his fair share, and no more than his fair share ; and it was bordering on midnight when the party separated."

The price of the dinner was twenty francs a head, not including the wine, and D'Orsay and Hayward were jointly responsible for the *menu.* " The most successful dishes were the *bisque,* the *fritures Italiennes,* and the *gigot à la Bretonne,"* so says Hayward.

In his latest days he still retained a keen zest for the good things of the table, as is shown by this letter of his to Hayward :—

"Paris, 1*st May* 1852.

" I must confess with regret that the culinary art has sadly fallen off in Paris ; and I do not very clearly see how it is to recover, as there are at present no great establishments where the school can be kept up.

"You must have remarked, when you were here, that at all the first-class *restaurants* you had nearly the same dinner ; they may, however, be divided into three categories. Undoubtedly, the best for a great dinner and good wine are the Frères Provençaux (Palais Royal) ; Philippe (Rue Mont Orgueil), and the Café de Paris ; the latter is not always to be counted upon, but is excellent

when they give you a *soigné* dinner. In the
second class are Véry (Palais Royal), Vefour (Café
Anglais), and Champeaux (Place de la Bourse),
where you can have a most *conscientious* dinner,
good without pretension ; the situation is central,
in a beautiful garden, and you must ask for a
bifstek à la Châteaubriand. At the head of the
third class we must place Bonvallet, on the Bou-
levard du Temple, near all the little theatres ;
Defieux, chiefly remarkable for corporation and
assembly dinners. . . . The two best places for
suppers are the Maison d'Or and the Café
Anglais ; and for breakfasts, Tortoni's, and the
Café d'Orsay on the Quai d'Orsay. In the vicinity
of Paris, the best *restaurant* is the Pavilion Henri
Quatre, at St Germains, kept by the old cook of
the Duchesse de Berri. At none of these places
could you find dinners now such as were produced
by Ude ; by Soyer, formerly with Lord Chesterfield ; by Rotival, with Lord Wilton ; or by
Perron, with Lord Londonderry. . . . You are
now *au fait* of the pretended French gastronomy.
It has emigrated to England, and has no wish to
return. We do not absolutely die of hunger here,
and that is all that can be said."

A few other friends were faithful. There was
Eugene Sue, a much read man in his day, but his
name drags on a precarious existence now as the
author of *The Mysteries of Paris* and *The Wander-
ing Jew.* Probably his chief claim to immortality
will be found to be his friendship with D'Orsay,
who indeed inspired him with the central figure
of " Le Viscomte de Letocère, ou L'Art de
Plaire." He was quite a dandy in his way,

though of course not comparable in degree
with D'Orsay, and, strange combination, was a bit
of a Communist. He gave vent to the true saying that "No one had any right to superfluity"—
not even excepting D'Orsay?—"while any one
was in want of necessaries." Yet this is a description of his manner of "doing himself:"—

"It is impossible to convey an idea of this
luxury, of the sumptuousness of those caprices, of
those whims of all kinds: here a dining-room,
where the sideboards display plate, porcelain, and
crystal, with pictures and flowers, to add to the
pleasures of the table all the pleasures of the
eyes; there an inner gallery, where pictures,
statuettes, drawings, and engravings, reproduce
subjects the most calculated to excite the imagination. Here is a library full of antiques, whose
bookcases contain works bound with unheard-of
luxury, where objects of art are multiplied with
an absence of calculated affectation, which appears
as if wishing to say they came there naturally.
Daylight, shaded by the painted glass windows,
and curtains of the richest stuff, gives to this place
an air of mystery, invites to silence and to study,
and produces those eccentric inspirations which
M. Sue gives to the public. A desk, richly
carved, receives sundry manuscripts of the
romance-writer, the numerous *homages* sent to
Monsieur, as the valet expresses himself, from all
the corners of the globe. . . . Everywhere may
be seen gold, silver, silk, velvet, and soft carpets.
. . . A vast drawing-room, furnished and decorated with all imaginable care, exactly reproduces
that of one of the heroines of romance of Monsieur

Eugene Sue, and there have been carved on the
woodwork of a Gothic mantelpiece medallions
representing the Magdalen falling at the feet of
our Saviour, who tells her that her sins will be
forgiven her, because her love has been strong.
. . . A small gallery, lined with odoriferous
plants, leads to a circular walk, which surrounds
a garden cultivated in the most expensive manner,
and there is a fine piece of water, with numerous
swans in it.   The walk is a *chef-d'œuvre* of comfort,
for it is alike protected from the wind and the
rain, being covered with a dome.   It is enclosed
with balustrades, covered with creeping plants of
the choicest nature.   It is a sort of terrestrial
paradise. . . . and beyond it is a park, admirably
laid out with kiosques, rustic cottages, elegant
bridges, and a preserve for pheasants, which
secures myriads of birds for the shooting ex-
cursions of the illustrious Communist, whose
keepers exercise a severe look-out to prevent any
person from touching the game." A paradise
almost worthy of being the home of D'Orsay!

Sue rightly appreciated D'Orsay, and wrote
thus of him to Lady Blessington : " Je quitte
Alfred avec une vraie tristesse ; plus je le connais,
plus j'apprecie ce bon, ce vaillant cœur, si chaud,
si génereux pour ceux qu'il aime."

Arsène Houssaye had seen D'Orsay at a dinner
at Lamartine's, but had not spoken with him.
Houssaye wrote him down as a very fascinating
man, "with a smiling air which comes from and
speaks to the heart."   Rachel came into Houssaye's
office to meet him.

" It's natural I should find you here," he said,

"for it was to see you I came to see Arsène Houssaye. You play *Phèdre* to-night; I should count it great luck to be there, but there's not a single seat to be got either in the stalls or the balcony."

"True," said Manager Houssaye, "but there's my own box, which I offer you with all my heart."

"Good! I accept it as an act of friendship, for it's the best in the house. I'll offer it to the Duchesse de Grammont, who will come with Guiche."

The evening was a great success for all concerned, and Rachel gracefully said—"Comment ne jouerais-je pas bien quand je vois dans l'avant-scène deux Hippolytes?"

D'Orsay and Houssaye became quite good friends, and the latter frequently visited the Count in his studio, which he describes as "being at once the *salon*, studio, work-room, smoking-room, fitted with divans, couches and hammocks." D'Orsay made a small medallion portrait of his visitor, and chatted much about Byron, from whom he showed a curious letter in which the poet says: "If I started life again, I would live unknown in Paris; I would not write a word, not even to women; but one cannot start life afresh, which is lucky!"

A very different view, however, is that which now follows:—

Count Horace de Viel Castel notes: "The journals say that Count d'Orsay has received the commission for a marble statue of Prince Jérôme to be placed at Versailles. So much the worse for Versailles.

"The Count is an old 'lion,' whom nobody now knows or receives. He has lived with his mother-in-law, Lady Blessington, the blue-stocking of the *keepsakes*, and with everyone but his wife, Lady Henrietta d'Orsay, who was the mistress of the Duke d'Orleans, of Antoine de Noailles, and a host of lesser stars.

"Count d'Orsay for twenty years lived on the aristocracy and the tradespeople of London. Steeped in debt, he has now turned artist, backed by a following of nonentities. . . . Every year he disfigures some contemporaneous celebrity either in marble or plaster ; last time it was Lamartine.

"D'Orsay has still great pretensions to ele-gance, and dresses like no one else, with a display of embroidered linen, satin, gold chains, and hair all disordered."

Accusations of a more serious character also he brings against him, even that he tried to persuade Jérôme Bonaparte that he was his son, so that he might receive some place or promotion.

Then on December 2nd, 1851, came the thunderclap of the *coup d'état*, when the Prince who had become a President created himself an Emperor, and at the same time appears to have put an end to his friendship toward D'Orsay. Shortly after the event, D'Orsay was dining with a large company, and naturally the *coup d'état* came up for discussion and comment. D'Orsay was quite outspoken in his condemnation, and said : " It is the greatest political swindle that ever has been practised in the world!" Which remark very naturally created considerable dismay in the circle ; it is not wise to express too freely adverse opinions of emperors—while they are alive.

In Abraham Hayward's *Correspondence*, considerable light is thrown upon D'Orsay's opinions of Napoleon and the political situation in Paris. On 17th January 1850, he writes from 38 Rue de la Ville l'Evêque :—

"Mon Cher Hayward,—J'aurois dû vous répondre plus tôt, pour vous remercier de l'article que vous m'avez envoyé. J'attendois d'avoir vu Louis Napoléon. Nous voici de retour à Paris, établi pour l'Hiver qui est des plus *rudes*. Les affaires ici vont mal ; l'amour propre en souffrance fait tous les grands révolutionnaires en France, il n'y a pas dix hommes de bonne foi dans ce beau pays ; les gens opposent dans la Chambre les lois qu'ils avait eux-mêmes proposées anciennement. Thiers et Berryer, bavards de profession, sont si versés d'être mis de côté, qu'ils combinent une conjuration de Catalina. Les élections de Paris montreront définitivement de quel côté est le vent ; en attendant, dans le midi, le gouvernement est obligé de donner son appui à des candidats légitimistes, plutôt que de voir des extrêmes rouges remporter la victoire, c'est bien tomber de Charybdis dans Scylla. Napoléon a le plus grand désir *to run straight*, mais les *crossins* et *jostlings* cherchent à l'empêcher, vous devez vous en apercevoir. . . . Rappelez-moi au bon souvenir de mes amis d'Angleterre, j'y suis souvent en pensée, et malgré que cela soit toujours avec un grand sentiment de tristesse je préfère cela aux gaietés de Paris. Votre très dévoué,

D'Orsay."

Then on the 5th, possibly the 6th, of December 1851, D'Orsay sends over to Hayward for publication in the English Press, the letter published in Paris on the 4th by Jérôme, which was scarcely calculated to please nephew Louis. Two lines in D'Orsay's covering note are striking :—" I always think of dear old England, that one must like every day more from what we see everywhere else."

On 2nd January, of the year following, D'Orsay writes a long and interesting letter to Hayward, in which he says emphatically that he was and is strongly opposed to the *coup d'état*, and that on account of it Louis Napoleon had sunk in his estimation, as he had believed him to be a man as good as his word. He held that Napoleon would have "arrived" without employing illegitimate means, and that Republicanism was an almost negligible quantity. After discussing the standing of various leaders and parties, he continues :—

" Vous voyez que je suis juste et impartial, quoique je suis reconnu, depuis 40 années, d'être le plus grand et le plus sincère Napoléonien qui existe." And : " Vous ne pouvez concevoir à quel point les gens ici sont courtisans et plats valets ; vanité et succès sont les deux mots d'ordres. . . . Tout marche à l'Empire." In conclusion : " Ah! if I were rich, I would soon be in London. Here I am an exile."

A few days later he writes again to much the same purport, and says : " J'ai l'air d'être dans une opposition, parce que je n'approuve pas la route que Louis a pris pour arriver où il en est maintenant." Who can doubt that Louis Napoleon blundered in not asking for and accepting D'Orsay's advice ? But then it was natural that he should not have done so ; the little seldom care to accept the aid of the great.

XXIX

In the early part of 1852 a trouble of the spine
became apparent, causing poor D'Orsay much pain
and sickness, which he bore with admirable and
uncomplaining patience. In July the doctors
ordered him to Dieppe, whither he went accompanied by the faithful Misses Power; but it was
too late; death was evidently at hand. At the
end of the month he returned to Paris, to die.

On 2nd August, the Archbishop of Paris
visited him, and on parting, embraced him, saying :
" J'ai pour vous plus que de l'amitié, j'ai de
l'affection." The next day he received the last
consolations of the Church at the hands of the curé
of Chambourcy.

Madden had visited him during his last weeks,
and has left a strange account of an interview with
him, which must be quoted verbatim :—

" The wreck only of the *beau* D'Orsay was
there.

" He was able to sit up and walk, though with
difficulty and evidently with pain, about his room,
which was at once his studio, reception room, and
sleeping apartment. He burst out crying when I
entered the room, and continued for a length of
time so much affected that he could hardly speak
to me. Gradually he became composed, and
talked about Lady Blessington's death, but all the

time with tears pouring down his pale wan face, for even then his features were death-stricken.

"He said with marked emphasis: '*In losing her I lost everything in this world—she was to me a mother! a dear, dear mother!* a true *loving mother to me!*' While he uttered these words he sobbed and cried like a child. And referring to them, he again said: '*You understand* me, Madden.'"

Madden believed D'Orsay to have been speaking in all sincerity. What are we to believe? There is something almost terrible in this scene of the dying dandy, broken down in body and spirits, making a gallant effort to clear the name he had for years besmirched. But the statements of the dying must not be allowed to weigh against the deeds of the living. And would the dead lady have been pleased?

Madden continues :—

"I said, among the many objects which caught my attention in the room, I was very glad to see a crucifix placed over the head of his bed; men living in the world as he had done, were so much in the habit of forgetting all early religious feelings. D'Orsay seemed hurt at the observation. I then plainly said to him :—

"'The fact is, I imagined, or rather I supposed, you had followed Lady Blessington's example, if not in giving up your own religion, in seeming to conform to another more in vogue in England.'

"D'Orsay rose up with considerable energy, and stood erect and firm with obvious exertion for a few seconds, looking like himself again, and pointing to the head of the bed, he said :

"'Do you see those two swords?' pointing to two small swords (which were hung over the crucifix crosswise); 'do you see that sword to the right? With that sword I fought in defence of my religion.'"

He then briefly narrated the story of the duel which we have already told.

During his last illness, D'Orsay received from the Emperor the appointment of Director of Fine Arts. The honour came too late.

At three o'clock in the morning of the fourth of August 1852, aged fifty-one, died Alfred, Count d'Orsay, the last and the greatest of the dandies.

He was buried at Chambourcy; the same monument covers his ashes and those of Lady Blessington. In the absence of the Duke de Grammont, who was confined to bed by illness, D'Orsay's nephews, Count Alfred de Grammont and the Duke de Lespare, were the chief mourners; the Duchesse de Grammont, his sister, was there, and among others Prince Napoleon, Count de Montaubon, M. Emile de Girardin, M. Charles Lafitte, M. Alexandre Dumas fils, Mr Hughes Ball, and several other Englishmen.

Gronow says: "His death produced, both in London and Paris, a deep and universal regret."

But one who did not love him, Count Horace de Viel Castel, whom we have before quoted, did not join in the chorus of regrets :—

"Count d'Orsay is dead, and all the papers are mourning his loss. He leaves behind him they say, many *chefs-d'œuvres*, and on his death-bed requested Clésinger to finish his bust of Prince Jérôme.

" D'Orsay had no talent; his statuettes are detestable and his busts very bad; but a certain set cried him up for their own purposes, and called him a great man. One newspaper goes so far as to affirm that on hearing of his death the President said : 'I have lost my best friend,' a statement which I know to be perfectly false.

" D'Orsay's friends were the President's enemies — the Jérôme Bonapartes, Emile de Girardin, Lamartine, etc. He never pardoned the Prince for not appointing him Ambassador to the Count of St James', forgetting, or purposely ignoring, the fact that such a thing was impossible. No Government would have received him. His debts are fabulous. . . . The papers inform us that he has been buried at Chambourcy (on the property of his sister, the Duchesse de Grammont) in the same grave as his mother-in-law, Lady Blessington. The incident is sublime ; to make it complete, perhaps they will engrave on his tombstone : 'That his inconsolable and heartbroken widow, etc. etc.'

" He died ten years too late, for he became at last merely a ridiculous old doll. The President does not lose his best friend ; on the contrary, he is well rid of, a compromising schemer."

Clésinger one day asked D'Orsay why he did not come to see him oftener.

" Because people say that it is I who make your statues," responded D'Orsay, with a smile.

" Really ! " replied the sculptor, " I will come and see you ; no one would accuse me of being guilty of *yours*."

Dickens wrote in *Household Words* : " Count

d'Orsay, whose name is publicly synonymous with elegant and graceful accomplishments; and who, by those who knew him well, is affectionately remembered and regretted, as a man whose great abilities might have raised him to any distinction, and whose gentle heart even a world of fashion left unspoiled."

Landor writes :—

"The death of poor, dear D'Orsay fell heavily tho' not unexpectedly upon me. Intelligence of his painful and hopeless malady reached me some weeks before the event. With many foibles and grave faults, he was generous and sincere. Neither spirits nor wit ever failed him, and he was ready at all times to lay down his life for a friend. I felt a consolation in the loss of Lady Blessington in the thought how unhappy she would have been had she survived him. The world will never more see united such graceful minds, so much genius and pleasantry, as I have met, year after year, under her roof. . . ."

Macready :—

"To my deep grief perceived the notice of the death of dear Count d'Orsay. No one who knew him and had affections could help loving him. When he liked he was most fascinating and captivating. It was impossible to be insensible to his graceful, frank, and most affectionate manner. . . . He was the most brilliant, graceful, endearing man I ever saw—humorous, witty, and clear-headed."

D'Orsay's good friend, Emile de Girardin, wrote in *La Presse* of August 5th, 1852 :—

Le Comte d'Orsay est mort ce matin à trois heures.

"La douleur et le vide de cette mort seront vivement ressentis par tous les amis qu'il comptait en si grand nombre en France et en Angleterre, dans tous les rangs de la société, et sous tous les drapeaux de la politique.

"A Londres, les salons de Gore House furent toujours ouverts à tous les proscrits politiques, qu'ils s'appelassent Louis Bonaparte ou Louis Blanc, à tous les naufragés de la fortune et à toutes les illustrations de l'art et de la science.

"A Paris, il n'avait qu'un vaste atelier, mais quiconque allait frapper au nom d'un malheur à secourir ou d'un progrès à encourager, était toujours assuré du plus affable accueil et du plus cordial concours.

"Avant le 2 Décembre, nul ne fit d'efforts plus réitérés pour que la politique suivît un autre cours et s'élevât aux plus hautes aspirations.

"Après le 2 Décembre, nul ne s'employa plus activement pour amortir les coups de la proscription : Pierre Dupont* le sait et peut le certifier.

"Le Président de la République n'avait pas d'ami à la fois plus dévoué et plus sincère que le Comte d'Orsay ; et c'est quand il venait de la rapprocher de lui par le titre et les fonctions de surintendant des beaux-arts qu'il le perd pour toujours.

"C'est une perte irréparable pour l'art et pour les artistes, mais c'est une perte plus irréparable encore pour la Vérité et pour le Président de la

* The well-known poet and lyricist.

République, car les palais n'ont que deux portes ouvertes à la Vérité : la porte de l'amitié et la porte de l'adversité, de l'amitié qui est à l'adversité ce que l'éclair est à la foudre.

" La justice indivisible, la justice égale pour tous, la justice dont la mort tient les balances, compte les jours quand elle ne mesure pas les dons. Alfred d'Orsay avait été comblé de trop de dons—grand cœur, esprit, un goût pur, beauté antique, force athlétique, adresse incomparable à tous les exercises du corps, aptitude incontestáble à tous les arts auxquels il s'était adonné ; dessin, peinture, sculpture—Alfred d'Orsay avait été comblé de trop de dons pour que ses jours ne fussent pas parcimonieusement comptés. La mort a été inexorable, mais elle a été juste. Elle ne l'a pas traité en homme vulgaire. Elle ne l'a pas pris, elle l'a choisi."

There is one more general summary of his character which must be given. Grantley Berkeley tells a pleasant story of a dinner at the Old Ship Hotel at Greenwich :—

" I remember a dinner at the Ship, where there were a good many ladies, and where D'Orsay was of the party, during which his attention was directed to a centre pane of glass in the bay-window over the Thames, where some one had written, in large letters, with a diamond, D'Orsay's name in improper conjunction with a celebrated German *danseuse* then fulfilling an engagement at the Opera. With characteristic readiness and *sang-froid*, he took an orange from a dish near him, and, making some trifling remark on the excellence of the fruit, tossed it up once or twice,

Death

catching it in his hand again. Presently, as if
by accident, he gave it a wider cant, and sent it
through the window, knocking the offensive
words out of sight into the Thames."

Then he continues :—

"D'Orsay was as clever and agreeable a companion as any in the world, and perhaps as in-
ventive and extravagant in dress as Beau
Brummel, though not so original nor so varied in
the grades of costume through which his imagination carried him. There were all sorts of hats
and garments named after him by their makers,
more or less like those he wore, and a good many
men copied him to some extent in his attire. He
and I adopted the tight wristbands, turned back
upon the sleeve of the coat upon the wrist, in
which fashion we were not followed by others, I
am happy to say. . . .

"Among the peculiarities and accomplishments
for which D'Orsay desired to be famous was that
of great muscular strength, as well as a knowledge
of all weapons, and when he shook hands with
his friends it was with the whole palm, with such
an impressive clutch of the fingers as drove the
blood from the limb he held, and sent every ring
on the hand almost to the bone. The apparent
frankness of manner and kind expression in his
good-looking face, when he met you with the
exclamation, '*Ah, ha, mon ami!*' and grasped
you by the hand, were charming, and we, who
rather prided ourselves on being able to do strong
things, used to be ready for this grasp, and
exhibit our muscular powers in return. There is
no man who can so well imitate D'Orsay's method

of greeting in this particular as my excellent friend, Dr Quin.

"Poor dear D'Orsay! He was a very accomplished, kind-hearted, and graceful fellow, and much in request in what may be called the fashionable world. I knew him well in his happier hours, I knew him when he was in difficulties, and I knew him in distress ; and when in France I heard from Frenchmen that those in his native country to whom he looked for high lucrative employment and patronage, and from whom D'Orsay thought he had some claim to expect them, rather slighted his pretensions; and when in his last, lingering, painful illness,* left him to die too much neglected and alone.

"That D'Orsay was unwisely extravagant as well as not over-scrupulous in morality, we know ; but that is a man's own affair, not that of his friends. His faults, whatever they were, were covered, or at least glossed over by real kindness of heart, great generosity, and prompt goodnature, grace in manner, accomplishments, and high courage ; therefore, place him side by side with many of the men with whom he lived in England, D'Orsay by comparison would have the advantage in many things."

* An amazing version of D'Orsay's death has recently been made public ; namely, that in addition to the disease of the spine, the Count suffered also from a carbuncle, which " was a euphemism for a bullet aimed at the Emperor as they were walking together in the gardens of the Elysée."

XXX

WHAT WAS HE?

WITNESSES have been heard for the defence and for the prosecution; the defendant himself has been examined and cross-examined; what is the verdict?

Lamb has told us that we must not take the immoral comedies of the Restoration seriously. His argument does not bear precisely upon the case in point, but it is of assistance. Lamb, speaking of plays, whereas we are writing of history, says: "We have been spoiled with—not sentimental comedy—but a tyrant far more pernicious to our pleasures which has succeeded to it, the exclusive and all-devouring drama of common life." For "comedy" substitute "history"; for "drama" put "psychology" and we can fit our text to our sermon, a thing often more easy to achieve than to fit one's sermon to one's text. We had been surfeited with sentimental history, with the white-washing of sinners and the super-humanising of saints; we therefore turned to what we are pleased to call real life, and taking everything seriously have made everything dull.

Let us return to our Lamb for a moment :—

"I confess for myself that (with no great delinquencies to answer for) I am glad for a season to take an airing beyond the diocese of the strict conscience—not to live always in the precincts of the law-courts—but now and then, for a dream-while or so, to imagine a world with no meddling restrictions — to get into recesses, whither the hunter cannot follow me—

'———— Secret shades
Of woody Ida's inmost grave,
While yet there was no fear of Jove.'

I come back to my cage and my restraint the fresher and more healthy for it."

That is the point of view we must take if we are to judge D'Orsay justly ; we must lock up our conscience for the nonce, we must get away from the unimaginative atmosphere of the law-courts, we must snap the shackles of convention which always make it impossible for us to form a fair opinion of the unconventional.

Judged by the standards of life and conduct which must control everyday men and women, D'Orsay was a monster of iniquity, and also, as *Punch* would put it, he was worse than wicked, he was vulgar. His friends cannot have weighed him by any such standards, or they would have condemned him and scorned him. They could not then have accepted him as one of themselves, as a man to be almost loved ; they would have turned cold shoulders to any ordinary mortal who treated the love of woman as a comedy and debts of honour as mere farce.

But your real dandy is not an ordinary man and must not be judged by common standards. He stands outside and above the ordinary rules of life and conduct ; he has not any conscience, and questions of morality do not affect him. All that is for us to do in viewing such a one as

D'Orsay is to weigh his physical and mental gifts,
and to examine the uses to which he put them,
to look to the opportunities which were given to
him and the advantage which he took of them.

Of the multitude of witnesses whom we have
summoned there is not one who denies that D'Orsay
was a man of supreme physical beauty, and the
portraits of him support their verdict. Good looks
that were almost effeminate in their charm were
supported by the physique of a perfect man, and in
all manly sports and pursuits he was highly accomplished. Of his mental qualities it is not so
easy justly to weigh the worth ; he was an accomplished amateur in art some say, others deny
it, but on the whole the evidence seems to be in
his favour ; he was endowed with a pleasing habit
of talk, though scarcely with wit. He was good-
humoured, a *bon garçon* and good-natured. He
was an accomplished *gourmet*. In the art of
dress he was supreme. He was more greatly
skilled, perhaps, than any other man, in the art
of gaining and giving pleasure. He was brave.

Morality, as has been said, does not enter into
the consideration of such a man ; he was above
morality, or outside it. There have been and
there are others like him. They are grown-up
children, utterly irresponsible ; not immoral but
unmoral ; they " please to live and live to please "
themselves. They do not realise that their actions
may prove costly to others and therefore do not
count the cost. They are children of impulse not
of calculation. They are emotional not logical.
Pleasure is their pursuit and they shun all that is
unpleasing and displeasing. They are so different

from us ordinary folk that we cannot appraise them or even fully understand them. Fear of consequences that would appal us have no terrors for them; they do not need to set them aside, they are not aware of them. Conventions which hamper us, for them do not exist. To fulfil the desire of to-day is their one aim and ambition and they take no heed of to-morrow.

It is as a dandy that D'Orsay must be judged, and in that *rôle* he achieved triumph. It was as a dandy he lived and as a dandy that he is immortal. Such men as he, if indeed there are others with his genius, should—as we have said—be pensioned by the State, should be set above the carking cares of questions of want of pounds—shillings and pence do not trouble them; they should be cherished and sustained as rarely-gifted and rare beings, to whom life presents not any serious problems, and to whom life is a space of time only too brief for all the pleasures which should be crowded into it. " Life's fitful fever" should be kept apart from such sunny souls, and our only regret should be that there are so few of them.

There are mouldy-minded people who put out the finger of scorn at D'Orsay. Is it not the truth that they are jealous of him, and that at the bottom of their hearts there is a muttered prayer: " I would thank God if He *had* made *me* such a man"?

Index

Index

COLSTONS LIMITED, PRINTERS, EDINBURGH